Sudden Death

Jim Kochanoff

Pregame

One of my teammates is a murderer.

That might not seem that unusual considering my team is called the Oshawa Assassins. In hockey, it's best to have a threatening name to draw fans and strike fear into the heart of your opponent. Although a logo with a hockey stick aimed at you like a gun really isn't that terrifying.

Over the last year, we have gone through some tremendous highs and lows. We fought for the survival of our team and played some really good opponents. We've been chased and questioned relentlessly by the police. It's true what they say; they won't stop until they get their man.

We haven't had a very good win/loss record (as the team's goaltender, I'll tell you it's not my fault) but we have a very interesting mix of guys. Some are talented, some try to make up for their lack of talent with the love of a good fight. But what's common in all of us is that we're all in it to win. With the low salary we make in this league, pride is the only thing that drives us.

Makes you wonder what drives someone to kill.

The Lineup

Welcome to the KHL. A bush league of players cut from the farm teams of the national hockey league. We traveled throughout the northern States of the USA and the provinces of Canada. Old veterans made up the bulk of the players but occasionally a young player used the league to propel himself into a farm team slot. The pay was horrible and the travel long. Players spend weeks on the road living on beer and fried food. Many players couldn't make a living doing anything else.

My team, the Oshawa Assassins, started this road trip crisscrossing five states and two provinces, traveling to a lot of cities. The team is away from our families for weeks at a time and the stress is non-stop. It was a tough life with the main reward being able to play the game of hockey. For most players, that was enough.

There were ten top players. Many had been given nicknames during their hockey careers and most have forgotten each other's real names. Some names were obvious; others had a story that had just stuck. These were the main guys who built the wall between the puck and me.

The Forwards:

Tunny was a brawler and a drunk. Not much talent but the meanest player on the team - if not the whole league. He was vocal and pushed the team toward extra curricular activities during our downtime.

Chilly was the most talented player but frustrated that he might never play professional hockey in the big leagues. He was a selfless player who tried to set others up with passes but was often stymied by the team's lack of ability.

Stefan was a bilingual hockey player from Montreal. He was very suave and always a hit with the ladies. He tried to impart culture on his less than receptive teammates.

Taj was the first and only hockey player of East Indian descent. He was the smallest player on the team but played with a lot of energy. Taj shot across the ice like a squirrel on speed.

Presley was the team captain and master of ceremonies. There wasn't a game or party where he didn't make a speech. He was always trying to motivate the team and relentlessly supported the Coach.

Dawson was the pretty boy; he spent more time on his appearance than his hockey skills. Problem was that both needed a lot of work. Lazy and always opportunistic, he waited for someone to set him up in front of the net.

The Defense:

Brick was a gentle giant. He would crush an opposing player and would then apologize as he picked up the broken body. Despite his size and crushing force, he was an overgrown teddy bear. Problem was, he didn't hit like a teddy bear.

Dozer played half the time high on weed. To be honest, he actually played better that way. He ate like a fiend, but never put on weight. He talked like a surfer, but his body rarely saw any water. Or soap.

Booker had a comment about everything. He thought himself as an intellectual and spent too much effort trying to educate his fellow teammates. He was a walking encyclopedia and explained everything in minute detail. Unfortunately, he often had the details wrong.

Rook was a young kid and first year rookie player, learning the ropes of the league. He tried too hard to be everyone's friend and took a lot of abuse from his teammates.

In addition to the top ten, there were five minor players who were so young that you wondered if they have even graduated from high school.

Dedication

This book is dedicated to John Bowman who passed away in the fall of 2007 after fighting a courageous battle against cancer. John was an organizer, webmaster, ace reporter, captain, rock of the defense and everyone's buddy.

He loved hockey and made the game a lot of fun with his infectious humor. He could turn a loss into a win by his careful selection of words in an after-game write-up. He had a great catchphrase that describes how we should all live our lives.

"Instead of being buried all neat and formal, I would rather come skidding around the corner in my coffin, slam into the hole disheveled and untidy and before I'm dropped in, say - Holy Crap! What a ride!"

All who played hockey with him, will miss him. Rest in Peace #7.

John "Sloop" Bowman
1955 - 2007

The Rules

Hockey is a simple sport if you can keep up with the action.

There are two teams – five players against five players on a sheet of ice. At each end is a goaltender that protects a net. All the players on the ice use hockey sticks that slap a small piece of rubber called a puck. There are three twenty-minute periods for each team to score in. The team who scores the most goals, wins. If at the end of the game the score is tied, then the teams can either have a shootout or play longer, considered sudden death.

The sheet of ice is divided up into lines, a centerline in the middle and two blue lines towards either net. To make sure the players don't cheat, several officials skate on the ice with the hockey players. An official called a linesman watches that players don't cross the blue line before they have the puck. This prevents players from staying in the opposing end if the puck isn't there.

The official called a referee is in charge of enforcing the rules. He watches that no one tries to hurt an opposing player or cheat to get the puck. It's the toughest job of the game and fans will always yell at the referee if he misses a call. If the referee catches a player doing something illegal, he will blow his whistle and call a penalty. The player then has to sit in a penalty box while his team plays shorthanded until his time is up.

But if the referee is not looking, a player can get away with *murder*.

First Period

October 13, 2006

Pain cut through his nerves like a razor blade.

Two teeth flew out of his mouth as his head recoiled from the punch. Darkness tugged at his reality, threatening to take his consciousness. He countered with a shot to his attacker's throat. His fist was rewarded with a slippery pop. Two glazed eyes stared back at him wishing for his death. The music blared and filled the stadium. The fans screamed for blood.

"Finish him off!" they yelled, "finish him off!" They stamped their feet and banged their hands against the boards. Their savage looks signaled that they only wanted one thing. BLOOD! He looked down at his opponent. His body was slumped on the ice like a rag doll. He felt the sweat from his opponent's greasy hair in his hands. He smiled through his bloody broken teeth and threw the knockout blow. The music peaked as the men in stripes came to separate the players.

A hand shut off the television remote. The huge plasma television screen went dark and the audio died. A spray of blood arced across the screen like a crescent moon. A woman's face was reflected in the dark screen.

"How do people watch that crap?" she asked.

"It's an exciting game, Lola," a tall detective entered the living room behind her. He ducked under the crime tape and checked the carpet for a weapon. "You really should give it a chance."

"I suppose you'd like to take me to a game, Brown?" She turned on her digital camera to take several pictures of the crime scene.

"Will you stop calling me Brown? And I've asked you out enough times to know when you're teasing."

"Are you sure? Maybe this time I'll say yes." She pouted her lips at him. Mitch sighed, knowing he had no choice.

"Lola, would you like to go with me to a hockey game?" Mitch faced away for fear of jinxing his request.

"I'll get back to you on that. If you were a hockey player, then you might have a chance." Lola smiled.

"Fascinating conversation, but can I find someone to discuss the crime?" Both officers jumped and turned to the sound of the voice.

Mitch Daniels regained his composure and looked up at a man in a suit. He stood well over six feet tall and was as solid as a linebacker. He stepped up to the crime tape and appeared ready to enter the room.

"This is a crime scene sir. I'm afraid I'm going to have to ask you to leave." The man flashed a badge.

"Special Agent Garson. What's wrong? Surprised a black man would come to this neighborhood?" he looked at Mitch.

"No sir, just doing my duty," he replied. He clenched his fist realizing that as the higher-ranking officer, Garson would assume command. *I'm sick of this bureaucratic bullshit, but better to be supportive now and still play a role in this investigation.* "Let me bring you up to speed." He pointed to the victim lying dead on the couch. His eyes were closed, and his fist grabbed an unfinished bowl of popcorn. "White male, about thirty-five, single. Looks like the victim was surprised, then killed and robbed." Garson put on a rubber glove and walked over to the TV. He looked at the blood splatter.

"Surprised is a bit of an understatement," Garson commented and looked back at the couch. "Do you mind kneeling down behind the couch?"

"Sure," answered Mitch. He stepped behind the couch and tried to imitate the killer's position.

"Okay, stand up," Garson commanded, "and step behind the victim." As Mitch stood, something caught Lola's attention.

"There's a lamp behind you. Wouldn't the victim notice the loss of light if the attacker stood up?"

"Good point," answered Garson. "Anyone have any ideas?"

"Yes, the lamp wouldn't be on. Any time I'm watching a game or a movie, I always turn out the lights. Better ambiance," Mitch looked over, but Lola was ignoring him.

"The light is on now – did either one of you turn it on?" Garson asked.

"No, we left the scene intact," Lola answered.

"So, he had company," Garson started -

"Looking at the mess of this condo, probably not a female," Mitch added.

"Or the killer turned the light on afterwards. Why?" Garson asked.

"Was the killer looking for something?" Mitch asked.

"Not the safe – that was in the bedroom," answered Lola.

"There's nothing behind the couch except a few magazines," Mitch pointed to them.

"Bag them and tag them," Garson replied. He stepped toward the victim. The blood had dried on the victim's head. "Pretty violent. Maybe the murder was made to look like a burglary." Garson surveyed a stack of hockey DVDs on top of the coffee table. *The Best of Hockey Fights - Part Eight* was placed on top. "Why do people waste their time watching this garbage?"

"Not a fan of hockey?" Mitch asked.

"I don't like a sport with white men beating a black object with a stick. It bothers me. Not the kind of sport a young boy plays growing up in the streets of Houston," explained Garson. Mitch decided against trying to argue about the merits of hockey.

"Well, the victim was definitely a fan. Besides the DVDs, he's has a collection of hockey caps and mugs in the kitchen."

"Who phoned this in?" Garson asked.

"The call came from the employer. Claims he hasn't seen the victim for two days, and he wasn't returning his calls."

"What did the victim do?" Garson looked the dead man over.

"Investment banker with Sterling and Scales. Apparently, he was a big money maker for them."

"Maybe he was a big money loser for someone else," Garson replied, holding his jaw.

"Patrol knocked on the door at 7:34pm. After getting no response they broke the door and found the victim dead. Three gunshot wounds: head, heart," Mitch pointed to the victim's crotch, "and you know. Wallet was taken and safe was busted open." They walked into the bedroom; the wall was blackened with explosives. "A neighbor thought she heard something but thought it was a sound from his television."

"How did he get out?" Garson was puzzled.

"Or she?" Lola replied. Garson looked at her.

"I don't have time to deal with your gender issues," he glared at her. "Where did the perp exit?"

"Door was locked with chain connected on the inside – had to go out a window," Mitch interjected. "No prints or sign of forced entry on the windows."

"And no one saw anything?" Garson asked.

"I've canvassed the neighbors," added Lola. "These condos are self contained and sound doesn't travel well. This hockey fight DVD has been blaring for days and no one heard it."

"No evidence, no witnesses, just a body and an empty safe. Should be a cakewalk. I love being handed these cases," Garson commented sarcastically.

"So why are you assigned to this case?" asked Lola. Garson turned to her.

"I've been working with the agency profilers and there may be a connection between this and a number of other unsolved murders. For the past four years during the fall and winter months, these unsolved cases take place in a variety of cities usually involving wealthy victims."

"How do you think they're related?" Mitch questioned.

"Not sure. On the surface they appear to be unrelated crimes - different methods of death, different cities. No similar relationship between the victims, only one common event. The victims are killed watching television."

"Could be a coincidence," comments Lola.

"Maybe. But my gut says you're wrong. Check with the employer, see the client list, and see if anyone was unhappy with the victim. Look at his bank accounts, see if he owed any money or was taking any large deposits."

"Where will we find you?" Mitch asked.

"At the office, I've been transferred here until further notice. Oh, and one piece of advice." Garson stared at them with a faint smile.

"Yeah?"

"Don't date your partner; it will compromise your working relationship. As long as you both work for me, keep it professional."

Lola suppressed a giggle as Garson left the room.

October 25, 2006

"This hockey game is a massacre! The Assassins are being killed!" the announcer yelled. He turned and slapped his partner who sat next to him in the press box.

"That's right, Doug," his partner answered. "The score is 7-2 with 8:15 left to play in the third period. The Oshawa Assassins are being slaughtered. They are running around because of the Albany Raiders superior puck handling ability. If the Assassins play this sloppy during the second half of the season, they aren't going to see the playoffs."

"Playoffs - this team is a joke! A basement dwelling joke," the first announcer yelled into the mike. The fans around the press box screamed their agreement.

"I wholeheartedly agree Bill! These losers don't even belong in the same rink as our Raiders," the first announcer replied.

A puck skimmed off the plastic window separating the press box from the ice and ricocheted into the stands. The announcer looked down into the waving hand of an Assassin player.

"Idiots! Those has-been announcers wish they had half our talent," the player yelled. A strong hand tapped him on the shoulder.

"Tunny don't waste your time on them. They still wish they could play hockey rather than sit up there and analyze it."

"Easy for you to say Chilly, you're still young enough to make it to the next division. This is all I've got and I'm not going to let those idiots ruin it." The linesman blew the whistle, stopping the play. Both players returned to the bench. The Assassin's coach, Joseph Munroe, provided advice for his players.

"This game is really simple: play your position, cover your man! Forwards - start coming back to help your defense! Defense - start passing to your forwards instead of trying to carry it up on your own!" The bench was quiet. "Are any of you listening to me?" He received fifteen blank stares and one nod. "Yes, Tunny, do you have a question?"

"Just one, Coach. After the game, can we go to that rib place we went to last time? They had the hottest waitresses." The whistle blew before the Coach could respond. The players skated back to the ice. The coach exhaled, resigning himself to a team full of misfits who listened to nobody. It was a paycheck for him, although he would still like to win a few games. He wished he could find a way to motivate his key players.

The forwards skated up to the center ready for the face-off. A bunch of teenagers banged the glass boards near the face-off circle.

"You suck Assassins. Your team sucks, your name sucks - hell your kids probably suck!" a skinny teenage fan laughed.

"Why don't you end the misery right now!" another fan yelled and tossed ice cubes from his drink onto the ice. One hit the back of Tunny's helmet and fell down the back of his sweater. The coldness was not pleasant as it sunk to waist. He rushed the glass screen and smashed against it with his body. Both kids were knocked back and their drinks went flying into the fans behind them. The surrounding fans around the kids screamed for blood.

"Why did you have to go do that? Now you're going to make them mad," pointed Dawson at the crowd.

"Bunch of trailer trash – give them something to talk about on the way home," Tunny grunted. He turned just as a huge yellow wad of spit hit his facemask. He looked up and saw the same kid standing over the plastic screen with a huge grin on his face. Without any thought for his safety, Tunny climbed the glass barrier and grabbed the fan by his shirt, pulling him over the boards onto the ice.

The whole arena erupted into pandemonium. Players from both benches jumped on the ice and started a bench-clearing brawl. Beer bottles, change and other debris flew onto the ice from fans in the stands. The three officials were overwhelmed. They called the game and signaled security to empty the arena. Within fifteen minutes, the local authorities had arrived and cleared out the arena, loading their paddy wagon with disruptive fans. Security directed both teams to their dressing rooms and the game ended in default.

"Quite a game today!" Tunny shouted to Stefan as they sat in the dressing room. Stefan grabbed a beer from the cooler and passed it to Tunny.

"A game? Mon ami! I think that is the worst game we have ever played, no?"

"If you mean hockey, yes. But for a brawl, I'd say that is one of our best." Tunny smiled and was decked in the back of the head with a newspaper.

"You idiot! We'll be lucky to leave this arena alive!" Coach said as he scratched his balding head.

"Relax. All the troublemakers have left. Well most of them anyway," replied Tunny, taking a swig of his beer. The coach paced the dressing room undeterred by Tunny's comments.

"Listen up everyone," the coach yelled. The dressing room went silent. "You are the most pathetic joke of a team I have ever had the misfortune of coaching in my entire career! I've seen women's teams with more talent," he yelled. The room erupted into laughter and cheers.

"Mon Dieu! You sure know how to motivate," replied Stefan. More beers were opened as the team took their after-game tongue-lashing.

"Speaking of women, I think our goaltender saw more rubber tonight than a condom vending machine!" Tunny yelled as everyone looked at me as I took off my goaltender pads. I smiled and nodded my agreement.

"You know, it wouldn't hurt some of you losers to come back to our end every once in a while," as I looked at the forwards.

"Enough!" The Coach interrupted. "That was the worst game I have ever seen you play! Do you want to see the playoffs?"

"We're trying Coach. I think we found the ice a bit soft tonight and it slowed our game," answered Dawson.

"If excuses were goals Dawson, you'd lead the league," commented Coach.

"It's barely November coach," Chilly replied. "It's a little early in the season to throw in the towel just yet."

"We should use the game to help motivate us to play better," interjected team captain Presley. "We can learn from this."

"Can we get a copy of the game tape today, Coach? I want to analyze the plays," asked Rook. Someone threw a dirty towel at him.

"No! For the thousandth time, we don't videotape the games. Hell, the way we play, we're lucky people even come to watch us!" the coach screamed.

"Hey that's not fair, Coach. We all know that the fans come to see me beat up the best players in the game," Tunny said proudly.

"Yeah, you stop their fist with your face," joked Dozer. The team roared.

"Is that why you are so ugly?" asked Stefan sitting next to Tunny.

"Enough!" the coach yelled. "Take a shower and pack your gear. The team bus leaves in an hour. It leaves whether you're on it or not." The coach took his clipboard and left the dressing room. Someone threw an empty beer bottle as the door closed. As the glass settled on the floor, the door reopened, and the Coach poked his head back in. "Make that forty-five minutes instead," he yelled and closed the door quickly before another bottle could connect.

The lights of Albany had long past faded behind the bus and the team was well on its way into its long drive back to Oshawa. A beer bottle rolled down the aisle before it rested next to a hockey bag. It was cold outside, but the windows were open to let the reek of hockey gear escape. The bus closed in on the Canadian border. The players were either drinking or sleeping. Dozer was playing hockey on his GameBoy; he scored a point, then jabbed his elbow into Dawson's back.

"Do that again and I'll shove that game down your throat," Dawson yelled." Dozer stood up and walked towards the back of the bus without responding.

"Don't you ever shower?" yelled Tunny to Dozer as he walked down the aisle.

"Yeah, dude! I showered yesterday with your mother. She says hello," he replied. Dozer took another seat and went back to playing his video game.

Dawson opened up the local paper. On the front page was an article about a break and enter and murder in Burlington, Vermont.

"What for you reading, mon ami?" Stefan asked as he grabbed a corner of the paper.

"Why, do you need me to translate for you?" Dawson answered. Chilly grabbed the newspaper out of Dawson's hands and threw it to the back of the bus.

"No making fun of our French friend. He's twice the player you are." Chilly replied. Dawson stood up and looked Chilly in the face.

"Why don't you and your girlfriend go find a room somewhere and leave me alone?" Dawson taunted.

"Can't we just all get along?" Presley said as he stepped between the two of them.

"Good job Presley. You're always the peacemaker," Booker yelled from the back of the bus.

"Thank you! Thank you, very much!" drawled Presley. He was almost knocked down by one of his teammates.

"Coming through!" as Taj ran to the back of the bus heading for the bathroom.

"Doesn't that guy ever slow down?" asked Brick.

"Not even in his dreams," Chilly answered. He folded his hands and started to close his eyes. Brick nudged him with his elbow. Chilly responded by opening one eye.

"What?" he asked.

"Do you think this is our last season? We lose more games then we win. I see less and less fans at each home game. If it wasn't for the fights, we'd have no fans at all," Brick commented. Chilly opened the other eye.

"I've played in this league for eight years and I've heard that question asked every year. Do I think this is our last year? Maybe. Kids are so caught up with their video games and surfing the net, they aren't coming to our games anymore. Our fans are mostly dads who can't afford professional sports tickets and come to our games to relive their old sports days. Even they won't last in our league forever. So, do I think our team is going to fold? Yeah, today, tomorrow. Who knows?"

"What you gonna do? Play hockey somewhere else?" Brick asked.

"Where? We're in last place and I doubt any other team would pick any of us up."

"Can you two shut up? All of your depressing talk is messing with my sleep," I yelled from a backseat.

"Why should you be tired? You let all the shots get by you tonight," Tunny shot back from the front. The bus eased to a stop as it reached the Niagara Falls border crossing. A female officer walked outside a gatehouse and looked up at the approaching bus. She was young and fit her uniform exceedingly well.

"All right! I'm gonna get strip searched tonight!" Tunny yelled and ran to the front of the bus.

"You be lucky she doesn't burst out laughing when she sees what you're packing down there!" Dawson called from the back of the bus. The driver stopped and opened the side door. The Coach got out of his car and came up the stairs of the bus.

"All right guys, you know the drill. Just a few standard questions and the bus can head home. Save the smart comments and we can skip any delays."

"I think I speak on behalf of the team, Coach, when I say that there will be no problems with us," said Presley. A second later a newspaper hit him in the back of the head. A large male officer and the female officer marched up the bus stairwell to address the team.

"Good morning, gentleman. A few questions before you proceed," the male officer stated. The female officer sat in the front seat and watched the hockey players. They returned her stare.

"Are you carrying any tobacco products?" the male officer asked. Stefan stuffed several packs of smokes into his hockey bag.

"No," answered several players.

"Are you carrying any alcohol across the border?" Booker stashed one of the empty beer bottles into his bag.

"No," again was the response from several players.

"Is anyone carrying any drugs," the officer asked. Dozer stuffed some grass into his pocket."

"No," the back of the bus responded.

"Is anyone carrying any firearms?" he asked. Before the group could respond no, Tunny stood up.

"I have a pistol in my pocket and it's about to go off," he stated expecting a huge roar of laughter from the bus. He was greeted with a mortified look of silence from his teammates. With increased border security, the players had learned to act serious and answer the questions in the negative. No one deviated from the script. The coach stepped in to try to ward off an embarrassing situation.

"I'm sorry. We've come off a hard game and he's trying to be funny. Trust me when I say there is nothing dangerous in his pants," the coach warned.

The female officer fell back into her seat and roared with laughter. Several of the team fell into the aisle, unable to contain their laughter, and one almost tipped over a case of beer. Tunny remained standing and was the only one not laughing.

"Laugh all you want you bunch of losers," he yelled to the bus. "But I'm in need of a strip search to disarm my lethal weapon. And I don't want no guy checking my pistol out," Tunny stated to the male officer.

"Very well," he answered and nodded to the female. She spoke into the walkie-talkie on her shoulder. "10-4, Control. Ready the room for a strip search. Over." She looked back to the male officer. Tunny could barely contain his excitement.

"Baby, you can take as long as you want with me," as he sidled closer to her.

"Oh, it won't be her," the male officer replied. "Officer Tenor is trained for vehicle inspection only."

"Then who?" Tunny started to ask and was interrupted by Stefan's yelling.

"Mon dieu! There is a beached whale coming out of the gatehouse. She looks like an opera singer who ate the whole opera house!" All of the players rushed to the side of the bus and looked out of the window. A very large, very masculine woman with pulled back hair and a severe look, stepped towards the bus. Her face was frowning, and she looked like she truly hated her job. The male officer grabbed Tunny and turned to the stairs.

"All threats must be treated seriously," he declared and marched him down the stairs towards the gatehouse. The female officer followed and looked back at the bus with a grin.

"Look," yelled Stefan. "Look at what she's wearing!" The large woman snapped a yellow glove on her left hand.

"A full cavity search gentlemen. We'll determine if this man has any dangerous weapons to declare," the large female officer growled.

Tunny looked back at the bus with a forlorn look. It would be several hours before the bus made it across the border.

October 26, 2006

Mayonnaise dripped down from the sandwich onto the photo. Mitch nervously looked around him and wiped it off with a napkin.

"Better hope Garson doesn't catch you," teased Lola as she entered the squad room door. Three walls were lined with photos of victims from several states and provinces. A boardroom table sat in the middle of the room covered with newspaper clippings and witness reports. A map in the corner held the locations of the crime scenes.

"I'll deny it if you say anything," Mitch replied nervously.

"Relax," laughed Lola. "I'm just jerking your chain." She sat down in one of the chairs and tossed an empty pop can into the garbage.

"Aren't you ever going to learn to recycle?" questioned Mitch as he picked the can out of the garbage and placed it on the windowsill.

"Give me a break. You'd recycle the bullets we pull out the bodies in the morgue. You're such a green freak," sneered Lola.

"Spoken like a true polluter. I can feel the temperature rising just listening to you," Mitch shot back.

Lola crumpled a piece of paper and tossed it at Mitch. She leaned back in her chair and reviewed another one of the folders.

"Do you really think all of these murders are the work of one psychopath?" she asked.

"Garson thinks so," Mitch answered, "but I don't see the connection. There are different methods of death, sometimes robbery, sometimes not. Victims are usually male but different ages and economic status. I don't see a common motive."

"Maybe there is none. Maybe this a wild goose chase," Lola said as she dropped the folder to the table and threw her hair back. Mitch walked over to her and placed his hands on her shoulders.

"You look tense, let me massage your back," he offered.

"Be my guest," Lola replied. Mitch pressed down hard on her shoulder blades. "A little to the right please." She motioned with her hand. "If there's no connection, how does Garson get all these resources to pursue these cases?"

"Because of his reputation. Before he was demoted, he was considered one of the up and comers in the department. That all changed on the Morchesti case." Mitch continued rubbing.

"The what? Oh, you missed a spot," joked Lola.

"Todd Morchesti. One of the lab techs told me about him." Mitch paused to gather his thoughts.

"You can keep massaging."

"Sorry," Mitch answered and pressed with his fingers. "Morchesti was a wealthy banker who was kidnapped about two years ago. Made the news because his wife was suspected of planning the whole scheme. Garson was chief investigator and believed it was someone else. He pursued a different angle. He believed the plot was the work of former employees."

"What happened?" Lola looked back at Mitch.

"Garson arranged for the money and exchange to be carefully controlled. Morchesti's wife was guarded at her home. Garson had everything analyzed to the smallest detail. The drop was watched from several directions, multiple agents, satellite tracking – the whole nine yards."

"Sounds perfect." Lola stretched her neck. "What went wrong?"

"Everything. The exchange never happened. They waited until two hours after the allotted time and packed it in. Garson and his agents went back to the Morchesti home. The wife was gone, and his agent shot dead."

"The kidnappers came back for her?" Lola asked.

"That's what Garson thought. They put in a missing persons report on her and waited three days for the kidnappers to call. They never did. Garson's team shut down operations and the case quickly became cold until one of the field agents noticed something odd about the briefcase used to make the switch. The case was smudged with a red substance – later analyzed to be lipstick. They opened the case and it was full of stacks of cut paper. The money was gone."

"What happened?" Lola turned her head with interest.

"Turns out the briefcase was switched. Apparently, the wife seduced the agent that was shot, and the plan was for the two of them to slip away to a foreign country. She may have been Todd Morchesti's wife, but she had no signing authority to release large sums of money."

"Except in a kidnapping – the bank would assist," Lola responded.

"Exactly. There never was a kidnapping – Garson and his team were on a false stakeout while she escaped," said Mitch.

"What about Todd Morchesti?"

"That was the kicker. They found his body later – hidden in an old oil drum in the basement. His body was covered in lye to prevent the smell of decomposition from alerting us any sooner. Dead banker, dead agent, lost money and escaped killer – Garson took a big fall from grace and never regained it."

"You missed one important point." Garson stood in the doorway of the squad room while Lola and Mitch jumped to attention. Neither replied to his comment. "I have prided myself on my ability to read people." Garson slammed the door behind him and sat down, turning his chair backwards. "When someone tells me their story, I always have them repeat it, again, again and again. And I ask slightly different questions each time to ensure sincerity. I have questioned a hundred people on a hundred different occasions, and I can always tell if someone is lying. She was different. I questioned her repeatedly, first thing in the morning, during a meal. I always watched for a variation in her story, a tremor in her voice – something to give away a lie. Not once did she falter, not once did I get the feeling that she was lying to me. She was the perfect psychopath."

"She had no remorse," Garson continued. "Criminals make mistakes because, for a split second, they feel guilty, or realize that they are telling a lie. It's that split second when you can spot their lie and their whole story comes apart."

"You can't hold yourself responsible for one mistake," Mitch stood up from his chair and faced Garson. "Chances are no one could have spotted her lie."

"You're wrong!" Garson slammed his hand into a desk. "If I didn't think I had an infallible sense for lying, I might have dug deeper into her past, her financial history, her relationships, and found something wrong. Because of my one mistake, an agent died, and a killer escaped. Both of you are here to make sure I don't make that mistake again." Garson stepped to the table and spread out several victims' pictures like playing cards. Their faces formed a gruesome collage of violence. Lola and Mitch stood around the table looking to Garson for direction.

"Over the last four years, sixteen murders have come to my attention – fourteen males and two females. Most had above average incomes; two were middle class. Most lived in major cities, three in rural areas within an hour to a metropolitan center. All reported as break and enters. The victims were at home and were killed either by fatal knife wounds, gunshot to the chest or asphyxiation. In all of these cases, some valuables and money were taken, not large amounts, especially to warrant murder."

"Murder is relative – some will kill for very little," replied Lola.

"We'll deal with the philosophical arguments later, Ms. Prince," Garson replied. "These deaths have a common thread. I know it. I can feel it, even if I don't why. I need the two of you to help me expose it!" He pounded his fist into the table.

"What if there is no common thread?" Lola was less than enthused by the pep talk. "What if these are common break and enters? We could add thousands more to this pile and it all could still be random," she pointed to several photos. She expected an impassioned response and was not disappointed. Garson's voice rose.

"There is a relationship, I'm sure of it! The murders always occur during the fall and winter months in the same cities for the last four years. They appear to be 'break and enter' but the method of death is too brutal, too professional for a burglar to use. Death always occurs in the early morning hours. If the intent was theft, why not rob the home during the day when the resident wouldn't be home?"

"Maybe the killer has a day job?" Lola added with a smirk. Garson ignored the comment.

"Why are the methods of death so different? Are we talking about more than one killer – maybe working collaboratively?" asked Mitch.

"What would they gain if the take isn't enough to support one theft?" added Lola. Garson looked at her.

"Find the connection and you'll find our killer."

March 28, 2007

Dawson's interrogation

Dawson stood in the interview room at the police station and looked into the mirror at his reflection. He pulled out a comb and fussed with his hair.

"Hey pretty boy, have a seat," Garson said as he entered the room and sat at the table holding a sandwich in one hand.

"I hope this isn't going to take long. We're heading back home in the morning," answered Dawson.

"Just a few questions. Should have you out in a few minutes." Dawson sat down. Garson took a bite out of his sandwich. Dawson looked concerned.

"What's in your sandwich?" he asked.

"Peanut Butter. Want a bite?" He pushed the sandwich toward him. Dawson almost jumped out of his skin.

"Get it away from me. I'm allergic to nuts!" He screamed.

"I didn't know that," lied Garson as he looked at a doctor's report on Dawson's condition. "Peanut allergies, who would of thought? Did you know that twenty years ago, peanut allergies were unheard of? In this state alone, all local school boards have banned peanuts from schools? Peanuts! Not guns, not knives. Peanuts! Can you imagine, instead of metal detectors, having peanut detectors at each entrance?" He leaned, his peanut breath coming a little too close for comfort for Dawson. "Do you know the penalty for bringing peanuts into the school?"

"No, what?" answered Dawson squirming in his seat.

"Expulsion! For bringing peanuts in a school. Can you believe it? What kind of world do we live in where a few people with an obscure allergy decide what the rest of us eat?" He waved the remainder of his sandwich at Dawson. Some peanut butter fell onto the table, Dawson jumped up.

"What are you, psycho? Are you trying to kill me? Do you know what that stuff does to me? How would you like it if your windpipe slowly constricted until you couldn't breathe? If you so much as come near me again with that peanut butter, I'll sue your department for everything its worth!"

"Relax. I won't hurt a hair on your head," Garson pointed as Dawson instinctively touched his hair to make sure nothing was out of place. "Now tell about your hockey life, have you hurt anyone?" asked Garson. Dawson's eyes looked puzzled.

"Is that why I'm here? Look, I didn't hit anyone at the bar. I was just minding my own business when all the fighting began," Dawson pleaded.

"You misunderstood me; I'm not talking about the bar."

"Then what are you talking about?"

"I'm talking about a person who obsesses with his appearance. I used to work a case that involved a serial killer who was always cleaning his hair and washing his hands to remove his victim's blood. Do you have a similar affliction?" inquired Garson. Dawson jumped out of his chair in rage.

"You're insane! I don't know what you are talking about. I'm not saying anymore until I have a lawyer present. And get that sandwich away from me!" Dawson screamed.

Garson finished his sandwich and tossed the wrapper in the garbage. He left the room and noticed Mitch who had been watching from the one-way mirror.

"Any thoughts?"

"He seems pretty adamant that he's not a killer," Mitch mused.

"Murderers usually are," answered Garson.

November 21, 2006

Sunbeams from the skylights flowed down through the tree. The grass was lush and well manicured. The smell of pine wafted through the air, bringing the scent of the forest to the facility. The Thousand Oaks golf course was one of the busiest in all of Southern Ontario.

"It is championship day. One stroke lies between a tie for the lead and utter disgrace. Will he be a hero or a zero?" Tunny talked into his golf club like a microphone. Brick stepped up to the green, laid his putter down flat to get the proper lie. "The crowd is hushed, watching his preparation with anticipation." Brick put one finger in the air to test the wind, there was no visible breeze from any direction. The perfect day. He looked right and then left. His opponent rolled his eyes, apparently unable to take more drama. Finally, Brick took the shot with his putter.

The golf ball rolled down the green, past the water trap, skirting the waterfall, and missed the windmill by the smallest of inches. It continued down the slope toward the gaping hole. Losing momentum, it slowed down, wavering on the edge of the hole. The ball stopped, unable to fall in.

"Crunch!" Brick's foot slammed the green, the ball teetered and fell into the hole.

"And the crowd goes wild," Tunny screamed. The hockey players yelled while families with their children looked on. One mother gave Tunny a disapproving look.

"What are you looking at?" he snapped back at her. She turned away.

The All-Star Thousand Oaks Miniature Golf course was a prime indoor entertainment in the tourist trap city of Niagara Falls. Along the water's edge was one of the most beautiful and breathtaking sites in the world. No wonder people called it the honeymoon capital. But drive a few blocks away from the falls and there were a number of sites destined to strip a tourist of his hard-earned dollar. Casino, wax museum, arcades, and of course, the king of all sports – mini putt.

The team was looking to kill some time before the evening's match. The winner got all the beer he could drink in the after-game festivities. For these players, that was the only motivation they needed. Brick and Dawson marched toward the last hole tied for the lead. The rest of the team followed behind.

"Hard to believe that Brick is going to tie the knot in another month," said Chilly to Rook.

"Not really, there are plenty of stupid women out there," responded Tunny. Brick turned around.

"I'm right in front of you, you know," he yelled back and turned back to his shot.

"They say there's someone for everyone," Booker said to no one in particular.

"Dude, if that's the case, let's take Tunny back to the border for another strip search," added Dozer.

"Shut up pothead, or I'll sick her on you next time," Tunny responded.

"The whole team's invited to the wedding?" Chilly asked.

"You know it, even the coach!" answered Brick.

"I hope Presley isn't going to make any speeches." Dawson stated.

"Why thank you, thank you very much," Presley mimicked making a speech at the head table.

"Hey guys, when can I play mini putt?" Rook inquired as he carried a golf bag with everyone's putters.

"Shut up kid and let the grownups talk!" sniped Dawson.

"You going to the wedding Stefan?" asked Chilly.

"Are there going to be any French woman there?" Stefan answered.

"The bride is from Montreal, what do you think?" responded Chilly.

"Mais oui – I will show the French women how to dance," Stefan continued.

"Maybe you could teach me some sexy French words?" asked Dozer. "Dude, nothing I try seems to work with the ladies."

"Sounds like your hockey game – your aim is so bad that you couldn't hit water if you fell out of a boat,' Tunny laughed.

Taj ate his chocolate bar and played through three holes during the conversation. He ran and bounced around the green like a ping-pong ball, hitting the ball quickly barely letting it stop. He accidentally bumped into Dawson.

"Does that chocolate bar have nuts?" Dawson asked with a trace of fear in his voice. Taj looked at the wrapper.

"This product may contain nuts or nut by-products. Why do you ask?"

"I'm allergic, just a trace of nuts and my throat constricts, and I can barely breathe," Dawson said.

"Well you did choke at the last hockey game," Booker commented. Taj ran away from Dawson, stepping on Tunny's foot.

"Slow down you little pip-squeak," yelled Tunny. "If you stood still for more than one second, I could squash you like a bug." Taj looked up to Tunny.

"In my home country of India, the bug is a revered creature," Taj commented in his Indian accent.

"Your home country? Jesus Taj, you were born in Toronto for crying out loud," Tunny responded.

Brick put his finger to his mouth. Silence pervaded the green. Behind them several teenage boys were laughing amongst themselves. The players looked back at the teenagers who immediately stopped laughing. Brick placed his orange ball on the mat at the front of the 18th hole. This was the toughest hole on the course. He took his well-used putter and lined up the ball. The wrap on the handle was starting to come off and the sticky residue made his hand itch. He looked ahead and saw an obstacle to be moved. He dropped his club and strolled ahead to the flag.

"What are you doing?" yelled Dawson. "Stop delaying the game!" Brick looked back and smiled. He stepped on to the green and pulled several dead pine needles off of the course. "There! Now there's no excuse for not taking your shot!" Dawson ran his hand through his hair.

"Listen to the metrosexual! Take the shot!" yelled Tunny. Brick concentrated and bent his knees. He hit the ball hard enough to go over an incline and it rested on the far right of the par four hole.

"Playing it safe, eh?" said Dawson. "Watch my shot. It's better to go big or go home."

"If you miss this shot, you better go home. I have money on you," yelled Tunny.

"Nothing like the added pressure of gambling," added Chilly.

"Did you know that unlike other sports, golfers only get paid if they win? Last year lots of professional golfers had zero tournament winnings. They basically played for nothing," Booker commented.

"It's a good thing hockey isn't golf," mentioned Presley.

"Watch, listen, and learn," Dawson hit the ball going for the shorter, riskier route through the water trap. The ball teetered near the edge but stayed on the fairway, significantly closer to the hole than Brick's shot.

"Booyah! And that, my friends, is how the game of golf is played," Dawson exclaimed.

"The hole is far from over," Brick answered.

"Hey Brick, this fiancée of yours. How long have you been seeing her?" asked Chilly.

"Couple of years, I guess. Why do you ask?" responded Brick.

"Just wondering what made you pop the question? You don't have a little one on the way, do you?" Chilly smirked.

"No, we just thought it was time. Oh, and she asked me," Brick answered. All the players looked at him in disbelief.

"Did she give up on you asking her?" questioned Chilly.

"Don't answer that mon ami," interjected Stefan. "Today's woman wants to be in control of her relationships. In control of her career. Today's woman is not afraid to take what she wants."

"Thanks for this month's summary of Vogue magazine, taunted Tunny. "The problem is that the man is supposed to ask the woman to marry, not the other way around. How can you look me in the eyes?"

Brick walked over to Tunny and looked down into his eyes. "She asked. I said yes. Deal with it!" Brick returned to the golf game.

"Wow! I wonder if I could get a woman to propose to me?" asked Dozer.

"Well if you took a shower, shaved that horrible beard, put on some clean clothes, replaced some of your broken teeth, flashed some money, wore some cologne, and said something intelligent for once, you might get a woman who wasn't disgusted by you," Tunny laughed. Dozer threw a club that barely missed the side of Tunny's head. Rook ran over to the neighboring green to pick it up.

"Trying to play a game of golf here," Dawson interrupted. He lined up his shot; there were little sand traps throughout the fairway ready to swallow his ball. At the end, the flag rested on a small green island where any shot hit too hard would be lost in the surrounding pond. Dawson aimed for the far right of the green trying to turn the corner for the home stretch. He took the shot, he hit it lightly, knowing that the gravity of the down slope would do the work. The ball moved slowly and stopped just before the corner, making it difficult to reach the hole in three strokes.

"Too bad – you're made yourself a tough shot," commented Chilly.

"Tell me something I don't know," yelled Dawson. He turned to see two teenage girls watching and straightened his hair for their benefit.

"Sweet onion ass," commented Tunny as the girls giggled at Dawson. "A butt so sweet it will make you cry."

"Cry? Those girls would laugh if you approached them Tunny – you're old enough to be their dad," said Rook.

"We'll see about that. Remember, what happens in Niagara Falls, stays in Niagara Falls," Tunny pointed with his finger to the team.

"If you pedophiles can keep quiet for a minute, I'm about to take my shot," interjected Brick. He lined up the shot and bit his lip as he composed himself. He swung his putter and hit the ball. The ball passed the water trap and missed the rock obstacle. It slid down the green before coming to rest four feet closer to the hole than Dawson's ball.

"Brick you're a genius. You could eagle this hole," Rook exclaimed.

"I don't think Brick has ever heard his name and the word genius spoken together. Anybody want to double or nothing their bets with me?" No one spoke until Taj whizzed by placing a twenty in Tunny's hand.

"I'll take those odds," Taj replied and disappeared.

"A fool and his money. . . ." Tunny started.

Dawson's putter took the approach shot. Unfortunately, a small rock caught the edge of the ball and spun it into the corner away from the hole.

"The biggest fool doesn't shut up when I'm putting," Dawson yelled, frustrated by the result of his shot. Tunny decided not to comment. Brick could barely contain his smile.

"Lots of game left," he commented.

"Whoa! This game can go either way dude," added Dozer smoking a joint while sitting on a nearby bench. He looked for a makeshift ashtray and flicked his ashes into a sand trap. "You guys should be this focused in a hockey game." Dozer took another drag and gazed up with a smile on his face.

"Is it just me or does it seem that every once in awhile, Dozer has something inspirational to say?" asked Booker.

"It's just you," replied Tunny.

"Can you guys hurry up and finish this game? We're supposed to be at the rink in half an hour," stated Presley.

"Keep your shirt on, what's the rush? Do you want to listen to one of the coach's pregame rants about how lousy a team we are?" Tunny asked.

"No, but it won't hurt to start taking the games more seriously. If we start winning a few games, maybe we stand a chance of making the playoffs," Presley shot back.

"We better start doing something different soon or we're going to be basement dwellers all season long," Tunny answered.

"Cry me a river. Can I take my shot?" Dawson asked.

"Go ahead. Don't choke like you do on the ice, pretty boy" yelled Tunny.

Dawson ignored the jibes and took the shot. He swung his club lightly and watched the ball head for the open hole. "Take out the flag," he yelled to Rook. Rook grabbed the flag and tossed it over to the side. The ball slid down the slope, veering left and right as it picked up speed hitting the little speed bumps. The ball swung toward the hole.

"Yes!" Dawson screamed. The ball flew toward the hole and sailed directly over it. It traveled past the hole and into the water, sinking to the bottom. "No!" Dawson cried. "That's not fair!"

"Welcome to an episode on my life," replied Rook and reached into the water to fish out the ball. He placed it on the green near where it went into the water.

"Better add a second stroke," commented Stefan.

"Thanks for stating the obvious," answered Dawson looking dejected. He looked over at the teenaged girls. "Hey Tunny, I think the girls are calling for you." The whole team watched as the two teenage girls left the green and headed for the concession stand.

"Come to Daddy," Tunny yelled as the girls ignored his call.

"Dawson's seeing things. It's your shot Brick," said Presley. "You stroke this, and the game is yours." Brick nodded and his face looked intense. He just had to make a short putt toward the fairway, away from the rock blocking the hole. One shot to victory.

"You can do it Brick!" Booker yelled.

"Stop yelling, you'll distract him," cried Rook.

"You know he's going to choke!" commented Dawson.

The ball rolled down the green to the island green. The hole was at the highest point – too hard and it passed the hole, too soft and it fell back. Brick's shot flowed nicely, dead on to victory. As the ball climbed to the lip of the hole, its speed slowed. Suddenly it stopped, hitting a small pebble. The ball's momentum halted and slid backward. It swung to the right and rolled into the water trap. Tunny was irate because he thought he lost the bet. He ran over to the hole and picked up the small stone.

"Who put that there!" he yelled while Dawson smiled. Tunny slammed his club into the water and the spray splashed a passing child. The incident caught the attention of the manager watching from the clubhouse.

"Relax, you almost hit the kids over there," warned Chilly.

"Relax? You expect me to believe that a stone happened to be placed in front of the hole during Brick's shot? Right when Dawson distracted the team with those girls? Dawson, you are the world's biggest cheater!" Tunny stabbed his finger at him.

"I didn't cheat," Dawson yelled. "Besides, we're even. We both have to putt to the hole to win. It's not over yet."

"I'm afraid it is," the manager stepped onto the green with Tunny's club in his hand. "I am asking all of you to leave."

"Oh, come on, is this for real? You are kicking us off a miniature golf course? You've got to be kidding." Tunny complained.

"Everybody calm down, I'm sure we can reach a compromise here." Presley looked at the Manager. "I am the captain of the team and I speak for the group. We'll just play two more shots and were out of here. No trouble! Okay?"

"Make it quick," the manager replied, "and no more trouble. Or I call the police."

"No trouble, you have my promise," Presley assured him.

Suddenly a yell of fire pierced the air. The manager turned to see hole seventeen on fire. Dozer was feverishly trying to pat the flames out that had spread from his discarded joint.

All the players ran over and tried to stamp out the flames on the green. In their enthusiasm, they split the green in two. Rook, Tunny, Booker, and Chilly fell into the water.

"Well, that's refreshing," commented Rook as the water only came up to his ankles.

"Don't move!" yelled the manager. "The police are on their way!"

The team sat on a nearby bench with their heads in their hands. Dozer tried to sit down on the bench, but Tunny kicked him off.

"Great. We must be the first hockey team that gets thrown into jail for destroying a mini putt. What do think the coach will say?" Tunny cried

"Nothing," commented Presley. "I've got a feeling that we not going to make the game tonight."

November 28, 2006

The car drove down the snowy suburban street. The cold winds blew off of Lake Michigan, sending a gust up against the car. Chicago was living up to its reputation as the windy city. Garson took another swig of his black coffee. He turned up the defroster, trying to heat up the car. He turned down Maple Crest Street – cars were parked in front of a small ranch style home. Half brick and half wood, the homes in this neighborhood were quaint, their architecture reminiscent of the eighties. Garson pulled his car to a stop and opened his door. It crunched against a crusty snowbank. He walked up the sidewalk and flashed his badge at a policeman guarding the entrance. He ducked under the crime scene tape.

The door was open, inviting him to enter. Red lights flashed behind him and a neighbor's dog barked across the street. Garson pulled out a pair of gloves and walked into the foyer. To his right in the hall sat a set of ladies' golf clubs. He walked forward and turned to his left, crossing into the living room. She was sitting on the couch. Her sightless eyes looked straight ahead to the opposite wall. A plastic bag was laying at her feet. He walked to the back of the couch and ran his hand along the top. The white leather was soft to the touch. Suddenly, something sticky caught his hand – he looked down and saw a black residue. He stood up and continued around the room. In front of the couch, some women's magazines were scattered on the coffee table.

Garson turned and looked at the dead woman. Thirty-five, athletic, red hair, pleasant looking, dressed in a sweat suit and sneakers. *Just back from a jog?* Beside the magazines sat a half-eaten bowl of pretzels and dip. *A snacker. At least she wasn't one of these women that starve themselves to death.* He looked again at her body. *Bad choice of words.* Her cheeks were pink and the blood vessels in her eyes had popped giving her a ghastly expression. *Did you even know your attacker was behind you?* He looked at her fingers – no sign of struggle. *Wouldn't she have fought her attacker?* Footsteps in the foyer interrupted his thoughts.

"Did anyone hear anything?" Garson asked.

"Nothing," answered Mitch. His jacket was tied tight around his chest as he looked in his notepad. "I canvassed the homes on either side and down the street. No one heard anything. None of neighbors saw anyone strange on the street over the last 24 hours. No deliverymen, paperboys, nothing. The neighbor across the street was the one who discovered her. Mrs. Palino, aged 64, walks her dog religiously every morning at 6am. When she walked by here, she noticed the door was ajar. She knocked. When no one answered, she walked in and found her."

"Did Mrs. Palino call 911 on this phone?" Garson motioned to the coffee table.

"No. She was so spooked that she went home and called from there. She hasn't come back since the discovery," Mitch responded.

"Door ajar, the killer wanted the body to be found," stated Garson.

"That's not all," both men turned to see Lola standing on the stairwell. Her face was serious as she tapped furiously into her phone. "The study upstairs is a mess, like someone was looking for something. Her purse was torn inside out and spread all over the floor. Her laptop was smashed into a dozen pieces. If there was anything valuable on the hard drive, it will be hard to retrieve. On one of the walls, every book is knocked off the shelf except one." Lola walked into the room waiting for the men to ask.

"Which book?" Mitch had to ask.

"*How to Stay Organized*," Lola replied.

"Our murderer is trying to be funny. It's almost like he gets a laugh by leaving us those clues." Garson shook his head

"What do you think he's looking for?" asked Mitch.

"Maybe just valuables or a wall safe? Maybe important information on the computer?" states Garson. "What did she do?"

"Current events writer – feel good stories for the masses, like dressed up dogs," answered Lola.

"That will make you some enemies," Mitch replied.

"Enough sarcasm. I want both of you to come into the living room. Lola go behind the couch, Mitch, get in front of the victim," commanded Garson. Both officers took their positions. Garson looked at Mitch. "What do you see?" Mitch looked at the victim.

"Victim is seated in the middle of the couch, slight abrasion on the left hand. Lipstick smeared on chin. Adjacent chair has a pile of workout clothes. She can't have too many guests over. There are chips, dip, empty glass, and couple of crumpled napkins. She may have worked out but liked junk food." Mitch looked up at the wall. "No pictures of family, but a few awards – mostly for local news stories. Probably proud of her work."

"Or narcissistic," added Lola sarcastically.

"Continue," Garson motioned.

"The bookshelf is mostly bare except for a few books on cooking, golf, journalism. No knickknacks. I guess she wasn't into trinkets."

"And we women love our trinkets," commented Lola.

"And what don't you see?" asked Garson. Mitch looked closely at her hands.

"Except for the left hand, there's no sign of struggle. For an athletic woman, I would have expected more of a fight. The bag at her feet couldn't have been put over her head easily. She would have fought back. How did her attacker get her so easily?"

"What are you missing?" Garson repeated. Mitch looked closely, trying to find the missing object. Then he saw it.

"The cup! There is food left over but the cup is empty. Maybe there was something in the drink to drug her," he answered.

"Exactly. Bag it and tag it. Make sure toxicology runs some tests," Garson spoke. He turned his attention to Lola while Mitch gathered evidence. "Tell me what you see from behind the couch."

"White leather couch, she doesn't do a good job of vacuuming underneath. I can see dust bunnies and some loose change. There is sticky black residue near the bottom of couch, possibly transfer from the attacker. I'll cut a piece of the couch and send it to the lab. Victim's head has slight bruising on neck, possible pressure from attacker's fingertips when he had the bag over her head."

"Good. Now tell me what you don't see?" asked Garson. Lola looked around the room trying to spot what's missing. Her eyes scanned the coffee table. *Magazines, food – what isn't here?*

"Did the officer on the scene touch anything in this room?" Garson asked.

"No. Once he established the victim was dead, he put up the crime tape." Lola answered.

"Was the TV on?" Garson questioned.

"No. Why?" Lola responded.

"The victim was likely watching television when she was killed. Otherwise she might not have been surprised. Why is the television off?" Garson asked.

"Because the killer didn't want to alert the neighbors with the noise?" Lola stated weakly.

"Then why leave the door open for the neighbor to pop in? No, I don't buy it. Besides what's missing if the TV was turned off?" growled Garson.

"The remote. Where is it?" she asked. Garson reached into the drawer of the coffee table and pulled out the remote.

"Dead people don't put away the remote."

"Why bother putting away the remote or shutting off the TV?" Lola was puzzled.

"Check the station on the satellite tuner and see what was playing last night," said Garson.

"You think the killer didn't want us to see what was on when she was killed?" asked Lola.

"That is what you have to find out. When the coroner gives the time of death, get a list of stations and the shows playing around that time." Garson walked toward the door.

"Jesus, Garson! The woman has a satellite dish, could be hundreds of channels broadcasting at that time," Lola added.

"Don't bring me problems, bring me solutions," answered Garson. "If I don't show some progress on this case soon, my captain is going to shut us down. Get a profile of our victim – I'm sure there are a lot of shows that she wouldn't watch. Narrow it down to the ones she would. Do you still think this murder is random? A burglar caught in the act?"

"My intuition agrees with you Garson, but I'm not sold that the other murders are all connected," Lola answered.

"One murder at a time," stated Garson as he walked out the front door. "One murder at a time."

March 28, 2007

Chilly's interrogation

"Think you're a good hockey player, don't you?" Garson looked straight at Chilly.

"Pardon me?" Chilly answered.

"Some of the other players say you're the player to watch. If anyone has a chance to advance to the next level, you're the one."

"My teammates are being generous – nothing is guaranteed," Chilly asked.

"Sounds like you'll be moving on soon. I hate to see someone drag your career down," said Garson.

"Drag me down? How?" Chilly looked confused.

"When one of your teammates goes to jail, I'd hate to see you brought down as an accomplice," Garson took another drink of his coffee.

"Goes to jail? That doesn't narrow it down on my team. Do you know much about the Assassins, Officer Garson?"

"Why don't you enlighten me?" asked Garson.

"My team has trouble with the law on every road trip. We've been stopped at the border, arrested for attacking our own bus, brawled at taverns in both countries. We've been kicked out of hotels and restaurants, stopped for speeding, and charged with lewd conduct. Trust me, no behavior is too juvenile for the Assassins. So, if you want to ask me about what could cause one of our players to go to jail, you're going to have to be a bit more specific." Chilly was faintly amused.

"I see," Garson scratched his chin and decided to pursue another line of questioning. "Tell me, how much does a bush-league hockey player make these days?"

"In this league, not very much. Maybe 30 grand for the season. We get meal and hotel allowances but they don't always cover everything. Most of the guys go back to work in the summer, some to family businesses. Why? You thinking of leaving the police force and joining up?" Chilly smirked.

"You have a tough lifestyle to resist. Low pay, living out of cheap hotels and eating badly. I already live that lifestyle now," Garson smiled. "Why drives you guys to play?"

"I take it you never played hockey before?" Chilly asked.

"Not a lot of interest for a young black boy living in Houston, Texas," said Garson.

"Then you wouldn't understand.," Chilly shot back.

"Try me." Garson asked. Chilly stood and paced the room.

"Have you ever had a moment when you forgot everything around you? All your problems seem small. You truly live in the moment. That's what the game of hockey is like. One puck, a little piece of frozen rubber determines whether you win or lose. Have you ever had something that gave you such purpose?" Chilly asked.

"I used to think police work gave me that same kind of feeling. Now I'm not so sure," Garson answered honestly. "Breaking down the details to find the truth. To catch the bad guys. I may not understand your love of hockey, but I think I understand why you play. What I don't understand is why people kill?"

November 29, 2006

"The score is tied after five minutes of overtime," the announcer yelled to the half-filled hockey rink. The fans milled around excited by the thrilling climax to the game. "The best three shooters will take turns skating against the opposing goalie. As visiting team, the Assassins go first." Both benches gathered around their coaching staff.

"We've been in Chicago for two days now. We have a chance to pick up a road win tonight. We need this!" The Coach bellowed as the Assassins players formed a semi-circle around the bench. "I want my best three forwards setting this up. Tunny, Presley, and Chilly – don't let us down."

If I make this, maybe the scouts will finally take me up to the farm club, thought Chilly. *If I ever wanted a chance, this is my time . . .*

"Hey superstar. Get your head into the game. Why don't you watch how a real star sets up a penalty shot," taunted Tunny. Chilly sat up on the bench as all eyes watched Tunny skate to center ice. An elbow jabbed Chilly in the side.

"Quite a game, eh?" asked Rook.

"We've played pretty good. Doesn't hurt that the Chicago Fire are missing a few key players due to injuries."

"Shush!" yelled Taj. "Tunny is taking the shot."

The referee blew the whistle. Tunny circled center ice as the fans screamed obscenities. Tunny looked up – *stupid fans*. He focused on the end of the ice. The goaltender slapped his pads with his stick. He stood slightly off center, favoring the right side of the net. Tunny smiled. *Like taking candy from a baby.* He stick handled past the blue line as the goaltender slid back into his net. Tunny lined up his shot for the top left corner. The goaltender anticipated and came out of his net to cut down on the angle. Tunny noticed the motion and tried to deke around. He saw empty space and turned as a beer bottle hit his face screen dead on. He shot the puck, but the distraction made him miss the empty side of the net. Tunny was furious and charged the stands trying to find the offender. The referees came and pulled him off the glass screen.

"Call the cops, I was robbed. I had that goal! I'll kill you. I'll kill all of you!" he screamed. Rook and Chilly grabbed him from the referees and took him to the bench.

"Come on ref," screamed the Coach. He yelled so loud his face turned red. "That's interference! The goal should count automatically." The referee ignored the coach's screams and skated over to the timekeeper's box. This infuriated the Coach even more and he jumped on the ice. His shoes were flat soled and had no traction. He took two steps and fell flat on his back. The coach exploded. Presley and Taj grabbed him under his arms and lifted him back to the bench.

"Don't take me there," he screamed. "Take me to the timekeeper's box!" Presley shrugged his shoulder and nodded at Taj as they carried him over. They dropped him off in front of the referee, but unfortunately, Coach still had terrible balance in his shoes. This time he fell forward and his hand grazed the ref on the shoulder.

"You're out of this game! Go to the dressing room immediately!" the referee pointed to the bench, thinking the coach was attacking him.

"It was all a mistake," the Coach wailed. "I have no balance," as he fell back to the ice.

"If you say one more word," the referee answered, "I will call the game and the Fire will get the automatic win!" The Coach tried to answer but Taj covered his mouth. They tried to slide him back to the bench. He fell twice more before Taj pulled him the reminder of the distance.

"What are we going to do?" Brick asked as the Coach walked by him towards the dressing rooms.

"Hope to God your other teammates don't miss! Presley you're in charge while I'm banned from the ice," Coach yelled to his captain.

"You had better win!" as he marched through the access way under the stands and into the dressing room. He smashed a hockey stick into a garbage can and then slammed the dressing room door shut behind him.

"He didn't have any luck pleading our case to the referee," Presley said to the team.

"This rink is a rip-off!" Dawson replied.

The whistle blew and the Chicago Fire sent one of their young scoring aces to try to beat me. I was unsettled in net and the young skater closed the distance in seconds. Everyone on the bench watched me in anticipation, unsure of my goal tendering ability. The player came on my right and motioned to the top right-hand corner. I reacted and the player faked left as I scrambled to recover. As the player backhanded his shot, it bounced harmlessly off the post. I was lucky.

"All right," yelled Stefan. They say a goaltender's best friend is his goalpost."

"Everyone gather round," asked Presley. The team gathered around him from the bench.

"I think you should go high," commented Dawson.

"No way, deke around him. The goalie won't expect the same trick twice," Rook added.

"Go to the low side left, he's got a weak glove hand," mentioned Brick.

"Watch out for bottles," advised Tunny.

"Guys – thanks for the advice but I'm just going to wing it. I'll see what opening the goalie gives me," Presley confidently replied. "Just remember, a third of the time, goaltenders drift to the left side," Booker slapped Presley on the back as he skated to center ice.

The fans screamed and banged on the glass trying to distract him. Presley looked over at the official. *Come on, blow the whistle!* The referee skated to the far boards and motioned for play to begin. Presley stared at the goaltender and pushed the puck ahead with his stick. *Time to make my team proud.* He skated in, hoping the goaltender would make a mistake. The goaltender slowly skated back into his crease. *Come on, show me an opening!* He skated closer to the goaltender's left, heading toward the right. The goalie moved his stick to check the puck away.

Ah-ha, Presley thought. He pulled the puck back as the goalie stick came forward. The momentum of the stick pulled the goalie from the net. The stick missed the puck and Presley skated around the goalie to bury the puck high into the net.

"Clang!"

The puck rebounded off of the crossbar and into the glass behind the net. The Assassins groaned from the bench. Presley skated back to the bench with the weight of the team on his back.

"I'm sorry guys. I should have found the back of net," he offered.

"Thanks for missing an empty net," commented Tunny.

"Dude, shut up," replied Dozer. "Chilly still has his shot."

"Oh, thank God, we're saved," Tunny mocked as he gestured with a hand over his heart.

"Will you guys stop jawing? The Fire is sending their youngest center to take the next shot," said Rook. The team watched the young player, Arnold Avery, or as his teammates called him – Double A. He was a forward with definite potential to make the farm club and beyond. He skated to center ice and awaited the whistle from the referee. For the first time, the stadium was quiet, as the fans pinned their hopes on the shot of a nineteen-year-old.

"I hope he misses," whispered Brick.

The whistle blew and Avery skated around the puck while I looked out at the incoming sharpshooter.

"He's dead!" commented Dawson on my chances to stop the puck.

Avery skated at breakneck speed closing the distance between him and the net in seconds. All watched as he approached halfway between the net and the blue line. He placed the blade of the stick on the puck forcing it to rest on the stick blade instead of the ice. He skated forward with the puck off of the ice. I looked at him like he was out of his mind. Avery twisted his body around and brought the stick blade to his shoulder and angled it down like a swing of tennis racket. I was caught totally off guard as the puck sailed by my face and into the back of the net. The rinks roared its approval.

"What a hot dog! That's not a legal goal?" yelled Tunny.

"Wait, the ref has his arm up! What's the call?" Taj yelled excitedly. Presley skated over to the timekeeper's box where the ref and the Chicago Fire's captain were heatedly discussing the goal.

"What do you mean the goal is disallowed? That was a beautiful goal!" Avery yelled.

"The stick went above the shoulder! No goal!" the ref answered.

"It was so obvious that the stick was too high – I can't believe we're even discussing this," Presley yelled, making sure the ref's decision stands. Presley skated back to the Assassin's bench where everyone looked at him with excitement.

"Goal doesn't count," he pointed to the scoreboard as the timekeeper dropped the goal off the scoreboard," Presley answered.

"Dude, about time we caught a break," replied Dozer.

"Chilly – you're up." Presley pointed to center ice.

"You can do it!" Dawson slapped his back.

"Look for an opening. Most of the time, a goal is scored below the waist," advised Booker.

"Be the puck," Taj offered his Zen like advice.

Chilly ignored it all, trusting his instincts to take him to the net. There was a time as a kid, if he thought too much about the play beforehand, he'd end up screwing it up. But when he was in the zone, that perfect playing moment when time slowed down, his instincts kicked in and served him well. He skated to center ice awaiting the whistle. It was hard to hear anything as the fans screamed for his blood. *Well, here's a chance to become a hero.*

The whistle blew and Chilly attacked the puck. Unlike the previous players, he headed neither left or right, but straight at the goaltender. He stared in the goaltender eyes. His body shifted back and forth from the exertion. The noise from the fans was deafening. His teammates yelled and the opposing players tried to shake him from his target. He crossed the blue line and immediately pointed his stick to the upper right-hand corner. He pumped his stick to slap the puck to that target and the goaltender reached with his glove to cover the hole. Chilly faked the shot causing the goaltender to overextend. Before he could recover, Chilly slapped it into the low left-hand corner. The red light flashed. He scored!

He skated to the Assassins bench and was mobbed by his teammates.

"You did it!"

"Beautiful shot!"

"I knew you could do it!" Before Chilly could enjoy more congratulations, a beer bottle hit the back of his helmet. And then another and another. The sky was awash with pop and beer bottles flying from the stands. Tunny swung his stick and hit one back at the fans.

"Take that!" he yelled at no one in particular.

The referee blew his whistle repeatedly and gestured his arms.

"The game is called! The Assassins are the winners!" The referee pointed to the Assassin's bench. "Go to your dressing room. Now! Security will take these fans out." The Assassins exited the bench. A rabid fan reached down and tried to pull Taj upwards. Brick slapped the fan's hand causing him to drop Taj. The team retreated through the hallway under the stands and into the dressing room.

"Yo Coach," yelled Dozer, "we won!"

"I knew you could do it! Now get inside and lock the door," answered the Coach.

"Why?" asked Rook as he latched the bolt across the door. The hammering at the door answered his question.

"Those fans are insane. We have to hold them off until the cops come," Stefan commented as he helped push an equipment locker against the door.

"I say let them in and I'll take them out one at a time," Tunny bragged.

"Sounds like something a rock head would say," added Dawson.

"Can you guys talk after we finish moving the locker in front of the door?" Stefan asked, finding it hard to lug the locker by himself. Three other players helped him.

"That should hold them. Now everyone get your gear off and get dressed. We're getting out of here!" Presley commanded.

"In most reported crimes, police response is less than fifteen minutes. We should be able to hold out that long," Booker described.

"That's fascinating, Poindexter. Why don't you go out and tell those fans that they better attack us quickly," Dawson replied pulling off his skates.

"Can you guys hurry up?" Taj answered changing to his street clothes.

"How does he do that? I barely have my skates off!" Rook exclaimed.

"I swear the guy wears a Velcro one piece for all his gear that he pulls on and off," answered Chilly. The banging at the door continued.

"You'd be smart to undress as quickly as Taj. All the gear in the world is not going to protect you from that mob," yelled the Coach. Dawson turned on the shower.

"Do we have time to shower?" Rook asked.

"No, but little buttercup can't go outside without his hair all primped." Tunny laughed.

Stefan stepped next to Dozer.

"Mon dieu! Do ever you stink!" Stefan cried.

"Dude, we all stink. No time for a shower. Gotta save our lives," said Dozer.

"The banging's stopped. See if anyone is outside." Coach motioned to the door. Since Taj was dressed, he ran over.

"I'm not seeing anyone," Taj says quickly as he peered under the door.

"Well, I'm not sold!" added Booker and took his hockey stick and slid it under the door. He slid it right and then left.

"What are you looking for?" asked Brick. The stick stopped as it hit someone's boot. Many hands pulled the stick from Booker's hands out from under the door. He heard the stick break in half and the pieces were thrown at the door. Booker jumped back.

"We're not going that way. Anybody have any ideas?" Everyone looked around. Hockey dressing rooms were notoriously small – one entrance, one exit.

"We could go high," offered Dozer.

"Getting high and pretending nothing's happening isn't going to help," yelled Dawson.

"No, go high," as Dozer pointed to the ceiling and the multipaneled ceiling tiles. Chilly jumped on the player's bench and pushed one of the tiles up. He accessed the dark crawlspace and then turned back to his team.

"Leave your gear behind and follow me."

Minutes later, Chilly pulled up a tile and looked down an empty hallway. *I can't see anybody.* He almost slid down when a security guard rushed by underneath.

"Code blue, I repeat code blue," the guard yelled into the walkie-talkie. "Get the city police in here pronto. These fans are about to break down the dressing room door!" His voice faded as he rushed down the corridor. Chilly motioned to Rook.

"We have to get out of here now!" He cracked open the tile and jumped to the floor below. Behind him, tiles cracked and broke as team members tumbled to the floor, some not very gracefully. The Coach winced as he fell on his tailbone. Brick and Presley hoisted Taj down to the ground. The whole team halted in the corridor as they heard their dressing room door splintering into pieces.

"Which way is out?" asked Rook.

"I think it's the corridor to the right," offered Booker.

"You think? Well, we know from firsthand experience how good your advice is," commented Tunny. Tunny barely finished his sentence as he rounded the right corner and watched about twenty fans smashing the remains of their door. One turned to see Tunny gawking at them.

"It's the hockey team. Get them!" yelled a large fan wearing a trucker's cap. Tunny was indignant.

"We can take them," he yelled. He turned and saw the rest of the team stampeding away in the opposite direction. Tunny followed them into the tunnels of the stadium. They quickly sped out into the loading zone area.

"There's the exit," Booker pointed. The team rushed through into the back parking lot of the stadium.

"There's the bus!" yelled Stefan.

As they approached the bus, they could see another angry mob was pelting it with rocks. The mob turned to face the team.

"Oh crap!" Brick said. Coach ran at the mob full tilt.

"He's going to get killed!" Presley yelled and chased after him. The Coach stopped in front of about twenty angry fans that were ready to attack him.

"They're coming," he stooped over out of breath. "The Assassins hockey team – they're right behind us!" The Coach pointed back to the door as several pursuing fans came rushing through.

"Get them!" The mob yelled and the two angry groups of fans collided, neither side listening to the protest of the others. They were a sea of arms and legs, moving in all directions. They were all too angry to realize their mistake.

"Quick thinking, Coach," Presley whispered into his ear. Coach nodded and picked up a rock from the ground and tossed it at the bus.

"Take that you damn Assassins – you bunch of cheats!" The other players took the gesture and followed suit.

"Stupid losers," yelled Dawson.

"Couldn't fight your way out of wet paper bag," added Tunny.

"You have no talent," yelled Chilly.

"Bunch of no name drug users," cried Dozer. The rest of the team looked at him. "Hey its what I know," he answered.

Taj reached down to pick up a huge rock. "Take that you old, slow hockey team." A strong hand reached behind him and stopped him from throwing the rock.

"The lot of you are under arrest for public nuisance" the Chicago police officer commanded. The rest of team turned and saw several paddy wagons loading up the mob by the loading doors.

"Actually officer, you'll find this pretty funny. We are the team that everyone is trying to attack. We'd like to press charges against them," pointed Presley. The cop laughed.

"Good story. I'm sure the team's not stupid enough to be anywhere near this mess. You can explain it all to the booking officer downtown," the officer said as he pulled out his handcuffs.

Chapter 7   *The Kickoff*

November 29, 2006

The lights of downtown Chicago faded in the distance as Lola and Mitch drove along Lake Michigan. Traffic was light as the sound of container trucks headed towards the harbor. They passed the science museum and drove toward the University of Chicago. Mitch warmed his hands on the heater while Lola deftly handled the wheel.

"What's your take on Garson? Are all his murder cases related?" Lola asked.

"For his sake I hope so. He is so keyed into making these cases into a major serial killer. He really wants to redeem himself for his past case," Mitch answered.

"Do you think he's reading into the crime scenes?"

"The analysis of the crime scenes seems to prove that they are premeditated. I just don't see enough correlation to tell me it's the same killer. None of these people knew each other. What possible connection could all of these people have?" Mitch questioned.

"Maybe it's the random theory," Lola added as she turned down a side street. "What if the killer has no profile for his victims. He kills the people he meets on the street. Maybe these victims were just unfortunate enough to fall in the killer's crosshairs when he gets the urge to kill. He follows them home and studies their habits before robbing and killing them."

"But what would be the motivation? Serial killers always kill a specific type of person usually related to an earlier trauma in their life. Remember the Zygote murders? The guy killed college girls. He was enacting his rage at being dumped by his college girlfriend and saw her in each of his victims," Severn responded.

"Maybe he kills for the sake of killing. You can try to profile him all you want – who really knows what can drive a man to murder?" wondered Lola.

"Money and infidelity are the top two," Mitch answered, "otherwise the killer might just be sadistic. But that's the problem. You can't always wrap things up in a neat bow. Murder is messy, sometimes it just happens."

"Maybe, but my gut tells me that there is a connection, we just haven't found it yet." Lola drove the rental car into the hotel parking lot. She shut off the engine and turned to Mitch.

"What does your gut tell you now?" she asked.

"My gut tells me I missed supper," Mitch laughed. "You want to order some room service?" he said as they both exited the car and headed indoors to the lobby.

"Are you trying to get into my hotel room, Brown?" Lola smiled.

"Lola, why do you always call me Brown?" Mitch asked as they passed through the sliding doors into the heat.

"Didn't you ever read the Peanuts comic strip as a kid?" Lola asked as they entered the main lobby, walking by the main desk.

"Sure, I loved Snoopy lying on the doghouse. What does that have to do with me?" Mitch puzzled. He pressed the button for the elevator door.

"Don't forget his owner, Charlie Brown," Lola stepped into the elevator, and the door closed behind them.

"You're comparing me to Charlie Brown. The kid that nobody likes?" protested Mitch.

"No! That's not it," Lola chuckled. "I call you 'Brown' because he always tries but loses. Do you remember the girl Lucy who always sets him up to kick a football?" They stepped out of the elevator and walked down the hallway.

"Yes, and she always pulls the football away at the last second." Mitch's feet stopped in the hallway. "What are you trying to tell me, Lola? Every time I ask you out, you're going to turn me down?"

"No, silly," she said as she swiped her room key through the slot. "I'm just saying, keep trying, Brown. Maybe some day, I won't pull the football away," Lola blew a kiss as she closed her hotel room door behind her.

Mitch walked down the hallway towards his room. He walked through the door and took off his shoes at the side of the bed. He laid down and put his hands behind his head.

Why do I let Lola get the better of me? I'm pathetic! When will I learn that she's not interested? Mitch grabbed a menu and looked over the meal items, but he had lost his appetite. Both he and Lola had worked on and off together for the better part of two years. He was attracted to her at first sight. Police work put you in close quarters with co-workers for months at a time. You either grew very close together or you hated each other's guts. He put the menu down and looked out the window.

About a year ago, they had worked a case on the Boston waterfront. He looked out the window while remembering the first time he had asked her out

September 21, 2005

The gun pointed through the bathroom stall door directly at his chest. *Talk about a crappy day*, Mitch thought. He sat on the toilet and listened to the instructions given to him.

"Pass the courier bag under the stall door. Make any sudden moves and this toilet will be your final resting place. Understood?" the voice with the gun commanded.

"Understood," Mitch replied and slid the bag out of the stall. The washroom door closed seconds later as his attacker escaped. Mitch stepped out of the stall and spoke into his radio. "Target has the bag. Repeat, target has the bag! Maintain your distance don't spook him!" Mitch waited five seconds and then walked calmly out of the room.

"Target is heading towards the food court at Quincy Market. He is still carrying the package," Lola's voice came through the receiver.

The two of them had prepared a sting operation to catch the thieves of courier robberies around the Boston area. The criminals had targeted courier companies and had nabbed several expensive transfers. It was clear they had someone high up who knew the contents of the courier packs. Mitch made sure his bait would be too good to pass up. Dressed as a courier, he had given the target an easy opportunity to take the package.

"He's passing by me now," an uninformed cop named Murray spoke into his mouthpiece. He must have spoken too loud because the thief looked back and noticed the earpiece in Murray's ear. The thief broke out into a run, spinning around several tourists. "I've been made," Murray yelled.

"Take him down!" Mitch yelled as he nearly collided with a merchant in the stalls of Quincy market. Lola was ahead of the thief and saw him running towards her right. Before she could close the gap, the thief knocked a teenager off of his bike. He jumped on the bike and pumped the pedals furiously.

"Suspect has grabbed bicycle and is heading toward the waterfront. Requesting squad car backup!" Lola said. The thief pedaled the bike and then braked as he saw the approaching police car. He turned and headed back to Quincy Market. Murray was the first to approach the thief.

"I got him!" he yelled. As he ran over to him, the thief cocked his fist back. Murray turned the corner and with the forward momentum of the bike, the thief sucker punched him, and Murray went sailing into a T-shirt kiosk.

"Officer down, does not seem to be seriously injured," Lola yelled as she turned the corner of a fish vendor. She grabbed a pole with a hook at the end and charged towards the oncoming bike. Lola drove it into the front wheel before the thief could veer away. He went sailing straight in the fish bin and disappeared into their bodies. Lola pulled out her gun and pointed at the moving pile of fish as the thief tried to get up. "Buddy, you're going to stink in your cell." She didn't see the fish coming as it sailed at her head. *SMACK!* As she fell to the ground, she was dazed for several seconds. She looked up to see the thief with the fishhook pointed directly at her chest.

Before the hook could puncture her, Mitch slammed into the thief, sending them both into the vendor two stalls down. Mitch pulled his head out a contained of chocolate ice cream.

"Sweet!" he said. "But what is that smell?"

"Trust me, this ice cream is ruined," Lola replied. "But thanks for the save."

"You owe me for this one," Mitch answered as he lifted the thief to his legs. "How about a date?"

"You're not my type," replied the thief shaking fish and ice cream off his clothes.

"Shut up," Mitch answered cuffing the thief's hands. "Lola?" he turned and asked.

"What he said Brown," she smiled.

Mitch turned from the hotel window as the memory faded away. He grabbed the remote. He laid out on the bed and looked for something mind numbing on the television. *Women*, Mitch thought, *impossible to please and impossible to live with out.*

March 28, 2007

Rook's interrogation

Rook sat at the table, his forehead was sweaty, his fingers tapped nervously on the surface. He kept looking at the mirror, trying to see if someone was watching him. He almost fell out of his chair when Lola entered the interrogation room.

"I think there's been some kind of mistake. I haven't done anything wrong. What are you people charging me with?" he stammered.

"Relax," answered Lola. "As we explained downstairs, there are a few questions we need to ask, and then you're free to go. Okay?"

"Questions? Are you're trying to trick me into admitting something?" answered Rook.

"Do you think I'm trying to trick you?" she shot back.

"Maybe."

"Do you think I can get you to admit to something you didn't do?" Lola raised her eyebrow.

"Maybe."

"Do you have something to tell me?"

"Maybe."

"This is getting annoying. Do you want to know why you're here?" her voice rose.

"Yes!" answered Rook.

"Someone on your team has committed murder. I need you tell me who it is." Lola commanded.

"Murder. Wow!" Rook seemed more excited than scared that there was a killer on his team. "I bet it's Tunny!"

"Why do you think that?" she was puzzled.

Rook paused. "Well he's the biggest goon on the team. Always picking fights and shooting his mouth off. He's got a real mean streak. I bet he's your killer!"

"Now, think carefully. Has he ever exhibited any suspicious behavior? Done something that didn't seem right?" Lola asks.

"Every road trip. That guy is a magnet for trouble. Sometimes I think he does it for the attention," Rook rolled his eyes.

"Getting into trouble is different from suspicious behavior. Has he ever missed a game or disappeared in the middle of the night? Carried a weapon?" she queried.

"No," Rook looked at her intensely, "everyone makes the games. Even if you're sick you still have to sit on the bench. I've shared hotel rooms with just about everybody and Tunny has disappeared a number of times to the strip clubs. I've never seen him carry a weapon. The guy's such a brawler, he's always using his fists."

"That doesn't sound unusual for a hockey player. Is there anyone else on the team that could be a murderer?" she pondered.

"Come to think of it, Taj has always been a suspicious guy. You know, a foreigner. Maybe he's a terrorist or something. He's always buzzing around everywhere. Maybe he's planting bombs to kill his victims," Rooks said lightly.

"None of the victims were blown up," she snapped back.

"Oh," Rook shrugged. "In that case, it must be Dozer. I've seen him spark up an occasional reefer before a game to relax. He would know how to drug someone and then kill them in their sleep."

"Has anyone told you that you have a vivid imagination?" Lola asked.

"No, but thank you. Most the guys treat me like crap because it is my first year."

"How does that make you feel?"

"Like crap," he grunted.

"None of the victims were drugged," she stared at him.

"Okay. Okay. I know who it is! It's got to be Stefan. Oh, he comes off as charming and sophisticated. He probably charms his female victims up to his room and then… blam!" He jumped excitedly in his seat. "Probably smothers them in their sleep."

"I thought all the players shared rooms with each other?" she queried.

"Ah, that's right," he remembered. A rap on the window caused Lola to look behind.

"I'll be back in a minute." She stepped out the door and saw Garson standing by the mirror.

"Any luck?" he asks.

"None! This guy would incriminate his mother if she was on the team. He doesn't seem capable of planning murder," she said with frustration.

"Unless he's playing us," Garson was skeptical.

"What do you want?" she asked.

"Wrap up your interview," Garson turned around. "I want to compare notes. I believe that among the ten team members we interviewed, one of them is the killer!"

December 2, 2006

"Gentlemen – start your engines!" the voice boomed through the microphone. Rook looked over his console one last time while revving the gas with his left-hand throttle. He turned and saw Tunny, Brick, and Booker intent on the racetrack. The warehouse was huge. The track had more twists and turns than a rollercoaster. In the far end of the building sat a huge pile of tires - a cushion for cars to slam into if they took the corner too fast. Two teenagers, dressed up in racing gear, occupied the other two cars.

The team was celebrating Brick's bachelor party with a series of racing heats at the Kart World racetrack in the city of Cornwall. All but four of the teammates had been eliminated. Unfortunately, the hockey team hadn't bought the exclusive use of the track and the addition of the two teenagers was a sore spot for Tunny.

"You kids better not get in my way. If you do, I'll drive right over you," he growled at the teenager next to him.

"Don't worry about us old man. We'll be so far ahead of you that you won't even see us," The teenager with a maple leaf cap taunted from the other side.

"Old man! I'll still beat the snot out of you with one hand," said Tunny as he tried to pull his legs out of the car to get up." The pit chief walked over and put an arm on his shoulder.

"Excuse me, sir. Is there a problem here?" Tunny looked up into the kid's eyes and settled back into his car.

"No problem. Just stretching a kink out of my leg," Tunny responded.

"Okay, but once the race starts there is no getting out of the car or you will be disqualified," the pit chief walked back to the front of the cars while holding the checkered flag. Tunny scowled when the teenager in the red car gestured rudely at him.

"Tunny, relax. Those kids aren't even in our race. It's just between us four." Booker yelled over the engine roar.

"Hey, this is my bachelor party. Maybe you could have fun for once! For guys who lose so much, I can never figure out why you're so competitive," answered Brick as he adjusted the goggles on his helmet.

Rook looked back at the rest of the team screaming and banging on the plexiglass window at the watch room. Taj and Dozer traded money as if placing a bet. Rook sniffed the air. *Thank God these engines are electric. If they were gas, we'd all be dying from fumes by now.* Beside him the control light flashed green and the cars peeled onto the track.

Clank! Tunny's car grazed Rook as he passed on the outside. *Jeeze, that guy is an idiot!* Tunny smiled back as if able to read Rook's thoughts. The cars raced down the straightaway toward the first hairpin turn.

Maple Leaf hat charged his car to the lead with Tunny and Brick jockeying for second place. Rook, Booker, and the other teenager brought up the rear. Rook looked toward the glassed-in control room at his teammates jumping up and down. They looked like overenthusiastic mimes. *This is the strangest bachelor party I ever attended. Usually a guy wants to get drunk or see some strippers, but I never thought that I'd be racing glorified go-carts.*

Screech!

"Hey Rook. Get your mind on the race. You almost cut me off," yelled Booker from his car.

"Sorry," Rook yelled back as he shifted gears and slammed the accelerator to the floor. *I've got five laps to prove my worth. Maybe they'll stop calling me Rook if I win.* He sped ahead while passing Booker. He looked ahead and saw Brick's broad back. Brick turned around and smiled at Rook. He drove to the middle of the track, making it extremely difficult for Rook to pass.

"You're not getting by me," Brick mouthed under his helmet screen.

The pit chief watched Tunny and Maple Leaf racing neck and neck. He clutched the yellow flag ready to stop the race if the two of them became too aggressive. *Nobody is going to wreck my cars*, he thought.

"Stop hogging the road old man," Maple Leaf yelled trying to burn past Tunny. "You probably drive like this on the road."

"How would you know punk? You're probably too young to have your driver's license," taunted Tunny.

"Beginner's license," Maple Leaf shot back.

"Wow! That means you can drive with your dad. You and your buddies must really party it up!" Tunny raced around heartbreak corner; he narrowly missed a pile of tires but maintained a slight lead.

"Screw you!" Maple Leaf yelled and rammed into the back of Tunny's cart. Tunny suddenly found the steering wheel unresponsive. He looked back at Maple Leaf. "What's wrong, swallowed your dentures?" Maple Leaf jeered.

Tunny pointed to the back of his car. Maple Leaf frowned.

"You idiot! You've locked your bumper under mine!" Tunny tried stopping suddenly to shake him off. Unfortunately, Maple Leaf did the opposite and accelerated at the exact same moment. His car hit Tunny and they remained locked as they slammed into the tire border. The pit chief came running out waving his yellow flag signally everyone to slow down.

"You two are out of the race! Take your cars down crash row." Both Tunny and Maple Leaf got out of their cars and took off their helmets.

"Race you to the pit!" he pushed the car with all his might.

"You're on, roadkill." Tunny yelled back pushing his cart.

Rook watched the two of them compete yet again. *If Tunny had a son, that kid would be it.* As he looked ahead, he realized there was a lot more room on the track.

Now there were four.

The other teenager was in the lead with Brick, Booker, and himself rounding out the group. He had four laps left to make a play. *I'll show those guys that I can compete.* He gunned his engine and tried to catch up with Booker.

Booker cut his car to the left as if sensing Rook's approach. Rook took his foot off the accelerator to prevent a crash. The track was narrow and passing was difficult. It was hard to overtake the lead car.

Booker skidded to the left, barely missing a pile of tires. He recovered quickly and prevented Rook from taking advantage. *How am I going to get around him?* Rook thought. The remaining lap counter dropped to three. Suddenly he got an idea and drove as close to Booker as he could without making contact.

"Hey Booker," he yelled.

"Go away. Busy right now," Booker replied without looking over. Rook wasn't so easily brushed off. He knew how to distract Booker.

"Booker. I have a quick question – which is colder, the North or South Pole?" He knew how to appeal to Booker's intellect and the fact he loved to talk. Even under the goggles, Rook could tell Booker has lost his focus and was trying to answer the question. Booker's distraction caused him to miss seeing the hairpin turn. Rook almost felt regret over his trick. Almost.

"Booker, look out!" he yelled too late. Booker saw the turn, but his speed was too great. His brakes caused the car to spin 360 degrees and he slammed into a pile of tires. Several tires from the top toppled down and covered his car.

And then there were three.

Brick was rapidly gaining on the teenager who was looking increasingly frustrated in the lead. Several times, the teenager gunned the throttle and the car would lurch forward and back. Brick took advantage and pulled his car alongside the teenager. As the hairpin turn came up, there was only room for one. Suddenly the teenager's car sputtered and came to a stop in the middle of the course as Brick took the turn alone. The teenager tried unsuccessfully to rev his engine. Frustrated, he got out of his car and kicked the side of it.

"Piece of junk!" he yelled as pit chief came running over.

"Please leave the track. We'll move the car!"

"Move my car! I want my money back!" he said as he walked off the track.

And then there were two.

Brick's was leading by several car lengths as Rook circled around the stalled car and bore down on him. The team was pounding on the plastic window of the control tower. Rook floored his car, until he was one car length behind Brick. *I can do this*, Rook thought. *I'll win and finally have the respect of my teammates.* The flag was waved as the cars approached the final lap.

Brick looked back in mock fright at Rook's approach. *You should be scared. I'm going to catch you.* Brick accelerated and turned a little too hard, allowing Rook to catch up. For the final lap they were dead even. *To the winner went the spoils.*

Brick looked at Rook. Rook looked back at Brick. *There could only be one.* They both revved their engines racing down the laneway. With fifty feet left, Brick's large frame caused his acceleration to be a split second behind. The checkered flag waved as Rook narrowly crossed the finish line first. He leapt out of his car, his excitement bursting at the seams. He grabbed Brick by the shoulders.

"Check your pants for treads, cause I just kicked your ass!" Rook danced around the finish line as the rest of the team joined them. Rook turned and smiled, awaiting their congratulations. He got the exact opposite reaction.

"Way to go, Rook!" Dawson hit him in the arm. "It's Brick's bachelor party. You're supposed to let him win!"

"You are too competitive, mom ami. You must have learned playing on this team that winning isn't everything," Stefan commented.

"But no one told me! How was I supposed to know?" Rook cried.

"Dude you are such a rookie," Dozer waved his arm dismissively. Only Tunny came up to greet him.

"Rook, you may have a chance on this team. Way to show the 'groom-to-be' who's boss!" Tunny slapped him on the back and walked back to Brick.

Great, the only guy who likes me is the team jerk. Someone tapped him on the shoulder. Rook turned and saw Booker.

"Listen, sorry about before. I didn't mean to. . . ." Rook started.

"Nonsense, now about your question. . . ." Booker's bone-crushing grip on his shoulder left no room for negotiation as he was dragged away.

Great, I've gone from purgatory to hell, he moaned to himself.

December 2, 2006

Garson walked down the glassed-in hallway of the Chicago field office. Each window looked into an office or forensics laboratory. He remembered a seminar on the design - the glass windows were less about supervisors being able to find lab personnel, instead more to give staff the feeling that they were being watched.

As he toured the facility, he wondered if people were just giving the impression of being busy. He turned a corner and stepped toward a junior lab tech named Simon. Simon was typical of the young techs - unkempt hair, casual clothes, and bloodshot eyes from too much partying. Garson pondered how the tech got hired in the first place. Simon was so engrossed in his experiment that he didn't hear Garson walk up behind him.

"What have you got for me?" Garson asked. Simon jumped back and almost dropped the test tube in his hands. He recovered and turned to Garson with a half-surprised smile on his face.

"Sorry man, I didn't notice you coming in."

"That's why you're in the lab and I'm in the field," Garson joked good-naturedly. "Any luck matching the residue on the back of the couch?" Simon spun in his chair to a file on his desk. He opened the folder.

"Common adhesive residue. This is typical of packing tape, duct tape, sports tape, etc.," Simon answered. Garson gestured with his hands for more information.

"What type of tape is it?" Garson asked. Simon shrugged his shoulders.

"Don't know – our databases doesn't carry any data on common household tape." Garson leaned in closer to Simon.

"Then take a field trip – go to a hardware store, buy a bunch of industrial tape products and do the analysis. Don't tell me that I have to do your job as well?" Garson growled.

"No sir. That's a good idea. I'm a bit backed up right now though." Simon motioned to a pile of marked plastic bags that looked like it would take days to get through.

Great, Garson thought, *it will be weeks before I can get any useful analysis.*

"Okay let's move on. What did toxicology have on the drink found in front of the murder victim?" Garson asked. Simon pulled a printout by his keyboard. "Nothing mysterious here," he said and tossed a can of pop from his desk.

"No thanks, I'm not thirsty," Garson replied.

"No, not for you to drink, read the ingredients," Simon asked. Garson looked and saw about twenty different type of chemicals mixed to make up the soft drink.

"You're telling me that there was nothing added to the pop?" Garson asked.

"No uppers, no downers, no alcohol. Just 100% root beer. My favorite by the way. Simon smiled. "Hey, can I ask you a question?"

"I think you just did. Want to try again?"

"Okay," Simon gulped. "Why does the captain have it in for you? Some of the other techs were talking and they say he can't wait to shut this case down?"

"It's complicated. Let's just say I'm still paying for a past mistake. Now, what do you have on the laptop?" Garson asked.

"Not much," Simon shrugged. "Whoever took that thing apart, fried it real good. I was able to retrieve some banking information, a couple of dating sites, and a few personal emails. Nothing out of the ordinary."

"Okay. Have you got anything for me at all?" Garson asked, wondering if this visit was a total waste of time. Simon rolled his chair over to a filing cabinet and lifted a baggie with a woman's purse inside.

"Victim's car apparently was untouched by the killer and was parked on the street. I haven't gone through her purse contents yet. I figured you want to scan it first and see what you want to run through forensics." Garson nodded his head, pulled on a pair of rubber gloves and took the bagged purse over to a table. He pulled parchment paper down the length of the table to make sure nothing was lost. He dumped the purse contents and spread them out with gloved fingers. He looked at each item separately and then put them on the opposite side of the table.

Dark purple lipstick – Sorry that does nothing for me, Garson thought.

Visa card – I'll have to check her purchases. Maybe she bought something of interest that her murderer decided to take.

Interstate tokens – Makes sense as a reporter, she'd be on the road a lot.

Female hygiene products – Have to ask Lola about these, I'm out of my element.

Reporter's pad – Now this looks interesting.

Garson leafed through the pages. There were notes on a variety of local stories, public interest, sports, and feel good stories. A lot of it was in shorthand, but for the most part Garson could make out the writing. Nothing of any significance, notes about dog show winners and sport stars.

Not exactly the type of stories that people would kill to cover up. One page ripped out, could be nothing, and could be everything. I'll make a note for forensics to try to get a tracing from the missing page. Two pens – She obviously hasn't embraced technology, no phone to retain notes.

Poker chips – I don't know what casino has the letter N for a symbol.

Car keys – I'll have Mitch check all the keys – maybe one leads to something interesting.

Data stick – I knew she couldn't shun technology completely.

"Simon," motioned Garson. "Plug this into your computer, I want to see if she has any news stories that would be worth killing for." Simon grabbed the storage device and plugged it into the USB port in his computer. A folder named 'News stories' popped up with five hundred- and sixty-five-word documents.

"Great, this will take forever to go through. Can you organize by most recent?" said Garson.

"You bet, boss," Simon sorted the files. "I think I've seen this lady reporter on the news. Current event kind of stuff."

"Remember any of her stories?" Garson asked.

"Just one. I think she was interviewing some owner of a lingerie store. Some pretty wild adult toys," he added slyly.

"Now I know why you remember the story. I don't think lingerie is what our killer was looking for," Garson looked amused.

"I don't know, sir. Some of those models were pretty hot," Simon said enthusiastically

"Sorry to interrupt your important crime scene conversation, gentlemen," Lola said as she walked into the lab and dropped a folder in front of Garson.

"Speaking of hot," Simon whispered.

"Pardon you," Lola commented and glared straight at Simon who looked at the floor.

"Never mind the hormones, what do you have for me?" asked Garson.

"Maybe nothing. I've got a list of the victim's recent stories for the last few months. Seems she was making a transition from feel good people stories to feel good sport stories. She's covered baseball to racquetball and everything in-between," said Lola.

"Where are you going with this? Think she had a romance with one of the sport stars she interviewed? A jilted boyfriend?" Garson inquired.

"Like I said, maybe nothing. Besides, it doesn't explain why most of the previous victims are male." answered Lola.

"Maybe the killer's a baseball player that swings both ways?" offered Simon. Lola ignored his comment and pressed on.

"Problem is, many of the sports stories were from teams that were passing through. Trying to connect with all of them would take a lot of traveling."

"Well, how about we start with the phone calls and decide if travel is needed later. Call each team covered in the last six months – see if anyone mentions a relationship. Check her place of work, maybe a colleague can remember a friendly sports star," Garson added.

"Mitch's on his way to the paper now," Lola answered.

The lights from the warehouse gleamed through the side door. Mitch walked in past a forklift carrying several pallets of the next day's paper. He stepped toward a foreman feverishly writing on his clipboard.

"Newsroom?" Mitch inquired. The foreman barely looked up.

"Up the stairs," he pointed to glassed-in area that looked down on the warehouse floor. Mitch walked toward the metal stairs. *Never fails, the newsroom always looks down on the rest of the staff.* He climbed the stairs and opened a semi-translucent door. Inside, a perky administrative assistant greeted him.

"Hi, I'm Becky. Can I help you?" she smiled. Mitch flashed his credentials.

"I'm here to collect the belongings of one of your reporters, Amanda Cotter." Becky's smile faltered, replaced by sorrow,

"We heard about her death. One thing about working at a newspaper, bad news travels faster here than anywhere else," replied Becky.

"What was she like?" Mitch asked.

"Really nice. Always asked how you were doing. Everybody here loved her," Becky responded.

"Any boyfriends? Anyone extremely friendly with her, like her boss?" queried Mitch.

"Heavens, no," she replied. "We've very family oriented here. Relationships between workers are strictly forbidden at the paper. Ruins the objectivity of our stories."

Okay that means any relationships would be hidden from staff, thought Mitch. "Where's her desk?"

"Second desk, third row – down by the file cabinets," Becky pointed. "If you need anything, I'm at extension 335." Mitch nodded his thanks and worked his way down the aisle. Several reporters were on the phone or tapping away at their laptops. Still, the newsroom didn't seem as busy as he would have imagined. *I guess more and more people work from home these days and email their stories in.*

Mitch sidestepped past a young intern hurrying to his next assignment. He stopped in front of Amanda Cotter's desk. Clean, organized, no laptop – *guess the one smashed at her home must have been from work.* He rifled through the desk, looking for any personal effects.

No family pictures, some gum wrappers, feminine products, some receipts - MacDonald's, O'Toole's bar, Wal-Mart. Keys on a ring. Mitch took the keys and tried a locked drawer. The drawer opened and he was rewarded with a daytimer.

The lab boys can go through that he thought as he sealed it into an evidence bag. He sat at the desk – *no land phone, looks like all the reporters use their cell phones.* He looked around the room. Staff members typed away on laptops while others chatted to each other. Two employees tossed a nerf basketball at a hoop in the corner of the room. *Seems like a lot of camaraderie. Maybe someone can tell me something about Amanda.* As Mitch walked toward the nerf players, a kid in his chair sideswiped his foot.

"Sorry mister," the kid looked up. Mitch flashed his badge. "You're not going to take me to jail for bad chair driving?"

"Depends how you answer my questions," Mitch deadpanned. "What do you do here?

"I'm a production assistant. Basically a gofer for all the reporters. Maybe one day, I can cover one of my own stories," the kid replied.

"Did you know Amanda?" Mitch pointed to her desk.

"Oh yeah, man. Everyone knew her. She did all the fun stories. Made people feel good."

"Did she get any threats or hate mail?" asked Mitch.

"No way. She never hurt anybody's feeling. Nothing news breaking. Hell, she was the kind of reporter that if she was doing a food review and the place was a total dive – she'd still find something nice to say about the place," stressed the kid.

"Anybody jealous? Maybe have a grudge against her?" Mitch stared at him.

"In this place?" the kid scratched his head. "Look around you – it's pretty relaxed. The stress level rises as the deadlines get closer at the end of the day, but the only yelling that takes place here is with the editor, not other reporters. How would you like to have your work revised minutes before it goes print?"

"Police work may not be as different as you think," Mitch answered, thinking of his own pressures." What was she like? A bit of a flirt?"

"No, man. Salt of the earth." The kid leaned closer to whisper to Mitch. "Some of these reporters are real jerks. Give me their crap work. Not Amanda, she was a sweetheart. Except . . . . " his voice trailed off.

"What? No detail is too small!" Mitch said firmly.

"Well these last few months," the kid paused, "she was a bit more antisocial. Missed a bunch a mixers at the bar. Seemed to have more on her mind." Before Mitch could get him to elaborate, the kid's cell phone rang. "Gotta go!" He raced toward the reporters at the back of the room. Mitch gathered a few more items and bagged them up. He walked back to the front of the office and stepped in front of Becky. She looked up from her typing.

"Find what you're looking for?" she asked.

"Maybe. Can you tell me where I can find a bar by the name of O'Tooles?"

"Sports bar. Round the corner. A lot of staff spend their after hours there." Becky leaned in closer to Mitch. "I'm off in another hour. I could take you there if you buy me a drink."

"I'll take a rain check. I have to be back at the office in a half an hour," Mitch smiled.

"Your loss. Remember, in a sports bar, it's not whether you win or lose, its how you play the game."

"You're full of clichés. I suppose you'd tell me next that if I have fun, that I already won," Mitch pattered back.

"No, but that's a good one," Becky replied.

"If you think of anything else relating to Amanda, here's my card," Mitch passed it to her.

"I'm sure I'll think of something. See you around, sport," Becky laughed.

March 28, 2007

Presley's interrogation

"Can you state your name into the microphone please," asked Mitch. He motioned to the microphone stand on the table.

"Presley. John Allan Presley," the Assassin's forward answered and motioned to the bottle of water at the end of the table. "Would you mind passing the water?"

"No problem." Mitch replied and slid the water down the table.

"Thank you. Thank you very much." Presley answered.

"Your welcome very much," Mitch mimicked him. "Now can you tell me what your role is on the Assassins hockey team?"

"Absolutely. I am the captain of the team. I plan a lot of the team activities and keep the men motivated. I guide our team members," Presley replied.

"And how do you do that?" Mitch asked.

"By setting an example for my team to follow," Presley settled his gaze on Mitch. "I am the one on the team that everyone can count on. This team is a business and has to run efficiently. Some players will lose their tempers, others will have a bad game. The young players need a role model to follow and the veterans need someone they can depend upon. I am that leader." Mitch turned his head and rolled his eyes at the one-way mirror. Garson smiled from the other side at Mitch's expression.

"You must know your players pretty well then," he asked.

"How well do you know your family?" Presley answered.

"Well-" Mitch started.

"These players are my family and I know each one especially well. I know when they are home sick. I know if they are broke. I know when they are angry. And I know when they want to leave," Presley answered.

"If someone was committing an illegal act, you would know about it," Mitch turned his head to the side.

"Absolutely!" Presley stressed. A few seconds of silence and Mitch tried to elicit additional information.

"Such as …."

"Such as .. . .." Presley looked puzzled.

"You know," Mitch wondered.

"But I don't know," Presley stammered.

"If there's something illegal, you would know right?" pressed Mitch.

"Right!" said Presley

"Is anything illegal going on in your team?" Mitch's voice was rising.

"Pardon me?" Presley looked confused.

"Are you telling me *nothing* illegal is going on?"

"No," Presley hesitated as he tried to think. "What do you mean?"

"I mean, is someone on your team killing people?" Mitch yelled.

"You mean like a serial killer," Presley asked.

"Yes, one of your precious teammates is killing people on the side!" Mitch yelled.

"You're insane! This team is a lot of things, but they are hardly killers!"

"The team is called the Assassins!" Mitch shouted.

"There's a team called the Penguins, Lieutenant. I'm sure you don't take everything so literally," laughed Presley.

"You don't seem too concerned that one of your teammates is a killer," Mitch was annoyed.

"What proof do you have? If you're so sure why don't you arrest someone?"

"That's not your concern. As the team captain, who do you think it is?" pressed Mitch.

"Lieutenant – our team is made up of different types of men. Drunks, adulters, fighters, lovers. Some will always play hockey; others will move on. You couldn't find a more different group of men. But there is one common thread among the whole bunch of them besides their love of hockey. None of them are killers." Presley stood up to leave. "If you're so sure your killer is a hockey player – you better start looking at another team."

December 5, 2006

Presley rolled his hockey bag along the motel hallway. The wheels caught on a tear on the carpet and skidded into the wall adding another black mark. Several light bulbs were out making the motel look even seedier. In order to stay on budget, the team stayed at cheap motels, sleeping two to a room. Presley pulled out his key and realized that the door was ajar. Sensing an intruder, he tentatively opened the door. He soon wished that an intruder had indeed broken into his room.

"Presley! About time you showed up. Have a seat, the boys and I are just settling in to watch the news," Tunny replied standing by one of the beds. Laying beside him were several empty bottles of beer, chip bags, and an ashtray where something was smoldering. Most of the other team members sat with rapt attention fixed on the television screen. *My team doesn't watch the news,* Presley thought as he turned to the television.

"Welcome to another edition of Naked Newscast, I am your host – Priscilla Winters." Presley looked at the host, an attractive young woman.

"What's going on in the world today, Priscilla?" Tunny cried. She responded by taking off her blazer.

"In Asia, there were trade talks between India and China for new guidelines involving manufacturing conditions. . . . " Pricilla started to unbutton her blouse.

"You know in India, the women would never undress like this," Taj commented.

"Glad we're not in India," answered Dawson. Everyone laughed.

"What about women from Montreal?" Brick yelled over the bed to Stefan.

"Mon ami! This woman undresses too quickly. French women know how to draw it out. These news bimbos are a cheap imitation," Stefan replied.

"Cheap! This newscast is costing me $5.99," exclaimed Tunny. Priscilla proceeded to throw her blouse to the floor while revealing a red bra. "Ding, ding. We have a technical knockout!" Tunny faked fainting and fell on the bed.

Presley crossed the room while several players complained to him about blocking their view. He almost stumbled on Tunny's stinking gear.

"Tunny! Could you have at least put your rotten gear outside," he yelled.

"Sorry," he responded sarcastically. "Kind of busy right know," he answered while keeping his eyes glued to the television screen. Presley opened the patio door and pushed both his gear and Tunny's outside onto the balcony.

"Shut the door, it's cold out there!" yelled Brick.

"Actually the temperature today is about two degrees above average for this time of year. Due to global warming. . ."

"Shut up Booker!" three players yelled in unison.

"Yeah, if I wanted a weather report, I'd watch the news," said Tunny. A new woman came on the screen and began giving a local weather report. She undressed while talking about the likelihood of precipitation.

"Hello! I love the news!" Tunny replied. The latest striptease was interrupted by a knock at the door.

"Pizza delivery!" a voice yelled.

"Excellent! I have a major case of the munchies," Dozer exclaimed as he opened the door.

"That will be $49.58," the female delivery woman replied. Dozer looked up to see a young girl with red hair. He was tongue-tied; he never knew what to say around a woman.

"Ah, ah," he stuttered.

"Don't mind him. He's a bit touched," yelled Dawson. "And it's not by any freaking angel."

"Okay, who's going to pay?" she replied coolly.

"Take it off baby!" Tunny screamed. The delivery woman took a step back unsure of what was going on.

"Sorry, he's yelling at the TV, not you," Booker clarified.

"You guys are disgusting. Just give me my money and I'll go," she answered. Dozer checked his empty pockets.

"Does anyone have any money?" he asked.

"Not me," replied Chilly.

"I've got five dollars in change somewhere," answered Brick.

"My wallet is in the other room," offered Rook.

"Never mind. Take this," Presley handed her fifty dollars.

"Big tipper," she muttered as she handed over the pizza and stepped back into the corridor. Presley was immediately surrounded by his hungry teammates.

"Where were you guys when I needed money?" he asked. Slices of pizza disappeared, and Presley had to grab for a slice before it was gone.

"Ah, meat lovers!" Brick savored his pizza. "Bacon is the candy of all meats," he said as he stuffed the slice into his mouth. Dozer dropped his piece on top of the open garbage can. He quickly scooped it up and stuffed it in his mouth.

"Ten second rule!" he grinned.

"That doesn't apply when you drop it in a garbage can you idiot! The no second rule applies then," Dawson commented while watching Dozer take another bite. "Man, you are just nasty."

Chilly reached up to change the television channel. A hockey game was playing on the sport channel.

"Hey what do you think you're doing!" complained Tunny.

"Relax,' Chilly laughed. "Your strippers are reading the news all day. I just wanted to catch the scores for the pros."

"Still think you got a chance to make the big leagues?" asked Taj.

"It's why I keep playing," Chilly answered.

"You're kidding yourself if you think a scout is ever going to draft from our team. We're a bottom dwelling bunch of losers," Tunny explained.

"Well, you don't speak for the whole team," replied Presley.

"Hey! Check out the highlight reel," explained Taj. "Did you see that shot?" he motioned to the instant replay.

"Well, if you angle it like this," Booker tried to lift up a puck with his stick. The puck fell to the floor two seconds later.

"Dude, that shot was physically impossible," Dozer commented with a face full of pizza.

"Can someone teach me how to do that?" asked Rook.

"Pretty goal," commented Dawson while combing his hair for the millionth time.

"That goaltender was more flexible than my last ten dates," commented Stefan. Tunny surveyed his teammates with disbelief.

"You guys make me sick! The group of you are more excited over a hockey goal than women stripping off their clothes." He shook his head and walked over to the end table to grab his beer. "My team's a bunch of homos!"

"Well, they say that the ratio is one in ten," commented Booker. The rest of team looked around the room at Dawson who was still gazing in the mirror.

Brick changed the conversation.

"Look!" Brick pointed. "The sports channel has changed from hockey to baseball. They spent a measly two minutes going over the score."

"Check out current events," Dawson replied. "We are a distant fourth after baseball, football, and basketball. A lot of fans just don't get hockey. The further south you go, you're lucky if you can find a hockey rink."

"Hockey popularity is dropping fast. Back home in Toronto, all of my family and friends are soccer crazy. It's so much cheaper to buy a pair of cleats and shorts than deck kids up with all the hockey gear," offered Taj.

"Let's face it, boys. Kids are into other sports today. I'm just glad that I can scrape out a living doing what I love," commented Brick.

"If our checks don't bounce. You see how low attendance was at our last home game," Tunny said.

"We have to start winning. The fans will come if we can at least break 500," Presley exclaimed.

"If we don't win next Friday man, our season is toast," reminded Dozer. He accidentally knocked over his ashtray and almost started a fire on the carpet. Tunny put it out by pouring his beer on the carpet.

"No need to thank me. I'm available for parades, weddings, and bar mitzvahs," Tunny saluted the room with his other beer.

"Speaking of weddings, are any of you guys going to respond to the invitations I sent out?" Brick asked. "My future wife is on my case to finish the seating plan."

"I'll be there!" Rook answered.

"Me too!" Dozer yelled.

"Are their going to be any young ladies at this event?" asked Stefan raising one of his eyebrows.

"Yes, but I thought you were bringing a guest?" Brick replied.

"Mais non. You don't bring a sandwich to a buffet," Stefan pointed out.

"You'll be like Dawson," added Taj.

"What do you mean?" asked Rook.

"He won't have a guest either because he can't take anyone prettier than him," Taj laughed as a pillow meant for him struck Brick in the head.

"I'm warning all of you," Brick raised himself to his full height, "to be on your best behavior."

"Don't worry, I've never been kicked out of a wedding before," laughed Tunny.

"Dude, is it an open bar?" Dozer asked.

"No, I wouldn't make that mistake," Brick answered.

"Can we request specific foods?" asked Taj. "My diet prohibits eating anything that flies or swims."

"Hello? Nut job, party of one," Tunny spit out a mouthful of beer.

"Give the guy a break," Rook defended, "you need to be more culturally diverse."

"You're right, Rook" Tunny leaned back on the bed. "That's why I hate every culture equally."

"I'm just saying it wouldn't hurt to be more tolerate," Rook stated as if he was gaining confidence in his opinion.

"For a rookie, you don't seem to know your place on this team. Maybe it's time I showed you," Tunny glared and started to stand up.

"Better yet, maybe it's time we initiated him with the chicken ceremony," Booker stated.

The rest of the players responded with silence as if this was a tough initiation for a new player. Rook looked at their faces and decided to run to the washroom. The room was silent for a moment as all eyes returned to the television. A large woman came on a commercial and talked about the wonders of weight loss.

"Hey, is the Coach bringing his wife to the wedding?" asked Dawson.

"Why? Is she quite the beauty?" Stefan questioned.

"Beauty? Think the opposite of beauty. She's so ugly…" Tunny started.

"How ugly is she?" Stefan asked.

"She's so ugly a train would take a dirt road to avoid her," Tunny finished.

"She's so ugly she'd make an onion cry," Dawson added.

"What's worse is the way she dances. Her body convulses and twitches like she's going into shock. It's like a train wreck. Horrible to look at but you can't stop yourself," answered Dawson.

"Mon Dieu! Surely you exaggerate," asked Stefan. "Besides, none of you can dance anyway."

"Speak for yourself Frenchy. When I get on the dance floor, I'm 220 lbs. of dancin' dynamite with a ten-inch fuse!" Tunny spoke enthusiastically.

"I think you're off by about six inches," Chilly smirked.

"Try to remember who the wedding is for," Presley added.

"That's right," Brick said enthusiastically. "I'm looking forward to having my best buds with me," as he bear-hugged Booker, Dozer and Chilly like stuffed toys." Nothing's going to ruin the most important day of my life!" They were interrupted by another knock on the door.

"Pizza woman's back! Bet she was so impressed with Dozer's smooth talking she came back. Ah, ah," Dawson mimicked Dozer's stuttering. Several other players joined him and the whole room mimicked poor Dozer.

"Shut up!" Dozer yelled and wrapped a pillow around his head. Rook came out of the bathroom and answered the door. The Coach dashed in breathless, bent over with exertion while holding a cigarette in his right hand.

"What's wrong Coach?" asked Presley.

"Did taxes go up again on smokes?" jested Tunny. Coach held his hand up a minute to catch his breath. He walked over to one of the beds and sat down.

"I'm glad I caught all of you. It saves me explaining this more than once. Something awful has happened."

"Come on Coach, we only lost by two goals," defended Chilly.

"That's not the problem. I just spoke to the arena staff. Our low numbers have finally caught up to us. The arena contract will not be picked up at the end of the season. We no longer have a home," blurted out the Coach.

"Can't we go somewhere else?" Presley asked.

"Who else will take us?" the Coach sat down and folded his hands over his head. "We're a money-losing team in a declining league. Unless our owner can persuade another city into a contract by April, this team is done!"

Chapter 11   Women Work Harder

December 7, 2006

Lola sat at her desk as the janitor passed by her door on his way out of the office. He noticed her light and peeked his head around the door.

"Excuse me, miss? I've finished this floor and I'm moving upstairs. There's no one else here. Are you all right by yourself?"

"I am. Thanks for asking. I'll lock up," she answered.

"Good night!" he replied and continued to wheel his cart down the hallway.

I'm closing up shop again, Lola thought. *The only way to get ahead in a man's world is to work twice as hard. Doesn't help when half the men chasing after me, are slowing me down.*

Lola Price came from a long line of law enforcement. Her father was a cop, her uncle was a sheriff, and her grandfather was a police commissioner. They all had long distinguished careers – yet none of them supported her in her quest to serve the law. "Why don't you marry a cop – it's the next best thing," her chauvinist grandfather would say. *Bet he's turning in his grave now.* "Lola – why don't you go into a career more suited for a woman?" her uncle would tease. Only her father didn't put her dream down. He simply stopped saying anything at all. His disappointing silence was all she needed to motivate her.

She worked hard as a cadet - even harder as a beat cop - to prove her worth. She had given up almost everything - a social life, a family, and a boyfriend – all to prove to a disinterested father that she could make him proud. And everyday she questioned if her sacrifice was worth it.

October 3, 2001

When the football exploded near her head, she knew she was in trouble. She leaned against a mannequin, pulling her ball cap down as she hunkered down in a sport store. She tried to look through a rack of clothes to get a glimpse of her assailant. *Be calm, stick my head up at the wrong time, I can lose my head. Literally.*

She grabbed a hockey puck and tossed it into the aisle way. It disappeared in a cloud a dust. *Okay, he's not moving.* Lola looked around the store, trying to find an advantage. The shelves were stocked with shoes, snowboards and ball caps. In the corner, she saw a circular mirror that covered the back of the store. There was no movement, so she did the only thing she knew to draw him out.

He looked though the sight of his gun, waiting to catch sight of the officer. One shot is all he needed to bring this to an end. He caught sight of movement near the baseball display. The capped figure came into his sight, her head ready to be taken out. As he squeezed the trigger, he felt the baseball bat at the back of his head.

"Drop it! Otherwise the mannequin gets it," The sight focused on the lifeless victim.

"Time!" the voice yelled over the intercom. Other officers immediately surrounded the sports store set.

"Good job Price! That time will definitely get your detective badge," an officer congratulated her.

"You got me Lola. You did good," her sniper shook her hand. In the corner, an older man stood with his arms folded surveying the scene. Lola stepped towards him.

"What do you think Dad?" she asked. His face was a frown with little emotion.

"You were slow. You wouldn't have had that much time in a real gunfight," he replied as he stepped toward a door. Her arm prevented him from leaving.

"I don't get it! Would it kill you to give me a compliment once and while? Can you throw me a bone? When will I ever be good enough for you?" Lola yelled.

"Find another career. The police force is no place for a woman," he replied without a hint of emotion. Lola watched as he left the training area.

Dad's always been old school. The woman should be seen and not heard. In the kitchen, barefoot and pregnant is where the woman should be. Well, I'll show him. I'll show all men that I'm not just

Her cell phone rang, interrupting her thoughts.

"Price," she answered.

"Jesus, Lola – are you still at the office?" Mitch's voice rang through her phone.

"Yes, aren't you still working?" she replied.
"No. I gave up two hours ago and I'm just relaxing in front of the television. Want to come over?" he asked.

"Nice try. Why are you calling?" questioned Lola.

"Sorry. Something about the reporter's workplace just didn't fit in. Everybody liked her, I mean really liked her. It was almost as if she didn't have an enemy in the world," explained Mitch.

"Well she definitely had one," Lola answered.

"I've hit a dead-end. What did you find out canvassing the neighbors?"

"Very little. No one seemed to know her very well. Seems she was on the road a lot covering different news stories. Those that did know her, said she was friendly and likeable. No boyfriends, no late-night visits, no family dropping by. She seemed to live a lonely life."

"So how does she compare to the stockholder victim?" Mitch asked.

"Surprisingly different. Much higher income than the reporter. Friends and co-workers describe him as aggressive but effective in his job. Arrogant, tended to rub people the wrong way, except his boss who made a lot of money off of him. Didn't travel much, his condo was his castle."

"Amanda played golf - what about the stockbroker?" Mitch queried.

"Armchair athlete," answered Lola. "Guy liked to watch sports, didn't play any of them."

"Is there anything similar at all between the two?" Mitch asked.

"Not that I can tell. The fact that one was killed by a knife and the other was suffocated might suggest two different killers."

"Not according to Garson." Mitch was quiet for a moment. "Have all the victims been single?" Lola leafed through the list of statistics on the victims.

"No. Four of the 16 cases had families. Each time they were killed, the victim was in a separate room and the rest of the family never heard a thing."

"I give up. I'm going to sleep on it and review the evidence again tomorrow with a fresh mind. You'd be wise to the same," Mitch offered.

"Yeh, I'm closing up," Lola hit the power button on her computer.

"You know, I don't feel any closer to an answer for this case than when we started back in October. How much more rope are we going to be given to make this case work?"

"As much as we need. Especially if we hang ourselves with it. Garson has a lot riding on this. I don't think the higher-ups want to take the case away from him unless they are absolutely sure that the crimes are not related."

"Lucky us," Lola answered.

"At least it keeps us at the crime scene – better than being stationed at a desk."

"I just wish we had something to offer Garson instead of spinning our wheels."

"You're working too hard, Lola. This killer or killers will make a mistake sometime – when they do, we'll be there to find it."

"Pretty sure of yourself. What if the leads and the victims just stop?" Lola asked.

"Doesn't fit the profile. The killer can't stop himself. Eventually they all get caught. It's just about how low we can keep the body count," replied Mitch.

"And how many serial killers have you caught?" Lola asked sarcastically.

"Never mind. Your negativity is wearing me down. Make sure you get some sleep. Garson wants us to go through the evidence room – make sure we haven't missed anything."

"That sounds exciting," Lola responded.

"Hey, law enforcement's not all about gun fights and car chases," offered Mitch.

"Then why do you do it Mitch?" Lola asked, an edge of tiredness creeping into her voice. "And don't tell me you do it to help people – this isn't an interview."

"I don't have time for this. You must be tired. Go to bed," Mitch answered curtly.

"Why can't you open up? I've worked with you for two years and I know less about you now than when we started?"

"Maybe you should go out on a date with me. Then you'd learn more," he replied.

"Good night, Mitch."

"Good night, Lola." The phone went dead.

Men. They show more emotion watching a hockey game than they do in a relationship. No wonder the news always reports on men that go on a berserk rampage taking everyone with them. She grabbed the files on the latest murder. *Yep, there's no doubt in my mind. Our serial killer is definitely a male.*

First
Intermission

December 8, 2006

The dressing room shook from the skate sharpener vibrating loudly. The stone spun round and round as he placed his skate blade along the edge. He pulled the shake away and ran his finger along the polished edge. *This blade will definitely draw blood,* the killer thought. He reached into his duffel bag and pulled out a knife. Its edges looked dull. He slid the blade along the stone until the edge of the knife shone like polished metal. *All tools must be in working order*, he thought.

It was getting more difficult to execute his orders. Although, he had been very careful not to leave any evidence of his identity at the victim's homes, the sheer number was piling up.

This is my last year. My discovery will happen if I continue indefinitely. They will match the cities with the ones our team have visited. After that it will only be a matter of time before they discover me. We just have to make it to April.

The door to the dressing room squeaked and the killer quickly hid his knife back into his bag.

"How come you're still here?" asked the Coach as he reached for some keys on a hook.

"Just doing some last-minute preparations for tonight's game," the killer responded.

"Okay, make sure you lock up when you leave," the Coach answered. "and don't stay to long with the wedding coming up," as he walked out the door.

The killer zipped up his duffel bag.

With another victim coming up, the wedding was the last thing on his mind.

Second Period

March 28, 2007

Brick's interrogation

Mitch walked into the interrogation room. As he turned, he ran straight into Brick. At two hundred and fifty pounds, Brick was an immovable object. Mitch fell flat on his back. Brick reached down a hand to pull him back up.

"Sorry about that, officer. I didn't see you come in. Are you okay?" Brick asked.

"Thanks for your concern, but I'm fine. It's my own fault, I had my head down. Is it true what they say about you?" Mitch gestured to the chair as they both sat down at the table.

"I don't understand. Who have you been talking to? Have I done something wrong?"

"No, no," answered Mitch. "Your teammates describe you as a gentle giant. On the ice, you crush your opponent but then apologize and offer to help them up off the ice. Why would you apologize to anyone? You're the biggest man on the ice."

"That's the role I play, officer. An enforcer, to protect the team's elite players. To prevent our goaltender from taking a hit. To energize our team when the score is down with a well-placed hit. Just because I have the power to demolish doesn't mean I still can't be a human being. Hockey is a contact sport. Look at me. If I hit you, you wouldn't be moving anytime soon. But I don't have to be an animal about it."

"Let me make sure I understand. If you check an opposing player into the boards, rather than continue the play you would offer to help him up?" Mitch asked with skepticism. "Come on, I'm not buying this."

"You obviously haven't been to one of our hockey games. Yes, in the heat of the moment, I can become an aggressive hockey player. But I don't let that aggression consume me. I believe in fair play. There is no joy in crushing a hockey player knowing that he is too hurt to continue. I'm not an animal."

But you sure have the strength to be a killer, Mitch thought. He reached into an envelope and pulled out a number of crime photos. Several shots had very explicit images of some of the murder victims.

"Does anyone in these pictures look familiar?" He scattered the photos across the table. Brick gave a short gasp as he looked at the horrific photos.

"Who are these people?" he asked. His eyes were wide with horror but unable to look away from the pictures. "What does this have to do with me?" Mitch stood up from his chair.

"Look closely. Do you know anyone from these photos?" Brick looked down again and scanned the images.

"Sorry officer. I don't know any of these people. Why are you asking me?"

"Because someone on your team is a killer. Despite your teddy bear act, you are the most likely suspect." Brick stood up using his superior height.

"Based on what? Since I'm the biggest player on the team? You are out of your mind if you think I did this!"

"Maybe I should ask your new wife," Mitch asked.

"You leave her out of this!" He picked up Mitch and slammed him into the glass window behind them. The shatterproof glass held but the door immediately opened, and two uniformed officers ran in. Garson walked in behind him. Brick dropped Mitch slowly to the floor.

"I'm sorry. I didn't mean to lose my temper," Brick said to Mitch and raised his arms in the air. The two officers escorted him from the room. Mitch looked at Brick's eyes as he left. The big man looked like he was about to cry.

"You okay?" Garson asked.

"I'm fine." Mitch replied. "You think he's our man?"

"I don't know. Just because he has the strength and size to commit the crime doesn't mean he's our killer. Hell, all these guys are hockey players. They're all strong enough to commit murder; we just can't find a motive to tie them to it."

"I think I know," Lola marched into the room carrying a folder of papers. "I've found something common between all the victims. A reason that could explain what motivates our killer."

December 10, 2006

Light shone through the glass dome onto the dirt ground below. The air was full of fluttering butterflies circling the trees, looking for plates of fresh fruit set out by the park rangers. The arboretum was a showcase of beautiful and rare butterflies and the site of a special wedding. Brick looked down into the petite face of his lovely bride holding her tiny hands in his massive ones.

"I promise to cherish and hold you, through sickness and health, for as long as we both shall live." The minister smiled and looked up at the group in front of him.

"By the power vested in me, I now pronounce you man and wife. You may kiss the bride." Brick bent down to kiss his new wife. The guests clapped and several of the hockey players cheered.

"The romantic in me would like to settle down, with but one woman? Mon Dieu!" Stefan exclaimed to Chilly.

"Maybe you should be a Mormon," added Tunny standing behind them.

"How did they get permission to hold the wedding in here?" Rook asked Booker.

"The bride is an administrator for the dome and always wanted to be married here. Now be careful where you step, some of these butterflies are on the endangered list," Booker answered. A butterfly landed on Rook's arm and he tentatively tried to brush it off without hurting it.

"Dude! I must have smoked some powerful weed. They're little fairies floating around," Dozer commented, his face wide with awe. He tried to touch the butterflies fluttering in the air.

"For the millionth time, those are BUTTERFLIES! We aren't supposed to touch them," Taj knocked Dozer's hands.

"Where's the pot of gold, little fairies?" Dozer pleaded oblivious to Taj.

"Guys, line up!" Presley commanded. The hockey players lined up on two sides to allow the bride and groom to walk between them. "Raise the hockey sticks!" All the players except one raised their hockey sticks forming a triangular steeple for the happy couple to pass under.

"Do I look okay?" Dawson asked Chilly as he tried to see a reflection of himself in the glass.

"Buddy, if you're looking for compliments from another man, you're fishing off the wrong pier," Chilly answered.

"Dawson, stop playing with your hair!" Tunny yelled as Dawson slicked his fingers through his hair, like a cat grooming its fur.

"Sorry," he raised his stick at the end of the line. Brick and his lovely bride were all smiles as they stepped forward to walk down the line.

"Tunny stop shaking your stick, you're going to hit the bride," Chilly yelled.

"It's too late now to knock any sense into her. Besides these damn butterflies keep landing on my stick," Tunny responded.

"So what? They're not moths. They're not going to eat it," added Dawson.

"Actually, in Southern Kenya, there is a species of butterflies that eat small trees," Booker began.

"Everybody shut up and hold your sticks still," Presley commanded. Brick and his bride marched slowly along the stick-lined pathway. He had the biggest grin on his face. She was less than enchanted by the stick salute.

"I think she's enjoying the little fairies," Dozer commented.

The couple cleared the stick path and turned to face their guests. Brick and his bride waved back and everyone except the hockey player's clapped and cheered. Brick opened the tunnel to the outside and they stepped into a passageway that prevented the butterflies from escaping into the secondary greenhouse. The team continued to hold the sticks for the guests to follow the couple to the reception.

"Hurry up, my arms are getting tired," complained Rook.

"Steady men. Remember our promise to Brick," commented Presley.

"Well I don't remember asking to be crapped on by butterflies all day. I'm done," Tunny dropped his stick causing a gap in the middle.

"If he isn't going to, then I'm out too," whined Dawson. Slowly, the rest of team dropped their arms and guests sauntered out of the arboretum.

"Man, we never follow through with anything. You'd think we were still on the ice," yelled Taj.

"Stop your whining. Last one to the buffet table buys the drinks," yelled Tunny. The team broke into a stampede as they pushed past the guests into the next building.

The reception was held in an indoor botanical garden attached to the arboretum. The moist air rose up and frosted on the glass as it hit the cool December air. A huge fountain was in the center and the water gurgled into three separate pools. A large buffet table sat to the left with a dozen makeshift tables and chairs for the guests. A gift table sat in the corner. Surrounding the portable bar, the hockey team jockeyed for a drink.

"Light beer! Can I have anything weaker?" Tunny complained sarcastically as he watched the drinks being served.

"Stop you're whining, Brick gave us two free drink tickets," Chilly waved his hand at the bartender.

"Two drinks – that's barely a warmup," Tunny responded.

"Not everyone has the same tolerance to alcohol," answered the diminutive Taj.

"Check out the bridesmaids. Tres magnifique!" Stefan pointed to a redhead. "I believe she will have a partner for the first dance," Stefan motioned to himself.

"Unless smooth talking Dozer gets to her first," jeered Dawson.

"Dudes, I might ask her out. I'm feeling very mellow today," answered Dozer.

"You're not exactly high strung to begin with," commented Presley.

"What's your take on marriage," Chilly asked Taj.

"In India, a wife is like a sandwich?" Taj started.

"I like the start of this," interrupted Tunny.

"In the buffet of life, there are lots of sandwiches to pick from. Some are exotic, some are meaty, and some are very tasty," Taj continued.

"I like a big sandwich," commented Tunny.

"But once you start a sandwich, no switching to another one until yours is finished. You are true to that sandwich to the end," finished Taj.

"Spoken like a true romantic," Stefan commented.

Suddenly the reception was interrupted by an announcement from the DJ.

"Ladies and gentlemen, esteemed guests. Please direct your attention to the dance floor where the bride and groom will now have the first dance," the DJ directed. Brick and his blushing bride looked into each other eyes as they danced.

"I think I'm going to cry," Tunny said as he dabbed a napkin at the corner of his eyes.

"Stop being so sarcastic and be happy for them," said Chilly as he elbowed Tunny in the ribs.

"The bride and groom would like the rest of their guests to join them on the dance floor," asked the DJ. A spotlight illuminated the dance floor.

"Oh no!" Presley screamed.

"You don't think?" asked Booker

"I'm afraid it is," pointed Stefan.

In the center of the dance floor, the Coach's wife moved into circle. And she started to dance. Actually, it was more like spasming.

"Should someone call a doctor?" Rook asked

"No, that's the way she dances," Dawson answered.

"Where's Coach?" questioned Rook.

"Dude always disappears during these dances. Big surprise," Dozer commented.

"She's trying to draw the best man over to dance with her," Taj cried.

"Look away gentleman. This isn't going to be pretty," Tunny commanded. The Coach's wife started to shake around the best man, bumping and grinding into him

"Please somebody do something," cried Rook. The save came almost immediately.

"Ladies and gentlemen, it is now time for the bouquet toss," Brick grabbed the microphone and directed his guests toward his bride. He winked at the Assassins at the bar.

"That guy is a saint," Chilly raised his glass.

"I'll drink to that," answered Tunny. The rest of the team enjoyed their drinks. Unfortunately for them, their break was short-lived.

"Look at the other side of the reception," Dawson pointed.

"Who invited that piece of garbage?" Tunny yelled while drinking beers from both hands.

"I think he's friends with the bride's family," answered Taj.

"Who is he?" asked Rook.

"Tidwell. Thomas Tidwell. Calls himself TNT because he thinks he's so explosive. Nobody knows what his middle name is," Chilly answered.

"I heard its Nancy," said Tunny sipping another drink.

"God's gift to hockey if you ask him," Chilly continued. "He's the league leading scorer for the last two years and just biding his time before a call up to the pros."

"Mes ami! I think he sees us," mentioned Stefan. "And he must be very happy because he has the biggest grin.

"I'd like to wipe if off," Dawson said.

"Everyone be on their best behavior. We promised Brick no scenes, no fights. This isn't the hockey rink," admonished Presley. Tidwell broke through the crowd and greeted the team.

"Woo hoo. The Assassins! You kill anybody today?" Tidwell laughed at his joke and slapped poor Rook on the back.

"Day's young Tidwell! The day's young" answered Tunny. Tidwell ignored Tunny and motioned to Rook.

"Why don't you be a good kid and get me a refill? Do a good job and I might give you an autograph," he patted Rook's head and nudged him on his way. "It's going to be worth something someday. Some of us got to move on, isn't that right Chilly?"

"I'll give you a heads up when I get to the pros," answered Chilly. "Maybe I'll give you a little help to get noticed." Tidwell laughed his head off.

"You been drinking? I am the franchise. You're good but you're not TNT. The most explosive player in the KHL," Tidwell pantomimed as if he was talking into a microphone and his voice was loud and booming.

"Is he on drugs?" asked Dozer to Booker.

"We play you guys next week. You think the big guy," Tidwell motioned to Brick, "will be back in time from his honeymoon? Hate to see you without your enforcer. Wouldn't want to just walk through your defense," Tidwell laughed.

"Don't you get your panties in a knot, Tommy. With or without Brick, we'll shut your team down," answered Tunny.

"Oh really. And what was the score last time? 4-1 is my recollection. And I think my own defense scored on our goalie so you wouldn't feel bad," Tidwell sneered.

"Chilly scored," answered Presley. "I'm sure you don't forget your stats like that."

"Oh yes – leave to it Captain Elvis to look after his team," Tidwell motioned with his hand. "A captain always goes down with his ship. What's it like to live at the bottom of the league?"

"Just a different view. When I look up, I see a lot of assholes," Presley deadpanned.

"Tut, tut. There are ladies present," Tidwell responded. Before he could respond a large hand grabbed him on shoulder.

"Tidwell! So glad you could make the wedding," Brick said. "If I can pull you away from the guys for a few minutes, my wife wants to introduce you to some friends." He pulled Tidwell away from the bar before he could protest. Brick looked back while Chilly mouthed, *Thank you*.

"I hate that guy! He's so arrogant," Taj commented.

"Problem is, he has the talent to back it," added Chilly.

"Have we ever beaten his team before?" asked Rook.

"Not for as long as I can remember," Presley answered.

"8 losses, 3 ties and no wins," Booker stated as if reading an invisible statistic in his head.

"Just once, I'd like to beat him and his team. Wipe that crazed smirk off his face," sneered Dawson.

"What's stopping us?" questioned Rook.

"Talent, fitness, and fan support," replied Stefan.

"Bull! We 're not so unlike Tidwell. We just don't give our all anymore. Most of us had talent or we wouldn't be here," stated Chilly.

"If you guys would start working out again and not drink so much," Presley looked at Tunny, "we might actually start being competitive again."

"Fans might come back if we start winning again," stated Taj. "What are you saying Chilly?"

"The team's going to fold at the end of the year regardless of how we play," Chilly responded. "We have two options. We can give up now and go through the motions of playing the rest of the season. Or, since we have nothing to lose, we go flat out and make the rest of the league sit up and take notice."

"Dude, that sounds like work," stated Dozer.

"Alcohol consumption would have to decrease," said Booker.

"Everyone would actually have to start using the exercise equipment for something other than hanging their clothes on," commented Rook.

"Stop it! None of you guys are making this sound any better," yelled Dawson.

"Enough!" Chilly motioned everyone around him and held out his arm palm down. "Who's with me?" One, two, three hands stretched out until everyone had committed except one. Tunny was still holding two drinks in his hands and seemed unable and unwilling to place one hand to the circle.

"Come on, Tunny. We need everyone to commit," said Presley.

"Relax!" he put one of his drinks on the bar. "Play time's over. It's time to break necks and cash checks," Tunny placed his hand on top the pile.

"Then it's agreed," stated Chilly. "Drink up boys." Everyone placed his drink hand up in the air. "Starting tomorrow, the Assassins become a lean, mean, killing machine!"

Chapter 14   *The Familiar Faces of Death*

December 10, 2006

Garson leaned back in his booth; the sound of early risers chimed through the diner as the door opened for each patron. The sun was barely up, and he was drinking one of the worst cups of coffee in the world. The waitress placed a sizzling plate of bacon, eggs, hash browns, and sausage in front of him.

"Garson, how can you eat that? It's a heart attack on a plate," Mitch asked while drinking his coffee.

"The only thing missing is a greasy donut to put on top," commented Lola.

"When my brain needs nourishment, only grease will do," he answered. Garson looked at Mitch's empty plate. "Do you want some?"

"No thanks. I don't do breakfast."

"Fine." Garson glanced over at Lola's plate of fruit and whipped cream with a blueberry on top. "Lola, are you trying to make me feel guilty?"

"No, I don't have time to worry about your guilt," she answered, scooping up a spoonful of strawberries.

"Okay then let's talk about someone else's guilt," Garson downed his scrambled eggs. "What do you have for me?"

"Lola, you finish your meal. I'll go first," Mitch motioned while pulling out a folder. He placed it on the table and looked around to make sure no one could see the gruesome photos. "Possible sixteen connected cases over the last four years. Eight of the murders were asphyxiation; five were stabbings and three gunshot wounds. The murders took place in the fall and winter in eight cities and always involved a break and entry. Each time, the computer was smashed, and minimal items were stolen."

"Tell me about the three methods of murder. Any other commonalities?"

"Not that I can find. Asphyxiation victims were always the same – plastic bag over their head. There was little sign of struggle, no drugs in the victims' systems. Victim usually in front of television, two killed in bed, one on the toilet," Mitch answered.

"Killer has a dark sense of humor," Lola said between bites.

"Good point," commented Garson. "Why does he kill? Does he enjoy it or is there a reason he selects these victims?"

"We could be looking for a connection when there isn't one. Remember in the 90's, when they caught that serial killer, Frank Onyx. He picked victims at random from out of a line at the grocery store. The agency lost six months trying to find a relationship that didn't exist," described Mitch.

"That's where you're wrong! There is always a connection. The grocery stores were the connection. They missed it because the stores were in different locations, but it was always the same grocery chain. It wasn't until some unopened grocery bags were left at the victim's home did the police make the connection," Garson explained.

"What's common with our murders? Could our killer be a traveling salesman? There would be seven cities that he would canvas. Should we canvas the larger sales organizations in these areas and ask them to provide an itinerary for their salesman for the last few years?" Lola asked sarcastically.

"You know how long that would take and we don't have the manpower. And if it was a salesman, he could be from a smaller firm that doesn't provide that information," Mitch commented.

"You're right, we have to narrow down our focus. Tell me more about the knifing victims," asked Garson.

"I've been investigating them," Lola offered and pushed her mostly finished plate to the side. "The five stabbings were committed in four cities. Three deaths were in front of the television, one in bed, and one in front of the computer. Little sign of struggle, victims appear to have died immediately by a slash across the throat. Victims tended to be middle to upper class, all were male."

"Think we have the makings of a female serial killer? It's rare but maybe a woman is trying to make up for a past wrong," Mitch added. "In each case, the victim is killed quickly indicating speed. The victim was never moved, so we can't determine the strength of the attacker."

"Then what's the motive? Do the male victims have the same appearance?" Garson asked. Lola flipped through her notes.

"First victim blond, athletic, short, early twenties. Second victim balding, average weight and build, late thirties. Third victim long black hair, overweight, early forties. Fourth victim had gray hair, average weight, mid fifties. Fifth victim was a big guy, muscular, in his late twenties."

"Okay so they don't look anything alike. What about socioeconomic status?" Garson squirted ketchup on his remaining hash browns.

"Two of the victims were trades people, one was a teacher, one a wealthy businessman, and the last was an accountant," Lola reamed off.

"Doesn't sound like they travel the same social circles. Any common clubs? Fitness centers? Live in the same area?" Mitch asked and motioned to the waitress to replenish his coffee.

"Nada. Victims didn't frequent any common franchises. Some common mail – three had newspaper subscriptions to their local paper, two had subscriptions to sport journals, two victims had financial planners."

"Big deal," Mitch commented. "I get the paper and I have investments – doesn't make me the next victim."

"We're missing something. In each of the killings, the place is ransacked. The office, bedrooms torn apart," Garson commented, "as if the killer was looking for something."

"We assumed that the killer was looking for valuables – cash, jewelry, etc., to sell," Mitch added.

"But he doesn't search everywhere, usually the living room is left untouched," Lola mentioned.

"What if we are looking at this the wrong way. Maybe the killer is not looking for something, but is destroying something," stated Garson. "To always catch the victim off guard, it seems like he must know their habits beforehand. Wouldn't he know where their valuable were kept?"

"Okay, I'll bite. What evidence is he destroying?" Lola questioned.

"Each victim has had their laptop or computer smashed. Why destroy something that you could fence or sell?" Garson pointed out.

"That's pretty thin. Computers aren't very expensive. Why sell a computer and run the risk of someone discovering the dead person's files?"

"Fair enough. But why destroy the computer? Why not just leave it, or take it to search bank accounts?"

"Unless you have the password, the accounts are useless. Besides, carrying a computer with you from a crime scene is going to slow you down," Lola pointed out.

"Exactly, so why wreck the computer?"

"To destroy all of the electronic footprints of the user. Maybe the victims had some common files or searched similar websites. Any luck retrieving any data on the computer files?" inquired Garson.

"Very little," answered Mitch. "Some bank information, personal letters, some cookies on websites, sport pages, social groups. One victim was a fan of porn sites."

"That only applies to half of the male population," Lola added.

"In spite of that," Mitch fixed Lola with a stare, "there is too little information retrieved to find any common website's or programs that the victims might have shared."

"But since all the computers are busted, there is no true way to determine those similarities." Garson pushed his plate to the side.

"True – we're just speculating."

"Another dead end," Garson threw his arms up into the air. "Okay, who wants to tell me about gun shot wounds?"

"Got it!" Mitch answered while laying out three folders onto the table. "All three victims were killed in the evening hours - two in front of the television, one in the kitchen while taking a beer from his refrigerator."

"Alcohol will kill you eventually," commented Lola.

"The shots were three bullets to the heart – clustered perfectly for immediate death. The victim didn't suffer. Killer must be a good shot. The shots are almost identical each time."

"That or he shoots the victim from point blank range," Garson mentioned.

"Possible. Several bullets did go though two of the victims which could be because of close range."

"What is common with the three types of murders?" asked Garson.

"There are a few similarities," Lola interrupted. "They're always killed from behind. Gunshots are from the back, knife wound to the throat from behind, asphyxiation from bag over the head from behind. The killer might be afraid of detection if he faces his victim.”

“Either that or the killer is unknown to the victim. The worst killers are the ones that the victim already knows. They let their guard down and then it’s too late,” Garson stated. Lola scribbled in her notebook. “What else?”

“Neighbors never hear a sound. No gun shots, no screams from the victim. In the gunshot murders, the killer must muffle the sound of the gunfire.”

“Okay, but do the victims always live alone?”

“Not always. In four cases, the victim had either a roommate or family in the house. In three cases, the killer waited until the roommates were gone or the victim was separated physically in the house. In one murder, the wife noticed that her husband had been working in his office all-night and checked on him. He was lying in a pool of blood from a cutthroat with his computer smashed and books all over the floor.

“And she didn’t hear a thing,” Garson asked.

“Nothing,” Lola answered. “But it didn’t help that she had her music player blaring in her ear the whole time. A truck could have probably driven through the wall and she wouldn’t have heard it.”

“The hard drives must have the answer. Have the lab double and triple check that there isn’t something on them that we missed,” Garson motioned for the check.

“Okay, and what are you going to do in the meantime?” Mitch asked.

“Go see the Captain and ask for some advice,” Garson answered while handing his money to the waitress.

“The Captain! What advice is he going to give you except to shoot down the decisions you’ve made,” comments Lola.

“Actually, that is exactly the advice I am hoping for,” responded Garson as he left the diner leaving a puzzled Lola and Mitch behind.

Chapter 15   Survivor in the Sauna

March 28, 2007

Stefan's Interrogation

Mitch looked through the one-way mirror at Stefan. He turned and handed a file to Lola.

"You sure you want this one? The guy thinks he's a real lady's man."

"Are you worried that he will seduce me?" Lola questioned. Mitch's blush was the only confirmation she needed. "Relax partner. Garson thinks he'll open up better to a woman." Lola started to walk towards the door as Mitch put his arm in her way.

"You be careful in there. The first sign of trouble, I'm coming in," Mitch said.

"You will not! Just because I'm a woman doesn't mean I can't handle myself," Lola yelled.

"I'm sorry," Mitch apologized, as he stepped back "I don't want him to touch you, that's all."

"Maybe I do. Try not to be too jealous," she teased as she pushed him out of her way.

Stefan looked up at the female officer entering the detention room. *This won't be so bad after all* he thought.

"I'm Officer Price. You've been brought in here to answer a few routine questions.," Lola directed. "Think about your answers carefully and don't leave out any details no matter how small you think they are."

"Petite," Stefan offered.

"Excuse me?" Lola asked.

"Petite, it is a French word meaning small. You mentioned small details and I was giving you the equivalent word in French."

"And this is relevant because?" questioned Lola.

"You should know that we French people are very observant. We are connoisseurs of wine, food, and women," he looked at Lola to drive the point home. *I should be able to appeal to his ego,* Lola thought. She leaned in closer to show him some cleavage. She imagined Mitch staring at her as well.

"For the record, can I have your full name?"

"Certainment Madame. Stefan Fournier – born of the city of Montreal. Have you ever visited?"

"No, but maybe someday. Now back to my questions….."

"But if you do, you must come visit me in the summer. I will take you to a beautiful café. They have the best crepes. Magnifique!" He kissed his fingers towards her to illustrate their tastefulness.

"Fascinating. Now if you could answer some questions?"

"Absolutement, but have we meet somewhere? I never forget a face. Can you tell me your first name?" Stefan inquired.

"Lola," she answered. *Great. He's remembering me from the strip club. He's going to take twice as long to interview.*

"Lola," Stefan repeated. "Such a beautiful name," he motioned for her to sit next to him. "Please, sit down." Lola paused and then sat down to pacify him. He stood up almost immediately. "You look tired. Would you like a massage?" An evil smile crossed Lola's lips as she gazed at the one-way mirror.

"I am a bit tense. Please," Lola replied.

"That's a girl. Did you know I have skilled hands?" Stefan asked.

"I can tell," Lola answered pretending to really enjoy herself. She could imagine Mitch squirming in the other room.

"Such strong back muscles. Although it is very uncouth of me to ask, how old are you?" Stefan's hand dug deeply into her back. "Thirty-five?"

"I'll never tell," Lola responded as she made a face at the mirror.

"Thirty-two?" he asked as his hands caressed the small of her back. "Shall I go lower?" as his hands moved southward. A pounding sound came from the window. Both of them looked over and Lola realized that she had gone far enough. She stood up and walked to the other side of the table.

"Mr. Fournier, please. We have limited time," she pleaded.

"I'm sorry, Lola. I am being rude. Please ask your questions," Stefan looked charmingly into her eyes.

"Thank you. During the last year, have you noticed any suspicious behavior among your teammates?"

"Suspicious behavior? The stories I could tell you. You see, I play on a team full of men with something to hide. Some drink too much, some do drugs, some rent prostitutes, some start fights, other cheat on their wives, some drive too fast, and some don't pay their parking tickets. We travel eight months of the year visiting small and big industrial cities across the eastern seaboard. You want to hear about suspicious behavior? I suggest you get comfortable; I have a lot of stories to tell."

Lola cupped her head in her hands and gave Stefan a big blank smile to encourage him to relay his information. *I bet Mitch's getting the last laugh now,* as Lola glanced at the one-way mirror.

December 12, 2006

Stefan laced up his shoelaces and grabbed a towel from his locker. He passed through the change room and into the main fitness area of the club 'Strength Zone.' As he entered the gym, he immediately picked out the most attractive females in the gym. He spied a tall blond on a bike in the corner, and a small redhead working out on the mats in the center of the gym. He thought - *Who shall I hit on today?* His decision was interrupted as he turned to the free weights and listened to Tunny and Dawson's conversation.

"Do you think this shirt makes me look fat?" Dawson asked Tunny while watching himself in the mirror. Tunny didn't look up but responded with authority.

"No, your fat makes you look fat," and placed his dumbbell by his bench. Looking for a different answer, Dawson turned to Stefan.

"Does this shirt make me look fat?" he asked a second time.

"No, but your face does," Stefan answered much to Dawson's dismay. Without another word, Dawson grabbed his towel and headed over to the water fountain. Stefan sat down and placed his towel by Dawson's vacated bench. He looked at Tunny and shook his head to the left.

"Blonde at 3'oclock. Have you ever seen her before?"

"Yea, her boyfriend is the meathead on steroids benching ten stacks of weights in the corner," Tunny answered. Stefan was nonplussed.

"Okay, option number two. Redhead at 10'oclock. Did she come in with someone?"

"Not that I noticed. Did you see her with anyone Chilly?" Chilly pulled himself up from some crunches.

"No, didn't notice. I actually came here to work out. Besides Stefan, the redhead is out of your league. Your French accent will take you a long way but the rest of you is a bit," Chilly looked for the proper word, "underdeveloped."

"Mon Dieu! I'll have you know that I am in magnificent shape" Stefan was insulted.

"I don't think he was talking about your fitness," Tunny laughed. An arm slapped him on the back.

"Are you pumping up for tonight's game?" Presley asked the trio.

"Anything to give us an edge over Tidwell," Chilly replied.

"That guy really gets under your skin, doesn't he?" asked Stefan.

"If he wasn't so talented, I'd probably let it slide. There's no doubt, he's going to get the call one of these days. But each game my chances seem to diminish to make it to the pros."

"Don't worry, the rest of us will continue to make you look good," Tunny grunted after ten repetitions of his dumbbell. The four of them were interrupted by the arrival of another team member.

"Oh, non!" Stefan exclaimed. Dozer arrived with a towel over his back as if it were a superhero's cape.

"I am the Fat Assassin!" he yelled too loudly. Several patrons heard his comment and nodded in unison. "I will kill fat before fat kills you!" He struck a pose as if about to fly off in space.

"The only killing you're doing is the number of brain cells you have. What the hell do you want?" Tunny yelled. Dozer looked a bit deflated.

"Dude, the Coach asked me to come get you guys. We're having a team meeting in the sauna."

"The sauna! Is he trying to put us to sleep?" Stefan asked.

"Maybe he wants to toughen us up. Sweat out all the alcohol," Presley added.

"Then this is going to take a while," Tunny replied.

Five minutes later, eighteen men crammed into a twenty by ten sauna. They wore a variety of different colored towels around their torsos and several had sweatbands around their foreheads. Cedar walls reeked of sweat and the air was thick and heavy. Several players jostled for a comfortable position on the bench as the Coach, wearing his towel like a toga, studied his players.

"Welcome to the sweatbox! Where only the strong will survive! Months ago, I struggled to get your attention. You were lazy, uninspired, and had no drive," he began.

"This isn't very motivating," Taj complained.

"Bear with me, the good part is coming," The coach smiled. He surveyed his unruly bunch and continued.

"Now, with the team's future in jeopardy and the negative force of a certain hockey player named Tidwell. . ." Brick made a kaboom sound. Everyone laughed.

". . .You can become a team to be reckoned with. A team that wins. But it won't happen overnight. This next road series is crucial. We're playing the top three teams in the league in four nights. If we don't win at least two of those, we will be in a hole so deep that any shot at the playoffs will be nearly impossible. Remember, the two bottom teams in the division are eliminated. Cornwall's team is worse than us and will finish dead last. That leaves a race for the final spot between Albany and us.

"What are we going to do differently, Coach?" Brick asked.

"Get some new players," offered Tunny. Several players chuckled.

"That's one solution," smiled Coach. Most of the players looked nervous about Coach's apparent acceptance of Tunny's joke. Rook looked the most worried.

"Does this mean I'm cut?" he asked.

"Then who will wash our jerseys?" Taj remarked.

"Nobody is going to be cut. We win and lose as a team. You will find a way to become a winning club." He paced three steps forward, three steps back on the sauna floor. The heat was stifling.

"What do we have to do?" Chilly asked.

The Coach smiled as if anticipating the question, yet didn't answer.

"C'mon, tell us. Stop making us sweat," yelled Dozer, the master of the obvious.

"There is one thing we can do," Coach continued, "we retrain, we refocus, we rebuild. We work our asses off, and we go out with style. But I need to see if you really want it."

"I speak for the whole team, we want it!" yelled Presley.

"Yeah!" several players confirmed.

"Good. Prove it to me. Show me that you can face adversity together. I want to see if you can last fifteen more minutes together in this sauna as a team."

"Fifteen minutes! That's going to be murder on my hair," complained Dawson.

"Actually Coach, that's not real healthy for our hearts either. People have had heat strokes in these things," described Booker.

"Enough!" The Coach brought their whining to a stop. "Either work together to stay in here or fall apart. You decide." He pulled a stopwatch from his pocket. "You have fifteen minutes from now!" and he exited the sauna door.

"Hey, why does he get to leave," yelled Tunny.

"Probably heading out to get a drink," Brick added.

"I'm thirsty!" complained Dozer.

"Hold it together! We haven't been in here for more than a minute and already I want to kill someone," Dawson said. Several players watched Rook as he took a swig from his water bottle.

"Hey, the newbie has water," Taj commented. All of sudden seventeen pairs of eyes looked down on Rook like vultures ready to pick apart their prey.

"Does anyone want a drink?" he asked sheepishly. The bottle was swiftly taken from his hands and passed around the room.

"Liquid love," Brick said as he squirted water into his mouth.

"No, that would be a cool pint of beer," Tunny replied taking the bottle from Brick.

"Actually, alcohol dehydrates the body," commented Booker as he took the bottle. "In some survival stories, you can drink your own urine immediately before bacteria grows to replenish fluids."

"That's just nasty," asked Taj as he zipped across the room to take the bottle from Booker.

"Slow down speedy, you're generating more heat in the room," commented Chilly as he grabbed the bottle. He took a drink and passed it to Presley. "You're next."

"I'll go last. A good captain looks after his team first," and passed it to Stefan.

"Like the captain of a ship," Stefan commented while squirting the water into his mouth.

"Well, women and children first," Dawson took the bottle from Stefan. The rest of the players took a final sip and then handed the empty bottle back to Rook.

"Thanks guys – thanks a lot," he shook the bottle to confirm its empty.

"How much time is left?" Brick asked. As if on cue, the coach marched pass the glass part of the door with a whiteboard saying *ten minutes left.*

"Dude, this is too hot. I'm not going to make it," Dozer looked as if he was going to faint.

"Relax, we're all going to make it. Just be calm," commented Presley who looked at Booker. "How come you don't look like you're going to pass out like the rest of us?" All eyes turned to Booker who smiled.

"It's all about the ability to visualize, using your brain to trick your body. There was a story last year about a man found frozen to death in the back of a refrigeration truck."

"What's so special about that? Taj asked.

"The refrigeration was never turned on. The man froze himself with his mind." Booker responded.

"Get out of here – that's got to be an urban legend!" Chilly exclaimed.

"Can you show me this technique?" Rook asked.

"Me, too," asked Dozer. "I'm dying in here. Several others chimed in as well.

"Okay, but you must follow my instructions exactly. I need everyone to close their eyes and imagine they are standing in a middle of snowstorm."

"That's easy. I just shoveled my driveway," said Brick.

"Repeat after me – the wind is blowing, and I can feel the coldness on my face." The entire room repeated after Booker with their eyes closed. At this point, the Coach looked in to see his entire team in mediation. *I'll be damned, they are actually working together as a team.*

"Now feel the cold slide across your body, your teeth are starting to shiver."

"This is actually working," yelled Dozer. "I feel cold."

"Can someone give me their towel? I'm freezing over here," Stefan yelled.

"Simple minds," Booker commented.

"Oh yeah, visualize this," Tunny yelled. All the players keep their eyes closed. "In the middle of this storm, I want you to imagine two girls in fur coats."

"They must be freezing. I'll keep them warm," joked Taj.

"Don't you worry, it's about to heat up," laughed Tunny. "They open their fur coats, wearing bikinis that are so hot that they melt the snow. I'm talking beer commercial hot."

"Yellow bikinis?" asked Rook.

"No, red bikinis because they are red hot!"

"Hey, I'm sweating again. Cut it out," yelled Chilly about to open his eyes.

"These girls toss their coats into the sand dune and start playing volleyball. The sun is beating down and they start to sweat. . ."

"Tunny!" everyone yelled. They opened their eyes; the spell was broken. The Coach passed by the window in the door with a sign saying *five minutes left.*

"All right boys, we've got five minutes to go. This will be no problem," Presley said as he walked across the floor. Suddenly, steam from the center of the room increased as if the sauna rocks had grown hotter.

"What's going on? Did someone turn up the heat?" Brick asked. Outside, the coach looked back in. His sign now read - *Can you take the heat?*

"The Coach is an idiot. He's trying to kill us!" yelled Dawson and dashed to the door before anyone could stop him. He was met with further frustration. "The door is locked! We're trapped in here!" The rest of the team rushed the door.

"This time the Coach has gone too far," Tunny yelled and smashed at the door. Presley pushed everyone back.

"Everyone settle down. In a couple of minutes, this will be all over." He sniffed the air. "What's that smell?" Everyone looked at the source.

"Sorry guys, I have stomach problems," Stefan responded. Mercifully, the door opened and the Coach marched in. "Time's up." He stepped away from the stampede of players as they raced to the shower and pool to cool off.

"That was pretty risky, locking everyone in like that," Chilly said as the last man to exit.

"It was impossible for us to push the door out."

"The heat must have made your brains shrink," the Coach smiled.

"The door pulls in not out," he said as he tossed a towel over Chilly's head.

Chapter 16   *Following the Captain's Lead*

December 15, 2006

The stakeout had lasted for the better part of two hours. Five unmarked police cars were stationed around a three-block radius in a small suburban community. Garson hated this part of his job, the excruciating wait while the criminals watched movies and drank beer. He especially hated it because it had come at his Captain's request. Since progress wasn't being made in this investigation, the Captain felt it important for Garson to observe an operation in which progress was being made. It was like pushing a puppy's face down on a mess it made on the floor. Garson realized that with his Captain's ego, he was being taught a lesson.

Car Three was making a routine trek down the street. Inside the car were two plainclothes officers dressed as a couple. No radio contact was allowed until the house was secured. The female officer signaled Garson's car. No new activity could be seen from the house. Garson made no effort at small talk with his Captain. The time would come when his opinion would be necessary.

The suspect house looked extremely ordinary with green trim and an adjoining garage. The occupants inside were anything but ordinary. A series of bank robberies had occurred throughout the east coast from Maine to New York. The targets were always the same - rural banks with minimal security and generally inexperienced with armed robbery. The snatch and grabs were like surgerical strikes. The criminals always stayed a maximum of three minutes. All video cameras were blacked out. The robbers wore green army fatigues with black masks and gloves. They were forceful and quick and had managed to steal over half a million dollars.

Many banks had a small amount of marked bills to include with cash as a means of tracking down the criminals later. So far, the criminals had not passed any of the marked bills. Either they were well versed with identifying the marked currency or they were using a fence to exchange their money for new bills. For all they knew, the bank money could be floating around a country like Brazil where the currency could be cashed unnoticed. Everything had gone smoothly for the bank robbers until the last robbery in New Hampshire. An off-duty sheriff was putting money into his account when the three robbers entered the bank.

Police training teaches you that when no one is in danger, don't play the hero. Be observant, get as much information about the robbers as possible for future identification. Most importantly, don't draw any attention to yourself. Thieves just want to get in and out. Unfortunately, this sheriff must have flunked Police Academy 101 and immediately drew his gun on one of the robbers while opening himself up to the other two. The remaining robbers were forced to make a choice, which they reluctantly did.

One death later, the three bank robbers had moved to the top of the ten most wanted list and a special task team had been formed to bring them in. Captain Irwin was one of the lead investigators on the case.

"You're pretty quiet back there, Garson. Anything wrong?" The captain asked leaning back from the front seat

"No sir. I just didn't want to make small talk that might distract us from the stakeout," Garson answered.

"Don't worry about that. I've got eyes in the back of my head. Tell me more about the progress of your case."

"Everything's in my report sir. We're at a standstill until another murder is committed. I've had profilers, lab techs and other detectives review the facts. There is no correlating evidence to identify a probable motive for our killer. It's been a battle proving that the three types of murders are in fact done by the same killer."

"Have the profilers reviewed the possibility of three murderers acting in unison, almost like a murderers club?" asked the Captain.

"We've explored the possibility, but besides the three different methods of death, all other aspects of the crime have been identical. It's difficult to replicate the same crimes among different people."

"Difficult, but not impossible. Remember the Louisiana swamp murders. A group of young men executed tourists for years around Mardi Gras. They picked up tourists at the casino after a night of losing and promised them a big score for next to nothing."

"But their methods were sloppy. Each killer compared techniques and tried to impress each other. The crime scenes had as many differences as they had similarities. It always looked like several people from the start. They were eventually caught because of their need for attention and by talking to civilians about their murders," Garson defended.

"Keep your mind open. Don't judge from the start. That's what got your career sidetracked in the first place."

Great, another lecture on my past mistakes, thought Garson.

"If you read my case notes you know I've meticulously planned this operation from the start. These bank robbers are going to get justice tonight. Nothing will go wrong."

Suddenly, the suspect house's main window exploded. The lights in the house went dark, flashes of muzzle fire illuminated the night. Bullets slammed into the side of the car as Garson and the Captain dove to the street. Garson watched from the pavement as an escaping suspect ran and jumped into a neighbor's yard.

"You take care of your perfect operation, I'll take down the suspect," Garson yelled over the gunfire. He was gone before he could see the Captain's displeasure. Garson jumped over a hedge, barely missing a flower garden on the other side. A motion light flashed on three backyards ahead letting him know that his quarry was just ahead. The suspect looked to be in his early twenties, wearing a green hoodie with baggy jeans. He leapt through a sprinkler. Garson followed seconds later, getting his clothes wet. Moments later, he almost tripped on a hose laid across the lawn. *Keep your focus on the suspect or you're going to lose him.*

The suspect was young and athletic. Garson paced himself as best he could so his quarry didn't disappear. Garson resisted pulling his gun out. Too many cops fire their guns and usually end up hitting civilians rather than criminals. The kid was running on adrenalin and as soon as it gave out, he'd close the gap. He loved the chase. His heart pumped with blood from the thrill of the hunt. There were so many ways for the suspect to disappear and he hadn't gotten a good enough look at him. Garson leapt over a fence onto the sidewalk. Around the corner was a commercial district. More people and more opportunities to hide. Garson's legs were starting to feel the burn. He looked ahead and saw the Diamond Ville mall complex. The suspect burst through the Handy

Mart doors. The chase went from difficult to nearly impossible in a manner of seconds.

"Suspect has entered the mall complex on Blowers and Argyle. Entering main doors to department store – requesting backup." Garson yelled into his walkie-talkie. Something told him that the rest of the officers were busy at the scene and he was on his own. The main doors slid open, Garson stopped and bent over from exertion. He looked up into the aged eyes of the official greeter.

"Welcome to Handy Mart. Would you like a shopping cart?" the elderly woman asked.

"No thank you," Garson showed her his badge. "Did a young man in a green sweatshirt and jeans just run in the store?" She gave him a big smile.

"I'm sorry officer. I've been busy moving these carts. I haven't seen anyone rush in for the last half hour," she replied sincerely.

Great. The suspect was smart enough to walk into the store, not bringing any attention to himself. He could be watching me right now, learning what I look like. How am I going to catch him? He saw a department phone on nearby wall and grabbed it.

"Good evening Handy Mart Shoppers! My name is Special Agent Garson and I am looking for a suspect in the store. He is in his early twenties wearing a green sweatshirt with hood and blue jeans. Do not try to stop him. Please yell wherever you are in the store and I will apprehend him." He placed the phone mike back into his cradle and waited for any response. *Nothing. People probably thought he was playing a joke.*

"He's over here," yelled a woman in the grocery isle.

"I see him," pointed an elderly man. And the chase was back on.

The suspect was running down the left main aisle headed for the back of the store. An unfortunate couple was knocked down as he plowed between them. Garson jumped over knocked merchandise and shoppers froze in the aisle like rubberneckers at a traffic accident. He narrowly missed one woman and then slipped on some marbles as he rounded the toy aisle.

Great. The suspect is planting toy traps for me. A scream from the automotive section told him that his suspect was still close. Garson swung into the main aisle again and saw an object that instantly deflated him. Lying in the aisle was the green hoodie.

Damn it! If he's smart, he'll walk out of the store in a stolen jacket and I'll never know the difference. Only one thing left to do. He doesn't know that I didn't see his face and he can't run to the entrance without attracting any more attention. Garson ran back to the front and stood by the greeter.

"Did you find the young man?" she asked.

"Not yet," as Garson scanned the outgoing crowd, watching families leave the store. *Fifteen minutes left before the store closed. I hope he tries to leave sooner rather than later.*

It took years of training to read people. Some people were easy. You could literally read them like a book. They tended to be highly volatile and wear their emotions on their proverbial sleeve. It's easy tell if they were lying or feeling nervous. But most criminals didn't fall into this group.

The majority of criminals hide their emotions and nervousness from the untrained eye. Fortunately, to a trained observer they still gave hints of guilt. They tended not to be able to look you in the eye. Some had a nervous habit, such as rattling their keys or playing with their hat. Most of the time, you could catch their twitches.

The smallest group and the one that many criminals tend to dwell in, was the most difficult. They showed no outward signs of nervousness. Most had an air of disinterestedness, as if nothing really mattered. Some were bold enough to give a pleasant smile but did nothing to make them stand out in a crowd. They were remarkable for their ability to be unremarkable. I suspected my target was part of group number three.

I watched as a group of teens walked out talking and yelling. They were at that invincible stage where they couldn't get hurt. I almost missed the mother with her three kids.

"Excuse me miss, I need to speak to your oldest son," Garson pointed to the youth behind her. She looked back at the boy.

"Go ahead, he's not with me," she said and walked ahead with her two sons. Garson tackled the youth as he turned to escape. He struggled and Garson cuffed his hands behind his back while the remaining shoppers watched with interest.

"How did you know it was me?" the youth cried.

"I wasn't sure, but your pants are wet like mine from running through the sprinkler. Here's your sweatshirt," he threw at the youth. "Let's go!"

A few minutes later, Garson dragged the boy with him through the main door of the Handy Mart. The Captain stepped out of the squad car and walked toward Garson.

"Good job! We caught his partners at the house. They aren't making much sense right now, but I think we can finally put the death of the sheriff to rest."

"I wouldn't be so sure. Andrew here told me a little bit about his group. They're a bunch of potheads selling to the local high school. Apparently two of them won a pile of money in a poker game three weeks ago."

"But they attacked us first," the Captain replied.

"They were tipped off. A phone call told them they were going to be robbed by a rival gang. It's not too hard to make potheads paranoid," Garson pointed out while shoving his suspect into the back of one of the squad cars.

"That means… the realization began to dawn on the Captain.

"We were set up and probably watched the whole time ourselves. The bank robbers wanted to check if the marked money would get them caught. Now they have their answer."

"Tonight, was worthless and we're no closer to capturing the bank ring!" The Captain was furious and raced back to the squad car to get to the radio.

Thanks Captain. Your case may have stepped backwards but you given me an idea on mine!

March 28, 2007

Taj's Interrogation

"Can you repeat the question?" asked Taj, his face a state of absolute confusion.

"I asked if you killed any of the people in these pictures," Mitch pointed to the photos on the tabletop.

"I think you must have me confused with someone else. I'm here because my hockey team was involved with a barroom fight."

"Oh, we know why you were brought in. This is the reason you're staying. Let me understand something. Where the hell in India do you learn to play hockey?" Mitch asked skeptically.

"You don't understand. I may be of Indian descent, but I grew up in North America. My father, a doctor, moved here when I was four. I don't remember much of my life there," Taj answered.

"So how does a short Indian boy grow up wanting to play hockey?"

"I was raised in a small industrial town. In the winter, to fit in with the other boys in town, my dad enrolled me into minor hockey. I was small but fast. Other boys tried to hit me, but I could always evade them. In the beginning I played to fit in, but as I got older, I really I enjoyed the game. And I was very fast."

"How long have you played for the Assassins?" Mitch asked.

"About four seasons."

"Your father must be proud!"

"Just the opposite, he hasn't spoken to me years. In our country, all of our family are doctors. He was disappointed I didn't study medicine and decided to play hockey on a third-rate hockey team."

"So that's why you killed on the side? To impress good old dad?" Mitch leaned over the side of the table. Taj jumped excitedly up from his chair, knocking one of the photos to the floor.

"You are mistaken. My religion prevents me from taking a life. There is no honor in murder."

"Right." Mitch seemed less than persuaded. He shuffled some papers in front of him. Taj sat nervously back into his seat.

"Is there anything else?" Taj asked. Mitch was silent for a second – almost as if he didn't hear Taj's question. He pushed a bank statement towards Taj.

"Someone has deposited $10,000 in your account from a Madras Enterprises. Is that how much the price of murder goes for these days?" Mitch asked with dead seriousness. Taj gulped and looked awkward. "What's wrong? No fancy Indian metaphor to explain the money?" Mitch stretched across the table. His trap had been sprung.

"The money can easily be explained but is embarrassing." Taj answered.

"I'm listening." Mitch sat back into his chair.

"Playing hockey for the Assassins doesn't pay a lot of money. Occasionally I receive cash infusions to cover my bills."

"But you said you have no contact with your father. Who's your mysterious benefactor?"

"My mother has a catering company. More of a hobby than a real moneymaker but my father indulges her. He hasn't really embraced western culture, but Mom certainly has. She keeps in touch and gives me money when I need it."

"Listen Taj. This is reality check time. You are too small to climb any further in hockey. How are you going to support yourself without mom's generous deposits?"

"This is my last year. I can't go on anymore. I love this game and I've given my all to contribute to this team. I'm fast, the fastest on the team but the professional league wants larger players. My mother has saved money to buy a seat to go to medical school back in India. In the end, my father will get his wishes."

"Okay. We'll see if your story checks out. You're free to go back to your hotel. I may have questions for you later."

Taj stood up and walked out of the room. A knock at the one-way mirror caused Mitch to turn back and motioned his hand for the person to enter. Garson entered the door.

"Everything seem in order?" Garson asked.

"To a 'T'. These guys seem like nothing more than third rate players in a bad hockey league.

"Nothing except someone on this team is committing murder," responded Garson.

January 17, 2007   Oshawa Autodome Rink

"Hockey widow? What's that supposed to mean," asked Brick as he ripped off a strip of shin pad tape.

"Come on! As a recently married guy, your wife never used the term?" commented Taj as he hung up the last piece of his gear in his stall. "My wife complains that when we're on the road, she feels like a hockey widow. No husband for weeks and she always worries about what condition I'll be in when I return."

"Is she as small as you?" Tunny interrupted as he tossed a puck across the dressing room. Taj avoided it and picked up his stick.

"She may be small, but her heart is huge. I don't think she's missed a home game yet!" he answered with pride.

"Maybe she comes to watch a real man in action," Tunny posed with his bicep. He was interrupted by Coach's arrival. He carried a whiteboard under his arm and several dry erase markers.

"Everyone have a seat!" he yelled. Around the dressing room, players stopped their conversations and took seats in their stalls. The home dressing room had space for twenty players. There were hooks and shelves for all of their gear and sticks. A skate sharpener sat in the middle of the dressing room; its stone cracked from too much use. The Coach marked a number of X's and O's on the game board to outline the game's strategy.

"Let's keep the game plan simple tonight. The Birmingham Bats are the second-best team in the league. Taj – you're going to cover Tidwell like a shadow. When he's on the ice, you're on the ice. You're fast and can keep up with him. Don't let him get started or he can beat us all on his own. The rest of you," he pointed to his whiteboard, "I want you to trap their players in center ice. Don't let them get going with their speed or we're dead."

"I like your style Coach. Age and treachery will beat youth and speed every time," Chilly commented.

"Hands in the middle," Presley commanded. The team stood up and formed a circle, hands outstretched.

"Are you ready to win!" the Coach yelled.

"Yeah!" the team responded.

"Do I have a lady's team in here?' The Coach shook his head. "Take your purses off your shoulders and tell me, are you ready win?" he yelled again.

"Yes, sir!" they screamed with more enthusiasm.

"Well, don't just stand there. Get your gear on. Twenty minutes to game time!"

A car manufacturer built the Assassin's rink in the 70's. Concrete was a popular building ingredient at the time and architecture schools pumped out designs using it. Spectator stands covered the concrete with wood seats that were hard and cold. The roof was supported with steel girders and beams that allowed a maze of catwalks to flow overhead. The ice surface was regulation size, with boards that were well worn with multiple black marks from pucks. With the auto industry laying off people by the thousands, there were no longer any more donations for arena maintenance.

Tonight, the rink held about a thousand fans, enough to cover expenses for the team. The staff had been trying several promotions to fill its seats. During this game, the promotion was giving away white t-shirts with the Assassin's logo. The design consisted of a gun and a hockey stick forming an X over a white goalie's mask. On the back of the t-shirt was a bullet flowing right to left with the tag line – *"Another Game, Another Victim"*. Definitely not politically correct, but popular with a certain age group and demographic. The crowd noise died down as the announcers introduced the two teams.

"Ladies and gentlemen, introducing the league's leading scorer – Thomas Tidwell – and the visiting team – The Birmingham Bats!" The crowd roared its disapproval while the Bats skated onto the ice from the dressing room below the stands. Kids pressed themselves up against the glass trying to make a face. Tidwell hit the glass forcing them to sit back down.

"Bunch of monkeys!" he yelled at them. Tidwell skated around the ice, waiting for the Assassins to arrive.

"Ladies and gentlemen!" The announcer interrupted the crowd. The lights dimmed and a spotlight danced around center ice. "Please put your hands together and make noise for your Oshawa Assassins!" The spotlight illuminated a long tube from underneath the stands to the home bench. The tube was shaped like a gun barrel and multiple gunshots echoed through the arena's speakers. Tunny skated through the tube first and reveled in the fan appreciation.

"This almost makes the road trip worth it," Tunny yelled back to Chilly. Both teams circled their end of the ice in preparation for the puck drop. The Assassins went to their bench and a familiar visitor paid them a visit.

"Good luck tonight, Assassins," Tidwell yelled while skating past the bench. "I'd hate to see you guys get eliminated from the playoffs," he mocked and pointed his stick like a gun at the players.

"I'd hate to see my fist punch through your face," Tunny warned but Tidwell ignored the warning as he skated back to his bench.

"Concentrate on the game! A guy like that is trying to get under our skin," Presley warned.

"Let's score on them. That will put an end to his taunting, non?" commented Stefan. The Coach huddled them together. "We need a win or a tie tonight to stay in the playoff race. A loss and we're out. Play like your jobs depended on this game. Because they do." They put their hands in the center and yelled their pre-game chant.

"Let's kill'em!" they yelled much to the delight of the nearby fans.

The teams lined up for the face-off, the only moment of civility during the whole game. Chilly lined up at center ice to face up against Tidwell.

"Ready to lose?" Tidwell grinned.

"Not to you," answered Chilly as the puck was dropped. He flipped the puck Taj, who was promptly crosschecked to the ice by a huge lumbering player called Boudreau.

"More where that came from," taunted Boudreau slapping the puck into the corner. Taj picked himself up and limped back to the bench for a line change.

"It's going to be a dirty game, Coach," Taj commented before sitting down.

"Five minutes left in the first period and the game is scoreless." The announcer finished his beer before continuing. "Birmingham has had a few scoring chances, but the Assassin's defense has held them off. Unfortunately, the offense for the Assassins has been non-existent, only five shots for the period. Let's hope they have a better effort planned for the rest of the game. The face-off is in Oshawa's end."

After the face-off, the Bat's defenseman took a hard slap shot that rebounded off the net. Brick pushed Boudreau away from the goaltender's crease and was crosschecked. Unlike Taj, Brick could take the punishment and pushed back. Boudreau fell forward and pushed his stick into my knee above my goaltender pad. I fell down hard onto the ice. Tidwell picked up a rebound and lifted the puck into the empty net over my sprawling pads.

"And Birmingham scores with less than two minutes remaining. What a garbage goal! Looks like the Assassins have a few things to say about that," the announcer reported.

"Goaltender interference," Presley yelled to the referee. "Their player intentionally tripped our goaltender for the goal!"

"I saw two players fighting for position. It looked like your defenseman pushed their player into the goaltender. The goal stands!" the referee signaled for a face-off at center ice. The fans booed their displeasure. The announcer was obliged to give his thoughts.

"Looks like the referee needs a white cane and a seeing eye dog. What will he miss next? At the end of the first period, it is Birmingham one, Oshawa no score."

As the period ended, both sides skated off to their ends. Tidwell skated by and Chilly saw his mocking wide-open grin. *You'll get yours,* Chilly thought. As Chilly walked into his dressing room, he was almost hit with a flying goalie stick.

"He took me out by my knee. I need some support out there," I yelled.

"That's my fault," answered Brick. "I let him get in too close. I won't let it happen again."

"If it does, I'll take him out with a slash of my stick," I mimicked while swinging my stick.

"Enough. We're playing awful out there," Presley gestured while taking a seat. "Even with their cheap goal, we've had no chances to score on them.

"They hack and slash me before I can cross the blue line," complained Taj showing a mark on his wrist.

"Maybe we need to play with a bit more spirit. Anyone have a drink in their bag?" asked Tunny.

"I've been hanging by the blue line. When is a defenseman going to pass to me?" wondered Dawson.

"Dude, it would be nice if one of you forwards came back once in awhile," Dozer answered.

"Enough! Playing the blame game isn't going to do anyone any good," said the Coach coming in the dressing room. "You guys are lifeless. I'm changing the defensive pairs and the centers. Maybe different partners will change your attitudes!" The Coach marched back out of the room. Rook over at Booker.

"I've never seen the Coach that angry before. Why is he acting like that?" Rook asked.

"First time we've actually had a chance to make the playoffs," answered Booker as he snapped his helmet back onto his head and the team headed out for the second period.

As the team marched out of the dressing room, everyone seemed determined. Skating onto the ice, Stefan was almost knocked down by an overzealous Tidwell.

"Stay out of my way, French fry!" he jeered and skated over to his bench.

"He needs to be taught a lesson, thought Stefan.

"Halfway through the second period, Birmingham remains ahead 1-0. I don't know what the Coach said to his Assassins players in the intermission, but they look even worse," the announcer droned on. "The players are frustrated; the puck is just not bouncing their way."

"Coach! Let's go back to our old lines. I can't connect with guys I haven't played with before," complained Dawson.

"You'll switch back as soon you start showing some heart out there," he bellowed.

The teams skated to the circle for the face-off. There was a mismatch on the left wing as Taj and Boudreau lined up. Boudreau towered over his opponent and stood perfectly still as the linesman readied to drop the puck. With the linesman's back to them, Boudreau slashed Taj in the leg but Boudreau was the one who dropped to the ice. He gripped his knee. Taj's cry of pain was misinterpreted as a yell of aggression by the linesman.

"Two minutes for slashing – go to the box," the linesman pointed at Taj.

"Two minutes! He should get a major!" Tidwell skated in trying to sweeten the pot.

"That's a lie!" Rook yelled. "It was their player that slashed Taj!"

"Sure. That's why our player is lying on the ice," Tidwell yelled back. Brick had to hold Rook back.

I hate Tidwell, I wish he would go away, Rook thought.

"Control your player Brick! Otherwise I might make this his only season in the league," taunted Tidwell and pushed Rook into Brick. Brick had a slow fuse, but even he had a breaking point.

I'd like to throttle his skinny little neck, he thought.

"Okay, break it up!" the referee commanded. Taj was sent to the box while the teams lined up again with the Assassins at a one-man disadvantage. The linesman led both teams to the circle before dropping the puck.

Tidwell got the puck and passed it back to his defenseman, while rushing toward the net. Boudreau raced up the same side and blocked the linesman's view with his size. The Bat's defenseman passed the puck to Tidwell. Tidwell received the puck, but it was offside across the blue line. Both defensemen, Rook and Brick, relaxed and waited for a whistle from the linesman. No whistle came and Tidwell shot. I was caught by surprise, waiting for the whistle to be blown. The puck rebounded off the post and into the net.

"And the Bats score on the power play!" the announcer yelled, and the crowd was quiet with shock. The Coach almost burst a blood vessel as he charged onto the ice.

"The puck was offside by a mile," he ranted. No goal!"

"I couldn't see it," shrugged the linesman.

"Call the frigging cops," yelled the Coach. "We've just been robbed!" He stepped back into the bench to keep from falling on the ice. Presley went to the referee.

"The play was offside," he complained. The referee was less than sympathetic. "The linesman makes that call. No whistle was blown, the goal stands!" he pointed to center ice. The fans booed. Presley marched back to the bench as Tidwell skated by.

"Mess with TNT and it will blow up in your face," he mimicked an explosion with his hands.

I'd like to blow your head off your shoulder, thought Presley.

Taj skated back to the bench from the penalty box and Tidwell poked him with his stick.

"Hey Tiny. Thanks for the penalty. Looks like your team is going to choke again!"

That's funny, 'cause I would like to strangle you right now, thought Taj.

"With five minutes left in the second period, things are looking bad for the home team. Despite the bad calls, they have looked lifeless for most of the game," the announcer droned. "The face-off is in Birmingham's zone."

Chilly, Dawson, and Stefan were on a line together. Chilly looked back to Dozer.

"I'm going to win the face off. I need you to stand right here," he pointed to the line on the ice. "Got it?"

"You know it, dude! I'll slam that puck through that goaltender," Dozer responded.

"Just put toward the net, buddy."

The players lined up and Chilly and Tidwell faced each other.

"Don't worry, the game will be over soon," Tidwell mocked. Chilly didn't respond but when the puck was dropped, he rushed forward. He pushed Tidwell back while knocking the puck behind him. Dozer grabbed the puck and slapped it with all of his might. The puck careened off of the ankle of the Bat's defenseman and bounced past the goaltender. The goaltender couldn't see anything as it went into the net.

The Assassins scored! Boudreau gave a late hit to Dozer as payback for scoring. Dozer laid down on the ice. Tidwell knelt and whispered into his ear.

"Maybe you should stay down druggie!" he stood up and skated away.

Maybe I should put you down for good, Dude, he thought.

"Ignore him, Dozer. You did good!" Chilly congratulated him while the rest of his teammates helped him up to the bench.

"After two periods, the Assassins are showing some sign of life. Score is Birmingham 2, Oshawa 1. And now a word from our sponsor," spoke the announcer. Both teams headed to their dressing rooms. The Assassins were feeling buoyant from their goal. Booker was the last in from the ice. As he rounded the corner, he ran straight into Boudreau's fist. He fell down on the rubber mat and looked up to see Tidwell's face.

"You're supposed to be the smart one on the team. Tell your boys to roll over. We need the win to score home ice advance in the playoffs!" Tidwell poked Booker with his stick as he and Boudreau walked off.

I'd like to lay you out permanently, Booker thought.

The siren roared and the two teams returned to the ice. The fans were shaking the boards and cheered their team. The Assassins were only down by a goal. The Coach motioned his players into a semi-circle around the bench.

"Go back to your original line mates, prove to me want to win. Defense, do not let Tidwell pass the blue line. Do whatever you need to besides getting a penalty to bring him down. Get the puck in their end and shoot, shoot, shoot! Are you ready?" The players put their hands in the center and yelled their catchphrase.

"Let's kill'em!"

The third period was end-to-end action with scoring opportunities for both teams. The fans screamed their heads off. The tension in the air was so thick that several fans could be seen biting their nails. But the puck wouldn't go in the net on either side leaving most of the third period scoreless. With one-minute left to play, the game looked like it would slip away. When a whistle was blown in the Assassin's zone, the Coach called a timeout.

"I want Buck off as soon as you get out of our end and Tunny to go on as the extra man. It's do or die guys! Show the fans, show the Bats, and most importantly show yourselves that you can beat these guys! Let's do this!"

The teams lined up. Chilly and Tidwell jockeyed for the best position for this important face-off. They both stood tall, trying to push the other away before the puck was dropped.

"You two settle down or I'm throwing you both out," the linesman warned. He immediately dropped the puck and Chilly leaned down. Tidwell pushed on thin air and spun over top of Chilly. Before landing on him, Chilly tossed the puck to his right onto the waiting stick of Presley. Presley skated down the ice and crossed the blue line. The defenseman hooked his stick and pushed him towards the boards. I had already skated off the ice while Tunny rushed toward Presley. He grabbed the puck while skating toward the net.

He was about to take a shot when Boudreau slashed him in the arm causing him to yell in pain. The two of them pushed each other while Tunny kicked the puck to Dawson who was alone by the side of the net. He shot before the goaltender could cross the crease and hit the top of the net.

"The Assassins have tied the game! The Assassins have tied the game!" the announcer screamed.

Dawson was about to raise his hands in victory when Tidwell hit him with a crosscheck across his back that slammed him against the net post. He fell to the ice and felt a wet sensation on his face. His teammates rushed to his aid. Both teams cleared the benches and every player looked ready to fight. The referee feverishly blew his whistle, but he had lost control. Security streamed on the ice to break up the teams while the fans hollered with excitement.

"That's it, this game is over. No overtime. The score will be tied!" The referee yelled to the fighting mass. Security had to pull most of the two teams back to their benches

"You can't do that!" Tidwell complained to the referee. "We'd win in a shoot off!"

"Should of thought of that before you crosschecked their player!" the referee shot back.

On the ice, Dawson looked up in a daze and felt the blood on his face.

"Am I still pretty?" he asked.

"No, you're just as ugly as ever," answered Tunny. "Maybe a few stitches will finally make you into a man." As Tidwell skated by, Tunny gave him a cheap shot with his stick to the side of the head. Boudreau came back to return the favor, but two security guards held him back. Tidwell cupped his bloody nose.

"You can't do that. I'm the star of this league!" Tidwell screamed.

"Think again Tidwell. After this game, you're a marked man. And I can't wait to take you down!" Tunny yelled.

January 19, 2007

The wind howled down the city streets of Buffalo. Garson parked his rental car by the motel's front desk. He exited the car and slid under the caution tape as he entered the motel room. Lola and Mitch were examining the room where the victim was lying prone on the bed, his open eyes facing the television.

"What do we have here? Are you sure the victim is one of ours? It's always been in the home, never in a motel before," he asked Lola.

"Victim's name is Tidwell. Thomas Tidwell. A pretty good hockey player from Birmingham on a road trip through Canada and the States. Bit of a stuck up. Most players room together, but because of his status, he insists on his own room."

"And because he was alone, he was easier to kill," commented Mitch. "All the other players had a roommate."

"Tidwell was asphyxiated, identical to some of the previous victims. No sign of a struggle. Bag at his feet."

"Only two entries, the front door," Mitch pointed back to the hallway of the motel, "and the patio door. There is a fair amount of traffic in the hallway and the front desk can see down the length of the hall. The desk staff did not see anyone suspicious nosing around the front of his room."

"Which leaves the patio door," Garson commented.

"Unlocked. Since the room is on the first floor, anyone driving through the parking lot could get in. Television was on, sound could have masked any sound of a struggle," Mitch added. Garson looked at the television.

"What the heck is this?" Garson asked at the two beautiful women on the screen currently in different states of undress.

"Playboy channel. I guess our victim had an appetite for ladies," Mitch answered.

"Of course, Mitch hasn't stopped looking at the television since we got here," teased Lola.

"Just keeping the crime scene intact," Mitch replied and returned to examining the nightstand. Garson's gloved hand clicked off the television.

"This doesn't make sense. In this tiny little motel room, there is no way someone could sneak up behind you. Even if you didn't hear the patio door open, the bed is up against the wall. You can't get behind someone, unless. . . ."

"Unless you were in the bed with him," finished Lola.

"Well that puts a whole new spin on things," said Mitch. "Do you think the victim knew his killer?"

"If the killer was on the bed with him, I say he knew him pretty well," commented Lola.

"Does this mean that with all the other victims, the killer was sitting next to them?" asked Garson.

"Most of the victims were male, but there were two females. You think the killer goes both ways?" Lola batted an eyelash in amazement.

"If that's the case, he not only goes both ways, he's attractive to members of both sexes," she winked at Mitch.

"Lola, get on the bed," Garson asked.

"With the victim? That's just creepy Garson," she answered.

"No, the other bed! Mitch, get on there with her," Garson commanded while Mitch smiled.

"Don't get any ideas there, Brown," she teased.

"Mitch sit in front of Lola. Lola get behind him and pretend to massage his back."

"Actually, my left side is kind of tight," offered Mitch.

"Please concentrate. You have a dead man six feet from you," Garson asked.

"Well, that kills the mood," answered Mitch.

"Close your eyes. You don't want you to see what's coming," Lola mocked. Mitch faked closing his eyes, one eye peeked open as if sensing danger.

"Lola, put your fingers around his throat. Lightly," Garson added.

"That doesn't feel like a massage," answered Mitch jumping up from the bed.

"Exactly! If the victim was drunk - and I bet toxicology will confirm he wasn't - you would react the same way. There are no ligature marks on the victim's throat. He wasn't strangled."

"The baggy at the foot of the bed is big enough to cover his head." Lola pulled it up with her tweezers.

"Just like the stockbroker," noticed Mitch.

"Bag it and tag it," Garson replied. "Although you'd have to be pretty big to hold this over someone's head without a struggle." His analysis was interrupted by a knock on the door. A large, towering man looked into the crime scene.

"Someone was looking for me?" he questioned, his gaze carefully avoided the dead body.

"And you are?" Garson looked up at the big man.

"Boudreau. Brad Boudreau." The three-hundred-pound man looked strong enough rip off Garson's head with his bare hands.

"You knew the deceased?"

"Yes. Besides being a teammate, I made sure that no one touched him on the ice or…."

He hesitated, catching a glimpse of Tidwell. Boudreau looked visibly shaken.

"Or you'd hurt them," finished Mitch.

"Yes."

"Did Tidwell have any enemies?" Garson asked while opening his notepad.

"Sure, lots of guys were jealous of him. He was going to be called up to the pros before the year was up. He was good and he let you know it. But he was our gravy ticket to the playoffs. No one on our team would try to kill him."

"What about other teams?"

"Pretty much anybody in the league. We had an ugly game with the Assassins two nights ago. Anybody on that team would have wanted to kill Tidwell."

"Okay, thanks for your help. Go back to your room and stick around. We may have some more questions for you," Garson dismissed Boudreau, who returned to the hall. Lola suppressed amusement.

"Assassins? You men and your team names."

"Do you really think an angry hockey player killed our superstar?" asked Mitch.

"Seems unlikely. But I've learned to not rule anything out," responded Garson. Something caught his eye. "What is that in the corner?" Lola inspected the carpet by the corner of the bed.

"Not sure," she answered, "looks like something heavy was placed here and it made an indentation on the carpet."

"Cut out that piece of carpet and take it to the lab. Let the techs figure out what was there," Garson directed.

"Why did the killer choose the motel room? It's different from his previous victims," Mitch asked

"Maybe the victim is different. Get me all the information you can on Tidwell. Find out everything worth knowing about this guy. I think we've found the break we've been looking for."

Chapter 19   If You Can't Stand the Heat

March 28, 2008

Dozer's interrogation

"For the record, can you state your name?" Lola asked.

"Stephen Dozerwalis," Dozer mumbled.

"Can you speak up; I can barely hear you?" Dozer's shyness with women was evident to Lola.

"Have you ever been convicted of a crime?"

"No, dude," he answered a bit too quickly.

"Do I look like a dude?" Lola replied.

"Sorry," apologized Dozer with his head down.

"You know, we can look this information up?"

"Then why ask the question?" Dozer erupted. His shyness was replaced with frustration.

"You should try asking questions where you don't know the answers."

"Thank you for that insightful piece of information," answered Lola as she paced around the room. "I'll pass that on to my superior. Let me ask the second question again. Have you ever been convicted of a crime?"

"Yes, possession of marijuana when I was younger. And yes, I did inhale."

"Any other convictions?"

"None. You know that. What do you want? Why is the rest of the hockey team here?'

"Maybe you can offer a suggestion?"

"Between border crossings and arena fights, I can only imagine what the team is in trouble for now." Dozer answered. A rap on the glass window caused Lola to look up.

"One second," she motioned to Dozer and stepped outside. Garson was standing by the glass window.

"What's up? Did one of the hockey players confess?" she asked.

"No, but this guy has a record, right?"

"Possession of a narcotic. Misdemeanor. Doesn't make him a killer."

"No, but it gives you some leverage. Use it. If he's not the killer, then threaten to throw him in jail if he doesn't tell you who is."

"If he's guilty, I'll make him crack," Lola answered as she stepped toward the door and back into the interrogation room. She looked at Dozer fidgeting in his seat. "So how long has it been since you have stopped smoking weed?"

"Years," he stammered.

"You know we can do a blood test and tell if you've taken a bit recently," Lola commented leaning over the table showing her breasts. Dozer wasn't sure whether to be aroused or scared.

"Leave me alone! Can you at least tell me why me and my teammates are here?"

"I think you know," Lola answered while circling the table like a hawk moving in for the kill. "Why don't you roll up your sleeve and I'll bring a nurse in."

"Enough! What do you want to know?" Dozer voice trembled.

"Someone on your team is a murderer. I want you to tell me who." Lola pointed at him.

"Whoa!" Dozer almost fell out of his chair in amazement. "You've got to be kidding. There's no dude on my team that's a killer. You got us mixed up with some other team."

"Really? Tell me how you feel about Thomas Tidwell?"

"Tidwell? This is about him? He was a big jerk who made everyone feel small. If I meet the guy who took him out, I'll shake his hand and smoke a big fat one with him."

"Pretty coincidental that he died two days after your game. Maybe you wanted to settle a score?" Lola asked.

"Jeeze lady, this is hockey, not cage fighting. Our whole team hated him but so did a lot of other teams. Probably some of his own teammates hated him as well. Have you tried asking them?"

"I'll ask the questions. If you had to pick one teammate that hated Tidwell the most, who would it be?"

"You're sick, lady. You want me to point a finger at one of my teammates?"

"I want the truth, and so far, I haven't heard anything remotely interesting. Maybe you're the murderer. Got to feed that drug habit."

"Will you get off my case? Unlike my teammates, I know my rights. Unless your going to charge me with something, I'm free to go." He tried to stand but Lola's arm pushed him back down into his seat.

"Not so fast, we're executing a search warrant right now checking all of your gear. Think will find any drugs?"

"That's not fair. You can't do that!"

"I can and I am. But," she walked away from Dozer with her back to him, "I can make it all go away, if you give me a name." Dozer bowed his head in grief.

"Chilly," he mumbled. "Chilly has the most to gain. With Tidwell gone, he's more likely to be brought up to the pros."

"There. That wasn't so hard was it?" she patted him on the shoulder. "Sit tight, I'm going to pay this Chilly a visit," she said as she exited the room.

January 27, 2007

"Red 9!" The croupier yelled. Several players cried out in disgust as their money was taken away. Dozer had his money doubled up on the red square. He pushed the chips onto Black 25.

"Living dangerously," said Booker looking over his shoulder. The croupier spun the roulette wheel and the ball rolled around the edge.

"No more bets," the croupier yelled.

"You know the odds are stacked against you in roulette. Why don't you play some blackjack? At least you have some input. A rolling ball follows no one's wishes," Booker explained. The ball continued to spin around the wheel.

"Dude! In blackjack you beat yourself up if you go over or stay too low. Where's the relaxation in that? In roulette, it's all left to chance. You place your money on where you feel lucky and let the wheel decide your winnings.

"Black 29! Black 29!" The croupier called.

"Too bad you don't get anything for coming close," smiled Booker as he grabbed Dozer by the arm. "Come on, the guys are waiting for us in the bar." The two of them walked through the casino's aisles passing blue-haired grandmothers spending their old age security checks on the slot machines. A busload of elderly high rollers entered from outside and the sun temporarily blinded Dozer and Booker. The doors closed and as their eyes adjusted back to the dim light, they saw the rest of the team waving from the Neon Lounge.

"Did you win big?" Rook asked Dozer.

"Naw dude, karma wasn't going my way," he answered.

In the center of the table sat a basket of spicy hot peppers.

"What are you guys doing?"

"Hot pepper eating contest. Think you got the stomach to handle it?" Tunny asked.

"Is everyone going to try them?" Dozer questioned.

"Only the men will try them, mon ami," replied Stefan. "Have a seat." Both Booker and Dozer sat down.

"Is it true that red is the hottest?" asked Rook.

"Not necessarily," Chilly answered. "I've tried all types, purple, red, yellow, bright orange, lime green, and even black. It depends on the ribs and seeds inside for the heat."

"This stuff is foul. How come you guys like the heat so much?" asked Brick making a face while biting into a red pepper.

"Pleasure and pain," answered Booker sensing a need to impart his knowledge on the matter. "The chili pepper uses heat as a defense mechanism against animals to prevent it from being eaten. But for us, the wallop of heat is addictive and it makes you crave for more."

"In India, we cook it with our curry," Taj added, "but these peppers are child's play compared to the ones I used to eat. I've had ones that have stripped the enamel off my teeth," he exclaimed.

"Wow!" several teammates replied.

"You're full of crap, Indian boy," laughed Tunny taking a bite out a purple pepper. "This is one North American who can take more heat than you any day!"

"Sounds like a challenge," said Taj as he stood up. "I say we have the making of a hot pepper eating contest. Any other takers?"

"Not unless you force me," answered Rook.

"I'm out!" replied Dawson and pushed his chair away from the table. No other players stepped up.

"This makes it easy then. Taj vs. Tunny. T and T, mano-a-mano. May the man with the strongest stomach win." Presley signaled for the waitress and whispered in her ear. She nodded and headed to the kitchen.

"Speaking of TNT, anyone hear anything about Tidwell's investigation?" asked Brick.

"Not much. Heard the police don't have many leads," answered Dawson. "It makes your chances better in the league, doesn't it Chilly?"

"What's that supposed to mean?" questioned Chilly, not liking the tone of the question.

"Relax," Stefan put his hand on Chilly's shoulder, preventing him from moving forward. "Dawson's just acting like a jerk."

"Hey, I'm just saying what everyone else is thinking. With him gone, Chilly is the next player most likely to get pulled to the pros. Hell, our team just got a better chance to make the playoffs," commented Dawson.

"What do you think happened?" asked Rook.

"Who cares," said Tunny. "Trust me, the heat of these peppers is nothing compared to the heat where he's going."

"What is that?" exclaimed Brick as he watched the waitress return with a basket of black chilies.

"That is the king of chilies – El Diablo. So hot that it burns a layer of skin off as it travels down your throat. Are you gentlemen still game?" The waitress looked at Taj and Tunny.

"Yes!" they both responded as they glared at each other.

"Could you please sign these?" the waitress put a sheet of paper and pen on the table.

"What's this?" Dozer picked up the sheet and stared at the writing.

"A waiver," the waitress answered. "In case any of you big boys decide that the peppers get a little too hot, you can't sue." Both Taj and Tunny picked up a pen and signed their respective sheets. As they handed them back to the waitress, Tunny made a play to get her to sit in his lap.

"Why don't you stay. You can give a kiss to the winner!"

"No, thanks," she skillfully dodged his reach. "Swapping spit with chili breath isn't my idea of a good time," as she retreated into the kitchen.

"Crash and burn," Rook yelled excitably.

"Shut up! Or I'll force feed you all of these chilies at once," Tunny warned. The whole table hushed, ready to watch how much heat the two of them could handle. Dozer broke the silence.

"I'll bet $20.00 that Taj eats more chilies than Tunny!"

"I'll take that bet!"

"The smart money is on Taj."

"Can you give 2 to 1 odds?"

Chilly stood behind Tunny. "Looks like you may have bitten off more than you can chew, no pun intended. Taj has eaten hot, spicy food all his life, what makes you think you can take him?"

"Because I never back down from a challenge. And I'll do everything I can not to lose."

"I'll back Tunny. He's actually stubborn enough to win," Chilly nodded. Money traded hands. Presley held the bets. He explained the rules.

"Gentleman. The rules are simple. You keep eating hot peppers until one of you has to stop. To be fair, you have to eat the entire pepper at the same time and swallow the whole thing. You upchuck and you lose. You spit it out, and you lose."

"If you faint," started Booker.

"Then you lose," finished Brick.

"Any questions?" Presley asked.

"Yeah, can you shut up so we can go ahead and eat?" Tunny answered.

"Taj?" Presley asked.

"What he said," Taj answered. "You're going down white boy!"

"This is going to get ugly," commented Stefan.

"Begin!" Presley swung his arm down as if to start a race.

Both Tunny and Taj took a big black pepper each and chomped down hard on them. Neither one looked the least effected by the heat. They each grabbed a second.

"Dude, shouldn't you wash it down with some water?" he asked Taj.

"Actually," Booker interrupted, "water is not what you want to cool things down. Milk is a better choice, or the best is …"

"Bread!" Taj interrupted ripping a piece of bread and swallowing it to absorb the spices in his mouth.

"Ready to give up little man?" Tunny taunted as the two of them bit into their third pepper.

"Not a chance. Is that sweat on your forehead?" Tunny wiped the perspiration off with a napkin.

"Just a little warm," Taj replied as he stripped to his t-shirt. Both grabbed a fourth pepper.

Tears started to stream down both of their faces as the heat grew in their mouth and throat. "Ready to give up?" taunted Taj.

"And lose to you? I don't think so," Tunny grabbed his fifth pepper and Taj raced to keep pace.

The rest of the bar had taken notice of the competition. Several people yelled in the back, giving their support or taunting the participants. Both players looked as red as beets.

"We can call this a tie if the two of you are willing to both walk away," Presley advised.

"Never," Tunny and Taj yelled back in unison.

"Then eat up boys, there's lot more peppers in the basket," taunted Dawson getting in close to the table. Tunny grabbed a pepper with gusto and juices went flying. Dawson was sprayed in the face. "He got me in the eye! It's burning," he screamed. Dawson crumpled to the ground as the rest of the team surrounded him.

"He can wash it out with my beer," Dozer tried to hand it to Dawson.

"No, that will make it worse," cried Booker. "Get a glass of water!" Stefan grabbed one from the table.

"Brick, hold him down!" Stefan yelled. Brick put his massive arms on Dawson's shoulders to hold him to the floor despite his thrashing. "This will take a few seconds," he said as Stefan placed the glass over the eye and brought Dawson's head up. "Open your eyelid!"

"I can't! It burns!"

"Stop being a baby," Chilly put his hand above Dawson's eye and flushed it with the water. The water helped and Dawson struggled less. They placed him sitting upright in a chair. Rook handed him some towels to absorb the moisture and he placed it over his eye.

"Thanks," Dawson croaked to the team. "I don't know if I can see but at least it isn't burning anymore." The waitress returned and bent next to the table.

"Sorry guys. My manager says you have to go. You're scaring away all the older customers and they spend a heck of lot more money than you guys."

"But we haven't finished the peppers, yet!" Rook cried.

"You're just in time to see a winner crowned," a very sweaty Tunny gasped.

"Yeah. I'm about to put this lightweight out of the competition,' said Taj with tears pouring down his face. The waitress shook her head.

"You boys will both be losers tomorrow morning when you're sitting on the toilet. Trust me, by quitting now, I'm saving your butts, literally," she smirked and slid back into the crowd.

January 23, 2007

The gun muzzle flashed three times. Three bullets tore through her target's forehead. Lola smiled and blew the smoke from her gun barrel.

"Man, that's so cliché," remarked Mitch. "You watch too many action movies. Don't you know how dangerous it is waving your gun around like that is?" He holstered his gun and pressed a button to bring his target toward him. The gunnery range was located in a soundproof floor in the basement of the police building. Except for them, the range sat empty.

"You're just jealous of my kill shots. Look at this," she pulled her paper target off the clip and waved it at Mitch. "Two shots between the eyes and one in his throat. This is one serial killer that isn't going anywhere ever again."

"Lola, how many times will a killer stand still in front of you? On television, murderers get killed all the time. In real life you better injure your target first before using deadly force or you'll be serving your own time."

"Blah, blah," Lola responded unimpressed by the lecture. "Let's see your remarkable shots." Mitch handed over his paper target. There were two bullet holes in the left leg and two bullets in the left arm.

"The idea is to injure or disarm your attacker. This killer can't get away from me or shoot me."

"Doesn't mean he's not dangerous."

"Doesn't mean I have to kill him." Lola's phone rang interrupting their disagreement.

"Officer Price." She paused, listening to the caller. "No, no plans. Yes, he's with me. No, you're not interrupting anything," she said curtly. "Okay we're on it." Lola smacked the phone shut.

"What's up? Was that Garson?" Mitch asked.

"Yep." Lola holstered her gun and put her jacket on. "He's got an assignment for us. You're taking me out tonight."

Fifteen minutes later, the pair was driving through the suburbs of Buffalo. Traffic was slow as Friday night revelers rushed out to fill the bars.

"Garson wants us to do what?" Mitch exclaimed squirming restlessly on the passenger seat. Lola turned to him and smiled.

"All of the Birmingham's players alibi's check out except for one. Brad Boudreau. Apparently, his roommate said he slipped out for a few hours in the middle of the night. Exactly the time Tidwell was killed."

"Why didn't Boudreau's roommate say something when we questioned them at the motel?"

"Boudreau's a beast. The players were terrified with him around. He spoke later in follow-up when he was alone and particularly begged the officer to swear that he wouldn't tell Boudreau who told on him."

"Probably won't stay a mystery for long."

"Doesn't matter, we have to bring in him for more questioning. The team is finishing their supper now before heading back to the motel. They've canceled their road trip and are returning to Birmingham first thing in the morning. We need to get him now."

"Great! We get to pick up a guy who can break the two of us in half in front of his teammates. No problem. Piece of cake," Mitch replied sarcastically. Their car pulled up to the restaurant just as the Birmingham Bats exited the main doors.

"Want to get him here or at the hotel?" Mitch asked.

"Let's get this over with now," Lola answered and put her badge over her jacket. The players continued to file out and entered a few cabs. The large silhouette of Boudreau was noticeably absent. Lola prepared to open her car door.

"Give him another minute. Maybe he has to beat up some small children on the way out," Mitch commented. As if on cue, Boudreau emerged from the glass door on his own and signaled for a cab.

"Why do I get the feeling that he's not going back to the hotel?" Lola asked.

"Give him some space. Let's follow the cab and see where it goes. It may tell us more than questioning him."

They followed the cab to the nightclub district. It soon became difficult with the traffic to keep Boudreau's cab in sight.

"Get close Lola. We don't want to lose him!" Mitch yelled.

"I'm trying. I don't want to get too close in case he looks back and recognizes us from the crime scene."

Boudreau's cab stopped suddenly next to a club called the *Velvet Underground.* Boudreau exited his cab, walked down the steps and disappeared into the club. Lola and Mitch passed the club and parked down the street.

"Not exactly the type of club I expect the team's enforcer to be going to."

"What you'd rather a bar called *Rifles and Rednecks*?" mocked Lola.

They walked to the main door. A large bouncer dressed to look like a pimp approached them.

"Cover charge if you're without a costume," he asked.

"How's this for my costume?" Lola waved her badge.

"Undercover cops, now that's original," he responded sarcastically as they entered. The bar opened up to a huge dance floor with tables and booths surrounding the south and west sides. A large bar was to the east. Costumed revelers packed the dance floor. It was impossible to see Boudreau in the masses.

"Looks like Mardi Gras exploded in this bar," said Mitch.

"You circle to the right; I'll take the left. There's only one public entrance. Even with the costumes, Boudreau is going to stand out." Lola headed straight into the mass of partiers. Cigarette smoke hung in the air, forming a thick cloud over the dancers. *I'll need to wash the stink out of my clothes tonight,* thought Lola. She looked over at the booths in the corner and saw a large man from behind. He was sitting with a man and a woman who both wore dresses. *Must be a charming couple.* As she headed in their direction, an arm crossed her path and prevented her from moving forward. She looked up at a tall man wearing a bright fur coat.

"Where's the costume, baby?" He asked with an entourage behind him watching his every move.

"I'm a cop," she waved her badge on her necklace to him. "You're blocking my way." Either he was drunk or didn't believe her because his arm didn't move.

"Then I'd like to report a crime," he said without missing a beat. "You've stolen my heart," he placed his other arm over his chest. "How about I buy you a drink and you can fill out my report?" he smiled. His friends slapped hands behind him after his comment.

Lola smiled back, disarming him for a second and he relaxed his arm. She grabbed it and twisted his arm behind his back. She pushed his face onto the bar next to an ashtray.

"The bar is loud, maybe you didn't hear me the first time," she yelled over his prone body. One of his buddies advanced on her from behind. She kicked her leg back right into his crotch. He went down like a bag of dirt. Before his other buddies advanced, she pulled a tazer out of her belt and showed it to them. "First jerk with any ideas, gets a jolt of this." They got the message and backed off.

Great! Now I've probably tipped off Boudreau.

Mitch pushed through the dance crowd trying to see further in front of him. He caught sight of Boudreau sitting next to a provocatively dressed woman in a booth. *Glad to see someone is getting picked up.* His attention was diverted as he slid by a blond woman on the dance floor. She smiled at him and he smiled back. He turned into the path of an incoming fist that almost took his head off.

He flew though the air and landed on the dance floor as people parted the way between him and his attacker. He looked up into the angry eyes of Boudreau.

"Why are you following me? I saw you at the restaurant and now you're here. What do you want with me!" he screamed. Mitch's head was swimming, but he had the presence of mine to hold up his badge. "Officer Daniels. I'm here to bring you in for questioning about the death of Thomas Tidwell," said Mitch as he struggled to stand up.

"I've told you that I had nothing to do with his death. I was in my room that night."

"We have a new source that says otherwise," Mitch responded. At that, Boudreau exploded with new anger and pinned Mitch against the wall.

"Who said that? I'll kill him!" Boudreau's massive hands cut the oxygen to Mitch's brain as two bouncers stepped behind Boudreau. One put his hand on Boudreau's shoulder. Boudreau swung his arm without looking back and knocked the large man backwards against a wall. The bouncer fell to the floor, obviously knocked out. The second bouncer tried to grab Boudreau's thumb to bring the big man down. Boudreau sidestepped, letting Mitch go for a moment as he punched the bouncer in the gut. The bouncer's eyes went wide, and he dropped to the floor. Boudreau returned his attention to Mitch.

"Who told you I was missing?' he screamed, his grip like a vise on Mitch's throat. Mitch reached out in panic to calm the Boudreau down. He reeled from the lack of oxygen and his vision was going black. Suddenly, Boudreau's eyes went wide and his body limp. Boudreau's entire weight came crashing down on Mitch, pinning him to the floor. Mitch tried to pull himself out while gasping for air. He turned to his right and Lola extended a hand to help. In her other hand, she held her tazer.

"Had to use the highest level. The charge should have taken down an elephant," Lola said.

"I'd rather reason with an elephant," Mitch answered as he stepped up off on the floor. He held out his hand to signal Lola for a glass of water. She grabbed one from a passing waitress.

"Looks like we caught our killer," answered Mitch between gulps. "Nobody would have put up a struggle like this unless he's guilty."

"Actually," Lola smiled, "He has an alibi. I spoke to his date." She pointed back to the booth toward the couple wearing dresses.

"What did she say?" answers Mitch.

"She didn't. He did," she pointed to the man in a dress, "Boudreau was with him. Boudreau wasn't trying to hide the fact he's a murderer. He was trying to hide the fact that he's gay."

March 28, 2007

Tunny's Interrogation

Tunny leaned back in the interview chair with his feet on the table. Lola, Garson, and Mitch watched him from the window in the interview room.

"This guy looks like he is enjoying himself in there. Maybe he's our killer?" Garson commented as he peered through the window.

"Either that or he just doesn't care. Let me go in first and you follow," she pointed at Mitch. "I'll be the good cop." Lola replied and walked into the room. Garson sat down to watch the show. Tunny looked up at Lola as she sat down next to him.

"Officer, I want to make a confession." Tunny explained.

"You have my full attention," answers Lola.

"You need to know something about me. I'm a killer," Tunny said seriously and brought his face closer to Lola.

"What do you mean?" she answered trying to hear his next words.

"I'm a killer. A killer in bed!" he laughed and almost fell out of his chair. "How would you like to examine the evidence," He pointed to his crotch. Mitch slammed open the interrogation room door before Lola could give her response.

"One more stupid comment like that and I will charge you with obstruction of a police investigation! Do I make myself clear?" He smashed his fist down on the table. Tunny looked unimpressed. He leaned over to Lola.

"I take it, he's the bad cop?" Lola looked at him and smiled.

"For you, we're both bad cops." She stood up and walked behind him.

"Wow, just when I thought you couldn't get any hotter," Tunny exclaimed. "I'll answer any of your questions, but if this takes too long, you can always take me home afterwards," he leered at Lola.

"We'll keep you as long as we want. How quickly you leave depends on your cooperation," Mitch answered.

"You cops should really loosen up," Tunny replied.

"Where were you on the night of September 5th?" asked Lola.

"September? Jesus, that's six months ago! I can barely remember what I had for lunch," responded Tunny.

"Let me refresh your memory. You were in Manchester, New Hampshire, playing a team called…" Mitch mentioned as he leafed through a folder.

"Maniacs," completed Lola.

"Oh yeah, those bunch of losers," replied Tunny.

"You lost 5-2 that night," Mitch added.

"Sorry, we've lost a lot of times. They all tend to blur. What's so special about the Maniacs? Did I hit one too hard and he cried to you cops?"

"No, But a Francis Macdonald was killed in his sleep on September 5th at 1am. Three hours after your game."

"Jeeze, with a name like Francis, you sure it wasn't suicide," joked Tunny.

"This is not a laughing matter! You were in the area at the same time and are considered a suspect."

"Why? Based on what evidence? I'm a goon for a bad hockey team. Why would I want to kill some guy named Francis? Because I hate the name?"

"Why don't you tell me?' Mitch asked.

"You guys are insane. I think your female partner just wanted to haul me in so she could see what a real man looks like," Tunny sneered at Mitch.

"Shut the hell up," Mitch snapped and kicked the chair out from under Tunny. He fell to the floor.

"Brother, if you wanted a fight, you came to the right place." Tunny cocked his fist back. Before he could connect, Lola extended her hand.

"Sorry for the misunderstanding. You're free to go. If you think of anything, please call." She extended a card. Tunny read the phone number. He stood up and looked at Mitch.

"Oh, she wants me," he smiled and walked out of the interrogation room door.

February 16, 2007

Tunny ran through the warehouse; his breath came in short gulps. He stopped at a partial brick wall while he checked the gun in his hand. *Five shots left – that's not going to be enough to save my life!* He wiped the sweat off his forehead with his glove. The warehouse reeked of death. He had left the rest of his teammates behind him and he was sure they were all dead. He wasn't sure how many were stalking him, but he wouldn't go down without a fight. *I've got to find some place to hide, give myself a few minutes to think. I'm dead meat out in the open.*

He ran from the wall to a corner with some barrels and broken forklift palettes. *A dead end. No place to run but a good place to make a final stand.* Nobody could get him without Tunny seeing them. He controlled his breathing to prevent anyone from hearing him in his hiding spot.

The warehouse had poor lighting with no visible access to the outside. The floors were slick with moisture and Tunny had to clamp his jaw to prevent his teeth from chattering. He checked his pockets in the vain hope of finding something he could use against his attacker. *Nothing. If only we were still at the hockey rink. My stick would be perfect.*

Crunch! Footsteps on a broken board, the sound rang though the warehouse. Tunny cocked his gun and peeked through the slats of the palette. For a minute, nothing moved. Then to the far right, he saw a shadow of a foot behind an old oil barrel.

Come on, show yourself. Give me anything, your foot, an arm, your head! As if on cue, his attacker's foot poked from beyond the barrel. Tunny needed no further encouragement.

He fired his gun and the bullet flew straight to its intended target. He heard the sickening crunch of a bullet impacting skin.

"I'm hit!" a voice yelled in panic. Before Tunny could enjoy his kill, a grenade flew over his barricade. Without thinking, Tunny leapt over the other side before the grenade exploded. His gun went flying under a crate and several bullets fell out of his gun. He crawled, trying not to alert his attacker to his predicament. The gun was lodged deep under a palette. He stretched his fingers to grasp the handle. *Damn it! I can't reach it!* He stood up to go to the other side. The bullet hit him square in the back. He turned to face his fate.

"I'm dead!" he yelled as he received two more bullets to his chest.

"You're dead!" smiled Brick with a paintball gun in his hand. A referee with an orange vest stood between them.

"Game over! Red team wins," he yelled, and the lights went on overhead.

The warehouse was a war games business called Paintball Nation. The guns were pistols loaded with paintball pellets, a round colored ball with a thin plastic membrane that broke on contact. Despite their appearance, these bullets could hurt.

"Whose grenade was that?" Tunny complained. "I thought we weren't using them until the final game?"

"That was me," Rook popped out of a barrel with a fresh blue paint mark on his foot courtesy of Tunny. "I just wanted to see how they worked." They both looked in the area that Tunny had hidden in. The grenade was a long piece of plastic tubing with two holes in the ends. The tube broke on contact, any paint marks larger than the size of a dime, was considered a kill.

"Didn't realize you wanted me dead so badly," said Tunny.

"You'd be surprised," answered Presley walking out the safe zone where all the dead players watched the action.

"Dude, you were awesome!" Dozer slapped Tunny on the back. "How come you're so aggressive?"

"Simple," Tunny smiled. "Unless you want to be just another nerd in the herd, you got to take chances. Stick with me in the next game and I'll lead you to glory." Tunny's motivational talk was interrupted by the referee's announcement.

"Can I get everyone to gather round?" the referee motioned everyone to the safe zone. The hockey team formed a semi-circle around him.

"This is the last game before the field shuts down for the day. What game do you guys want to play?"

"Capture the flag!" yelled Chilly.

"Wanted Dead or Alive!" said Stefan.

"Medic!" rallied Taj.

"Kill the President!" screamed Tunny. There is silence as all his teammates look at him like a lunatic. "One team protects one of their teammates from the rest of us. It's a blast!"

"How about Speedball?" questioned Presley.

"What's that?" asked Dozer.

"Simple game," answered the referee, "but fun with loads of bullets."

"Count me in," replied Rook.

"Each team stands at opposite ends of the warehouse until the horn sounds. It's a race to the center to ring this bell," the referee held a gold bell on a stand. "I'll stand it on top of this spool. It's a race from your end to the center without being shot. First team member that reaches the bell alive, wins." The referee looked around and assigned the captains. "I want you," pointing at Brick, "and you," pointing at Booker, "to pick out your teams before we start."

"How about our goaltender? Are you playing this game?" Rook asked me.

"No, I'll sit this one out. Don't want to hurt myself before tomorrow's game," I answered. It was more fun watching these guys shoot at each other than playing. They divided up into two teams:

Brick picked Rook, Dozer, Taj, and Presley. Taj pointed to Brick. "I'm going to ask the referee if I can wear these for the final game," he pointed to a set of goggles. "I picked them up at an army surplus store."

"How will you use them?"

"You'll see," Taj answered as he went over to talk to the referee.

Booker picked Tunny, Dawson, Chilly, and Stefan. "I'm going to buy some more bullets for the final game. Up my kill rate," Tunny smirked. This started a stampede of team members rushing to augment their ammunition.

Minutes later each team stood at opposing ends of the warehouse, ready to break out into a run to the center. Each team had to touch the wall so neither side had an advantage. Both sides were tense, ready to react to the sound of the bullhorn.

"As soon as the game starts, I want Tunny to dash to the center first with the rest of you providing cover. In this kind of game, it doesn't hurt to play aggressive," said Booker.

"Almost matches the way we've been playing on the ice lately," commented Chilly.

"I know, and tonight we play against the Lewiston Bears. Our winning streak needs to continue," Stefan responded and patted Dawson on the back.

"Lewiston! Those guys are either drunk or inbred. I should know I'm from there," Dawson commented. His teammates laughed.

"What's so funny?" asked Dawson.

"You don't look drunk," answered Tunny.

"Boooommmm!" The air siren scream deafened all those around it. Before the teams could pounce, the lights in the entire warehouse went dark.

"What the hell is going on?" yelled Tunny. "I can't see a foot in front of my face."

"Hey, are you guys screwing with us?" Brick yelled from the other end of the warehouse.

"No! We thought you were," answered Dawson.

"Everybody stand still!" Booker yelled. "I don't want anybody to get hurt. Something must have knocked out the power." Suddenly several speakers pumped out instrumental music with a heavy dance beat.

"If the power is out, how come the music is playing?" yelled Stefan.

"Maybe this is part of the game?" asked Rook.

"If it is, I'm not liking it," Chilly said and took a shot into the wall. The glow of the bullet and its impact on the wall, lit up the warehouse.

"Whoa, Dude!" yelled Dozer. "They sold us glow in the dark ammunition. Righteous!" Several others fired off shots and the warehouse brightened up allowing the teams to see ahead of them."

"Watch out! You almost hit me," complained Dawson to his teammates.

"That's the answer! Use the cover fire to light a path to the center of the warehouse," Brick yelled.
The warehouse lit up like a fireworks display as the players sprayed their ammunition to light a path to the center. Unfortunately, the team's excitement turned to a lot of friendly fire shots. Stefan, Dozer, Rook, and Chilly were casualties in the first thirty seconds.

"I'd like to know who shot me!" complained Rook as the four returned to into the safe zone overlooking the playing field.

"Relax kid," answered Chilly. "Save your aggression for the ice." The game slowed as fewer players with less ammunition started to measure their shots out carefully.

"Shoot at the center," Booker yelled to Dawson. "Tunny go to the right. We'll try to blaze a path for you!" Tunny ran and jumped over a wooden spool, landing next to a metal barrel. Bullets rang off the side, bottling him in.

"I could use some help here," he screamed.

Booker leapt over his barricade and aimed at the enemy gun muzzle. "Pop!" His gun fired a bullet that barely flew ten feet. "Damn it!" he yelled. My air canister is nearly empty. My bullets have no power!" A bullet to his chest ended his cries. "I'm hit!" Booker looked down at the ground and walked out of the game.

"You shouldn't talk so much; you gave away your position!" Brick commented as Booker walked by. Brick turned to the center and was rewarded with two bullets to his chest. Dawson smirked. He made no comment, not wanting to make the same mistake of talking. Four left. They crept along in the dark, afraid to give away their positions. The observers in the safe zone were not amused.

"Can you do something to speed this up?" Stefan asked the referee. He nodded and spoke into the intercom.

"One minute left in the game!" He turned a dial and the dance music beat, that was adding tension to the game, was gone. Now all movements in the field could be heard. Tunny took this as a cue and jumped over the barrel spraying the air with bullets. He saw Presley hiding behind a barrel.

"Prepare to die!" he yelled as he sprayed Presley in the chest with five bullets.

"I'm dead! Talk about overkill," he groaned as he walked off the field wiping the bullet spray off his chest.

Your pain is my pleasure, Tunny smiled. He heard a sound behind him. Dawson appeared with gun in hand.

"Ready to finish this," he smiled as they walked to the center of the warehouse. Dawson shot two paintballs to light their way.

"The prize is mine," Tunny reached forward. Suddenly the lights came on and both were blinded.

"What the …?" he sputtered as two bullets hit Dawson in the back. Tunny and Dawson turned to see Taj's gun aimed squarely at them. Taj flipped up his goggles.

"Night vision," pointing to his goggles. "You guys were so easy to follow in the dark. Walk off Dawson. You're done," Taj commanded. He cocked his gun and aimed at Tunny's chest. "And then there was one." He fired and the bullet broke in the barrel. Taj shook his gun in alarm. He fired again and another bullet broke in the barrel. The broken paintballs had jammed the gun. Tunny smiled and aimed his gun. Three shots to his groin dropped Taj to the ground.

"Time's up!" yelled the referee.

"No fair! I was going to win if my gun hadn't broken down." cried Taj.

"You're unlucky, man. While I'm made for a game like this," Tunny crowed as he cocked his gun." I'm a natural born killer."

March 2, 2007

The two men in the squared circle looked at each other with unbridled hatred. The man with a long scar down his face charged forward, his heavy steps echoing throughout the building. His opponent, a giant of a man, held out his arm and clotheslined his attacker. Scar somersaulted backwards and slammed into the ring post. The giant lumbered forward and tried to crush the other man.

Scar moved at the last second and his foot swept the giant, knocking his mighty frame to the mat. The giant was dazed and couldn't regain his footing. Scar leapt to the top of the corner ring post and sized up the giant. He jumped seven feet into the air with a spinning back kick that caught the giant squarely in the face. The giant fell as if he had a glass jaw. Scar leapt on top of his unconscious body as the referee sailed in to give the count.

One-two-THREE! The referee hand slapped the mat and held up Scar's hand in victory. The crowd in the rink screamed its approval.

"Did you see that! Did you see that kick!" a fan screamed and jumped out of his seat.

"I saw it," answered Garson unimpressed. "You realize that wrestling is fake." The fan didn't answer, his attention again fixed on the ring. Garson took this opportunity to leave the stands and headed up to the announcer's booth. As he walked through the main concourse, vendors yelled at him to buy a program. Before he could answer, his cell phone rang.

"Garson here. Where are you two?"

"Downstairs in the dressing room area. I want to talk to the ice maintenance staff who worked the night before Tidwell was murdered." Mitch answered

"Get back to me if you get anything important." Garson flipped his phone shut and waved his credentials to a guard. He walked through the gate and climbed the stairs to the announcer's booth.

"Still think we'll find the killer at the last rink Tidwell played at?" Lola asked Mitch.

"Don't know. If we have a crazy fan, then who knows if he is here tonight. Hopefully the staff will be able to shed some light." The wrestler named Scar walked down the hallway. He turned back and looked at Lola.

"You're pretty. Every think of becoming a wrestler?" he commented as he opened a can of beer. Lola stopped, unsure how to take this inquiry. She pulled out the necklace with her credentials.

"You need another enforcer?" she joked. The wrestler seemed interested.

"We could always use more enforcement. You got the look. Put some meat on your bones and you could go far. Make a lot more money than a cop."

"Excuse me. We have an investigation to conduct," Mitch interrupted placing his hand on the wrestler's chest. Scar looked down at Mitch.

"Now your boyfriend here wouldn't last a minute in the ring. He doesn't have the look," Scar glared.

"Oh, he's not my boyfriend," smiled Lola egging the wrestler on.

"Oh really," he grinned back.

"Listen," Mitch looked up, "I'll say this slowly so even you can understand. Move along. We are on OFFICIAL business. Don't make me charge you for interfering with our investigation."

"Actually, you have no grounds. You're bluffing. If you try to arrest me, I'll have your badge and a civil suit against your office," Scar replied confidently. Lola giggled, then regained her composure.

"You're pretty sure of yourself," Mitch challenged and tried to stretch his six-foot height by another inch.

"Yale. Pre-law. Eventually finished a business degree. Trust me, with my contract and merchandising, I'll retire by the time I'm forty."

"Sorry, I jumped to the wrong conclusion because of your profession and that ugly scar," Mitch apologized.

"Scar?" The wrestler reached up, removed the fake rubber scar and placed it on Mitch's forehead. "Just a prop, I'm surprised it fooled a cop like you." He turned to Lola and handed her a card.

"If you ever consider a career change, give me a call. I'll introduce you to the right people." The wrestler turned and headed down towards the locker room. Lola watched him go.

"Guess you can't judge a book by its cover," Lola poked Mitch in the ribs.

"Hey, you thought the scar was real too," he complained.

"Looked fake a mile away," she answered as they headed to the maintenance office.

"Please have a seat." The announcer motioned Garson to sit on a comfortable leather couch. Garson looked through the glass overlooking the mayhem in the wrestling ring. He scribbled a couple of words in his notepad.

"Tell me about the game on January 17th between the Assassins and the Bats, Mr. Morrison," Garson started.

"Hank. Call me Hank." The announcer poured himself a drink from behind the bar. He was middle-aged, thin and wearing one of the ugliest suits sold to man - a combination of a Hawaiian shirt and rhinestones. You could get sick on this suit and never see the vomit.

"Ok, Hank. Tell me about the game. Anything unusual happen?"

"Unusual?" He motioned to the liquor cabinet to see if Garson wanted a drink. Garson declined. Hank poured himself a second drink. "How about that there was actually a good crowd to see an Assassin's game for once. It's been a while since I've seen so many fans for a hockey game."

"Anybody stand out as a troublemaker?"

"Troublemaker?" Hank had the irritating habit of repeating the words that were just said. "Officer Garson, I don't know if you watch many hockey games, but we had a home team with the fans screaming for the blood of their opponents."

"And Tidwell?"

"Tidwell would be at the top of any fan's list as #1 Most Wanted."

"Why did people dislike him so much?"

"Dislike?" Hank finished his second drink and started his third. "Try hate. The guy was a natural talent and cocky son-of-a-gun. He was good, and he didn't mind telling you how good he was. Then he asked you to tell him how good he was. Outside of his mother, I'd say anyone living who ever met him is a potential killer."

"What about yourself?" Garson asked. He loved to throw people off guard with this question.

"Are you kidding? I use a guy like that to charge up a crowd. People love someone to hate. Let me tell you something, Agent Garson. Most of the people who come to games are blue-collar. They probably just got off a twelve-hour shift at one of the auto manufacturing plants. They are constantly worried if they will have a job tomorrow. The hockey game is their release. They can curse, spit, and throw stuff. They channel everything they hate in their lives into the game and guys like Tidwell are the perfect target. Arrogant, skilled, and in your face. I miss him."

"Nice speech," answered Garson. "But you never answered my question." He looked directly at Hank.

"You're a bit thick," smiled Hank. "The answer is no."

"What about the Assassins? Anyone have a run-in with Tidwell that night?"

"Try the whole team. But seriously, if anyone was going to kill Tidwell, they would do it on the ice with a thousand fans calling his name. The local cable company tape the games. I'm sure you could get a copy if you wanted to look at your *suspects*," he added sarcastically.

"I might just do that." His cell phone rang. "Excuse me," Garson said to Hank and turned his back.

"What? I can't hear you, the reception in this building is horrible. Yeah? Ok, I'll come to you." Garson flipped his phone shut.

"Found your suspect?"

"Maybe. Here's my card. If you think of anything, call me."

"No problem," Hanks pocketed the card. "If you want to come see a game sometime, the bar," he polished off his third drink, "is always open."

Lola sat in a ratty chair while Mitch talked to the zamboni driver. Stuffing stuck out of the back of the chair like it was a loser in a knife fight. She looked at the numerous nude pinups on the walls of the zamboni driver's office. A particularly large breasted woman stood above the snap-on-tools box. *I take it that he doesn't get many visitors.* She looked around the dark dingy office. *Or they're all men.*

Mitch gazed into the weathered, friendly eyes of Sunny, the zamboni driver. He had been clearing the ice for over twenty years and knew the arena inside out.

"Preparing the ice is the most important thing in this arena," Sunny proudly said. "You need a minimum of three-quarter inch sheet of ice to play hockey. Can't have any concrete showing. Now for the wrestling match tonight, we had to cover it over and insulate against the cold. I'm telling you; the fans would never know they're sitting on ice." Mitch interrupted before Sunny had a chance to continue.

"Fascinating," Mitch rolled his eyes. Now the night of the Assassin and Bats match-up, did you see anything out of the ordinary?"

"Ordinary? Nothing about this job is ordinary. Why, I remember when I was younger and one of the female fans came down to visit. . ." He looked at Lola and decided to discontinue his story. "I remember that the rink was pretty full. That hasn't happened in awhile. The Assassins have actually started to play decent hockey. I didn't see much of the game, but there sure was lots of yelling going on." There was a knock at the door.

"Come in!" Sunny shouted. Garson stepped in and walked around the Zamboni to the office. He scanned around the office and smiled. He looked twice at the woman above the toolbox.

"You got something?" he asked Lola.

"Thanks for your time," Mitch handed a card to Sunny and the three officers stepped outside of the office.

"Was that old guy actually helpful?" Garson asked.

"No. Except for giving Mitch his jollies over the pinups. But he did give us this," Lola handed him a league schedule.

"I circled the dates of the murders since September. In every case, this team was in the same city on the same date." Mitch added.

"Which means we finally found a connection linking the murders. The victims may not know each other or be related at all. The crimes could simply be because of proximity, maybe they went to the hockey games?" Lola asked.

"Either way, it looks like our killer is either affiliated with the team or a player!" Mitch smiled.

"What is the name of the team?"

"The Assassins!"

Second Intermission

The green glow of the computer screen illuminated the room. The killer sat back in his chair. He had gotten sloppy. In the past, he had always stuck to the orders, never deviating from the assignment. He had played it safe; his methods couldn't be traced to a single motive. But Tidwell's death had changed all that. He had crossed the line from business to personal. And he could feel the police breathing down his neck. They never had a reason to suspect a hockey player. Until now.

The phone rang interrupting his train of thought.

"Yeah," the killer answered.

"Hey. It's me," the phone replied as the killer realized one of his teammates was calling. "Can you pick me up tomorrow? My car's in the shop and your house is on the way," the teammate asked.

"No problem. See you at ten," the killer answered and placed the phone down in the receiver.

His teammates were so naïve. They played hockey never realizing the intricacies of keeping the team running smoothly. The money needed to grease the wheel. Soon it would be all over, and he would move on. But before he did, he anticipated at least one more murder for the team to make it to the end. One more time. He just needed the contact to tell him, when and where.

And he was willing to bet, that it would be soon.

Third Period

March 28, 2007

Booker's interrogation

Booker was carefully studying the folder of evidence placed
before him on the table as Garson and Mitch entered the room. He
glanced up at them and then went back to the file. Mitch looked at
Garson in surprise.

"Excuse me, that is official police evidence. You should not be
looking at the material," Mitch commanded. Booker didn't even
look up.

"Then don't leave it sitting on a table and have me sit for an
hour. There are only so many times I can count the ceiling tiles,"
he answered.

"Do you think we placed this file on the table for you to read?"
Garson asked.

"That's obvious. You must think I can help. I always considered a
career in law enforcement." He tapped his head with his left index
finger. "Superior intellect. Unfortunately, a lot of my teammates just
don't get me."

"They're probably just jealous," Garson offered. Booker's eyes lit
up in acknowledgement.

"I think you're right. It's nice to be appreciated for once."

"Tell us who is committing the murders in these files?" asked
Mitch.

"Well, likely a male between 30&40, obviously abused as a
child…"

"I'm sorry, how did you determine that from these crime
scenes? We gave no details on the killer."

"Oh, I'm giving a profile. Trust me, I am well read. In most
murder mysteries I've perused, the killer is a white male." Garson
eyes blinked as he tried to choke back a comment. "Now, where was
I? Oh yes, there is no common method of killing, which leads me to

believe that there are three killers. Three very sick killers, with very little empathy for our fellow man."

"What do you think their motive is?" asked Mitch.

"Motive? Motive is a subjective thing officer. Most murders fall under three categories – passion, hatred, and greed. Sometimes all three combined. You want my guess; these are crimes of passion. Check to see if the victims had a common lover."

"You realize that several women were killed even though the majority were men," asked Garson.

"Men. Women. Maybe you haven't kept up with current events. There is a term called bisexuality that you might want to look up."

Jesus, this guy's full of himself. Same kind of profile as a serial killer, Garson thought.

"Let me get this straight, we have a bisexual white male," asked Mitch.

"No, no, no. There has to be three bisexual males traveling in a pack, maybe robbing rich people of their estate."

"Some of the victims came from very middle-income salaries. Not much for a lover to take," added Garson.

'They're research skills are poor. Chances are they are in the will."

"Most didn't have a will."

"Honestly officer, I can only do so much. You and your men will have to fill in the blanks. I think I have given you a great start."

"Possibly. Tell me – are any of the hockey players on your team bisexual?"

A half-hour later Booker was escorted from the interview room.

"Do you believe his scenario?" Mitch asked Garson.

"I think he's full of crap. The question is, does he really believe what he just recited or is he leading us on to cover his own guilt?"

March 13, 2007

The motel room was dark, lit with dozens of candles. The Assassin's team members stood in dark robes with hoods over their heads that shrouded their faces. The room was quiet except for a laptop in the corner playing some music with heavy chanting. In the center of the room was a cushion. The teammates stood around it in silence.

The door opened slowly, and a stream of light bounced off the white stucco walls from the hallway. Booker came in first, robed the same as the others, while Rook followed behind in a white robe that looked remarkably like a bed spread. The team members stepped aside so Rook could sit in the middle of the room. Rook felt nervous and tried to catch a smile on any one of his teammate's faces. They all looked solemn and averted their gaze to the floor. Booker raised his hands to gather everyone's attention.

"We are gathered here today to induct a new member into this hockey family. He has endured hardships over the year to prove his worth. Thus far he has succeeded. But he has never had to face the one true test of the Assassins. He has yet to complete the Chicken Ceremony." The hockey players began whispering around the room. A bead of sweat ran down Rook's forehead.

"Everyone in this room has had to face the chicken ceremony in order to make the team. Those that have failed are no longer with us." The rest of the team murmured its agreement. Booker raised his left hand and the room was quiet again.

"With life comes death. And with death comes life. Tonight, your life will begin with its death."

What the hell does that mean? Rook thought.

"Tonight, you will perform a very intimate ceremony for us and us alone. None of this will be videotaped. No one will talk about this to anyone outside of this room. This stays within the team. Tonight, you must prove your worthiness to us and to the Assassin franchise. You must kill another living being!" Rook mouth dropped two inches, as the rest of the team looked dead serious. He started to shake, and the uncertainty caused him to lose his nerve.

"What is it you want me to do?" he whispered. Booker gave no answer and signaled to the door. It opened and Dozer stepped though. In his hand was a cage, covered with a sheet. The sound of a bird clucking came from under the sheet. As Dozer set the cage down in front of Rook, several feathers fell to the floor. Booker looked Rook straight in the eyes.

"If you want to remain on this team, you must choke the chicken!"

"Choke the chicken!" the rest of the teammates yelled as their shadows danced off the candlelight in the room. Rook was petrified

"You want me to do what?" he screamed. The cage shook with the bird's frightened cry.

"Stop yelling! You're scaring the bird," Chilly complained.

"Scaring the bird! But you guys want me to kill it!" Rook answered.

"Hush," answered Booker as he put a calming hand on Rook's shoulder. "The choice is yours. If you want to remain on the team, you must perform the deed. It's you or the chicken."

"Come on," yelled Tunny. "Chickens die every day. You ever go to Kentucky Fried Chicken?" Rook's body was shivering from shock and his mind was reeling. *Why? Why is this happening to me?*

"To make this easier, we have provided you with a prop, so you don't have to look the fowl in the eyes," Booker nodded to his teammates. Stefan came over and placed a blindfold over Rook's eyes.

"This is the best thing for all of us," Stefan said before Rook's world went black. He heard the wire mesh of the cage squeak open and the chicken's wings frantically flapping. The team members chanted low but slowly built in intensity.

"Choke the chicken! Choke the chicken!" Strong hands on either side held him down on his knees and pulled his shaking hands forward. The bird's feather's flapped against his outstretched hands. Its cries increased in terror, as if it knew what was happening. Rook's body was racked with fear, aware of the penalty of not finishing the ceremony. His hands grasped the chicken's neck, it was cold to the touch. The team members continued their chant.

"Choke the chicken! Choke the chicken!" Rook began to sob uncontrollable as the chicken thrashed in his grip and he tightened his fingers. The neck gave easily under his hands.

"No!" he yelled and ripped off his blindfold. He stared forward to see the look of amazement on his teammates faces. His hands held the lifeless chicken. The poor lifeless rubber chicken. His teammates convulsed with laughter.

"Oh my god!" yelled Brick. "I thought I was going to burst my gut. The look on your face. . ."

"Are you kidding?" Taj snorted at Rook. "Your face got so red, I thought you were going to burst a blood vessel. I'm wouldn't want to explain to Coach tomorrow why Rook was in the Hospital."

"But I heard the sound of the chicken in the cage," Rook sobbed.

"You heard this!" Presley held a small tape recorder with a chicken clucking through the speaker. "Your mind filled in the rest."

"But I felt the chicken moving in my hands."

"Are you kidding? Tunny and I were shaking the rubber chicken in your hands to make it feel alive. It took everything I had not to pee myself from laughing," Dawson jeered.

"That's why I wore a diaper," Tunny screamed.

As it finally dawned on Rook that he had been duped, his body did the only thing it could in reaction to the shock. He fainted. He fell headfirst, with the rubber chicken breaking his fall. It squeaked on impact. The room went bezerk with several team members falling on the bed and floor with laughter. Only Booker remained composed.

"Welcome to the Assassins," he said calmly to no one in particular.

March 27, 2007

"Air Transit flight 439 from Houston, Texas has arrived at gate 58," came the announcement over the loudspeaker. Garson carried his luggage off the plane into the terminal. Lola and Mitch trailed behind looking at the gate information. Lola checked at her watch.

"What time is it here in Montreal?" she asked.

"1900 hours, adjust your watches," answered Mitch and he turned his watch back one hour.

"How's your French, Garson? Parlez-vous en francais?" Lola asked.

"We're in Montreal. The city is bilingual. I'm sure I'll get by," Garson responded. He pulled out a paper and read the first paragraph. "What was the Assassin's itinerary for today?"

"At 1930, they played the Montreal Mavericks at the Iceoplex on the eastern outskirts of the city," answered Mitch. Lola pulled out her computer printout.

"The team is staying at an inn not far from the rink and then driving four hours back to Oshawa in the morning," she added.

"Give me a list of the principal players," Garson asked.

"Ten players have been to all the locations that the murders took place. The rest of the team has either been injured or not brought up on those specific road trips. The Coach missed one road swing and the goaltender had a groin pull and another one was brought up from the minors for three weeks."

"Doesn't mean they still didn't follow the team," Garson added.

"True," Mitch answered, "but each one of the ten main players can be traced back to everyone of the murder cities on the same dates that the Assassins visited town. I say we start with them."

"Does the team have any fans that follow them game to game?" Garson looked at Lola.

"Not any that travel with the team," she answered. "Attendance is spotty, and fans and family tend to stay behind. But there is no way to track any fans that might drive on their own."

"Okay, I want full bios on these ten players. Where they went to school, where they were born, financials, any priors in their security check, if they had a tough childhood. You know the drill. I want to know these guys intimately before we decide to bring them in for questioning. If there is something to use against them, I want to know what it is." Garson stepped down an escalator and the three headed to the baggage claim.

"Think we're on another goose chase?" Mitch told Lola while Garson was picking up a baggage cart.

"Maybe. But it's the best lead we've had in the investigation. Seems like a huge coincidence that this hockey team has been in each city at the same time a murder took place," Lola answered.

"Possibly. But think of how many other sports teams, concerts, and other traveling shows were in these cities at the same time as well. We could be chasing ghosts," shrugged Mitch.

"At least we're chasing something. Even if we find who it is, the why still isn't coming together," Lola said as she sat down by the baggage carousel.

"I think we're wasting our time trailing this team. We should just bring them in and question them right away. We'll look for any guilty responses. Following these players is going to be boring," yawned Mitch. How much trouble, can a bunch of hockey players get into?"

The music blared on the stage as two strippers twirled through the curtain. Club Super Sexy was a two-story nightclub with a main stage, a side stage for select groups, and an upstairs champagne room for the wealthy. Two poles broke up the main stage with patrons lining the entire edge waiting for the show. The show rarely disappointed.

"Wow, are those two twins?" Rook exclaimed from the Assassin's table about twenty feet away from the stage.

"What are you drinking, mon ami?' Stefan asked. "One of those girls is five inches shorter than the other," he motioned the waitress for a drink. She carried a tray with a pitcher of beer and wore a t-shirt that left nothing to the imagination.

"How much for the pitcher?" Tunny asked while looking directly at her breasts.

"Tunny! Her face is up there," Presley pointed. The waitress smiled.

"That's okay," she answered. "As long as he tips, he can look at anything he wants."

"Well if you need some extra money, maybe I can make a suggestion," Tunny leered.

"Sorry, love. I don't need the money that bad."

Taj handed her a twenty as she placed the pitcher down and picked up two empties. "Thanks honey, this money will go toward my university education." She winked at Taj and headed over to the next table.

"Do you really think she's working her way through college?' Taj asked. Chilly shook his head.

"No," Chilly answered. She's playing you for sympathy, so you'll give her a bigger tip next time."

"Well, it's working," Taj answered. He looked over at Dozer whose eyes stared at the stage. Taj ran his hand over Dozer's face to see if he was still conscious.

"Good old Dozer. Always fascinated by what he can't touch."

"The guy's pathetic. Can somebody wipe the droll from his chin?" Dawson complained. "You know Dozer, they have stuff like this on the internet now." Dozer continued to focus on the stage while ignoring the comments.

"Where's Booker?" Brick asked.

"Out back playing the video slot machines," answered Stefan. "How he can pull on a metal handle for thrills when lovely ladies are dancing is beyond me."

"The guy's gay, pure and simple," Tunny laughed.

"Who's simple?" said Booker as he sat beside Taj, not catching the full conversation.

Before getting an answer, Booker plunked three twenties on the table. "I got lucky on the slots; drinks are on me!" Several hands patted him on the back while Tunny choked back a response in favor of more beer. Brick got up from the table.

"I've got to use the sandbox. Be back in a moment," he said.

"I need to use washroom too," Stefan followed behind. As they crossed the club, Stefan bumped into a woman rushing through the crowd. He smiled at her.

"Sorry," Lola smiled at Stefan as she continued to the back of the club.

"Le plaisir est le mien. The pleasure is mine," he said as he watched her backside as she disappeared into the crowd. "You know what they say about woman patrons in a strip club?"

"What's that?" Brick asked.

"They're here to take a man home. When the guys realize the stripper aren't leaving with them, they figure they can step right in."

"Good luck with that," Brick replied sarcastically.

Lola grabbed a seat next to Garson and Mitch.

"Sorry I'm late. I was checking out their motel rooms. Nothing was suspicious in any of their suitcases. I almost gagged on the smell of their hockey gear. Have you found the hockey team?"

"You just bumped into two of the team members. Thanks for staying inconspicuous," Garson complained. Lola put her head down on the table. "I'm sorry. Hopefully they saw me as some drunk bimbo."

"We'll see," Garson answered, not sold on her response. "Tonight's just about watching the players and seeing if anyone warrants further investigation. Did anyone catch your attention?"

"No, they're all a bunch of losers," commented Lola while taking a drink of water.

"There's the obvious drug charge on Dozeralis. There's some unexplained money in the account of the Indian hockey player. But there's nothing in anyone's past to make me think they're a serial killer," answered Mitch.

"Well, watch and observe. If one of these players is our killer, I only have enough resources for a week to prove to the Captain that this isn't a waste of time," commented Garson. Lola giggled. "Is something funny?" he asked.

"It just seems very typically male to have a stakeout in a strip club." Before Garson could respond, they were interrupted by a club announcement.

"In just a few minutes, our featured act will come on stage," the DJ's voice came from the loudspeakers. "Specially signed posters will go to members of our audience. Get a good seat and a refill of beer before the next act starts." As the DJ clicked the mike off, several guys from the first row got up and headed to the bar.

"Look dudes, here's our chance to get a good seat," Dozer said excitably, apparently the DJ's voice had broken his blank look. Neither Taj nor Stefan protested too much, and they accompanied him to closer seating.

"Remember, Dozer, just because we're close enough to touch the strippers doesn't mean you can. See the bouncer by the door?" Stefan pointed. Dozer looked nervously at the man who was as big as Brick.

"Ne pas faire de touche. Do not touch. One touch and he'll toss you out the door, no questions asked. Got it?"

"Got it, dude. I'm just here to watch. I'm just here to relax."

"You're such a tense guy to begin with," joked Taj. Before he could laugh, he received a shove from behind.

"You guys are in our seats. Get out!" a skinny college student with preppy clothes demanded.

"Did you old guys wait for us to leave so you could take our seats?" a shorter student with slick black hair complained.

"Last time I looked; nobody owned these seats. Maybe instead of all going to the bathroom like a bunch of teenage girls, you should have left someone behind," shot back Taj.

"Just get out of our seats, old man and we'll promise not to rough you up too much," the skinny student jeered, and his buddies laughed.

"Relax dudes. We're hockey players, we're just trying to have a good time," Dozer explained.

"Let me buy you a drink, mes amis. I'm a lover not a fighter," quipped Stefan. He motioned the waitress for a drink.

"You can buy us some drinks and then get out of our seats," demanded the shorter student.

"Is everything all right?" the students turned and looked at the massive form of Brick. The students had no wise remarks for him.

"Forget abut these losers," commented the skinny student and the group headed over to an empty table.

"Thanks, big guy!" said Taj. Brick saluted them with his beer as he sat back down at the table with the other Assassins. The music blared and another announcement echoed through the speakers.

"Club Super Sexy is proud to present to you tonight's featured act. She was Miss Nude 2006. Would you please put your hands together for, Megan Woods!" The lights went out immersing the bar into darkness. A spotlight flashed on stage and a tall, beautiful blonde strutted on stage. She wore nothing but a hockey jersey and carried a hockey stick.

"I'd like to play on her team," Dozer stammered as his eyes went wide.

"Don't get too excited. She's out of your league!" Stefan commented. "Besides, beautiful women like that always travel with a manager/boy friend. See him sitting in the corner?" he pointed to a young male with dirty blonde hair. "He's watching the guys around the stage and not the show. He's seen the performance before and he's more concerned that no one gets too close."

The stripper strutted around the pole, bending over at the appropriate beats in the music to give the patrons a closer look at her body. She took her hockey stick and started stick handling across the stage, much to the cheers of the Assassin's hockey team's table.

"She's got better moves than you, Chilly," teased Presley.

"She's got better moves than most of you jerk offs," Tunny chimed in.

The music stopped and the spotlight pointed to the stage ceiling. A large, plastic, domed semi-circle was wheeled on stage. Megan Woods deliberately stepped into the dome.

"What is she going to do, disappear?" Rook asked.

"Now that would be cruel," answered Dawson.

A rope was dropped from the ceiling and she reached up to pull on it. As she did, a torrent of water rained down from the ceiling, soaking her and her jersey.

"Dude! She's taking a shower," Dozer said excitably. Almost as if sensing his excitement, she tossed the wet jersey to the stage exposing her nearly naked body. She slid towards Dozer giving him his own personal dance. Dozer eyes almost jumped out of his head. "Quick give me some money," he held his hand out in front of Taj.

Taj reached into his pocket and gave Dozer five dollars. Dozer turned to receive a close up view of the stripper and took his money to place into her thong. Suddenly he was shoved from behind, turned around and his hand instinctively reached out to steady himself. Unfortunately, the only thing his hand could grasp, was the stripper's left breast. The music came to a halt.

"Freddy!" the stripper yelled. "The guy out front just groped me!" The bouncer at the back, waded his way through the crowd and grabbed Dozer by the shoulder.

"Time to leave!" he yelled, leaving no room for discussion. As Dozer resigned himself to his fate, Tunny blocked the path of the much larger bouncer.

"It wasn't his fault. The frat boys in the corner shoved him into her!" He pointed to the college guys who had been laughing and slapping themselves on the back. They turned and tried to look less conspicuous.

"Then I'll follow up with them after I throw this one out," the bouncer answered and pushed Tunny aside.

"Maybe you didn't hear me. I heard taking steroids can make you hard of hearing. Or maybe you don't speak English very well. This guy," pointing to Dozer, "didn't do anything. Let him go." Dozer shook his head to tell Tunny to leave him alone. The bouncer looked at Tunny and pushed him back again. He then motioned to the bar for reinforcements. Tunny shook his head. "You shouldn't have done that."

"Why, what's going to happen?" The bouncer responded.

"This!" Tunny punched him straight in the jaw. The blow should have knocked the bouncer off his feet but instead it barely knocked his head back. The bouncer returned the sentiment and Tunny went flying into an adjoining table. Before the bouncer could throw Dozer out, he ran straight into the fist of Brick. This time the bouncer fell to the floor.

"Why don't you pick on someone your own size," Brick yelled before two bartenders tackled him from behind.

"Can't we all just get along?" Taj asked. As he turned, he was sucker punched by one of the frat boys.

Stefan hit the skinny frat boy over the head with a chair,

"Guess I can fight," he said as the short frat boy jumped him from behind. Suddenly the whole bar erupted into chaos as patrons either picked a fighting partner or escaped through the main doors. Presley stood on a table trying to restore order.

"Fighting never solves anything," he yelled to no one in particular as a beer mug whizzed inches from his head. Chilly pulled him down.

"Are you trying to get yourself killed?" he asked while spying Dawson hiding underneath the table.

"Let me know when it's over," Dawson shouted and pulled a napkin over his head to hide from the rest of the bar.

The short frat kid kicked Stefan in the gut while another held his arms behind him.

"Stupid hockey players," he yelled at Stefan and was about to kick him in the head, when the edge of the table caught the frat boy in the chest.

"Dude! When I see you, I'm glad I never went to college," Dozer knocked the short frat boy flying into the next table. Three bikers sitting there didn't appreciate the interruption. They beat on the frat boy when he tried to stand up.

Stefan reached up from the floor and grabbed the balls of the taller frat boy above him. Frat boy number three fell to the ground, shaking with agony. Stefan looked down at his hand.

"I need to wash this. I've gone where no man should have to go." Suddenly the music stopped, and all eyes turned to the front door.

"This is the police! Anyone continuing to fight will be charged with aggravated assault and will face a minimum of two years in jail!" A large cop with cropped gray hair bellowed. The doors opened behind him and several dozen cops appeared. "Everyone will be escorted to the station where statements will be taken, and charges filed. If anyone has a problem with this, speak up." The bar went quiet until one voice spoke up.

"I want to file a charge against these hockey players. They started the whole thing," the whiny short frat boy whined. The older cop walked up to him and gave him a hand to stand up. The boy smiled, thinking he was being helped. The cop took his right hand and put him in handcuffs.

"Kid, you don't even look old enough to shave, let alone be in this bar. It's been my experience that the one's who complain the loudest, are usually the ones at fault." He looked behind him to a younger cop. "Take him and his buddies first. Then put the hockey players in the next van."

Tunny was about to say something when Presley shook his head and put his finger to his mouth. Tunny thought better of his comment and remained silent.

"All right ladies, make two lines at the door and we'll get this over with as quickly as possible," the cop commanded, walking by Garson's table.

"What are we going to do?" Mitch asked Garson.

"Let's go for the ride. Since the team is being booked for public nuisance, it saves us from bringing them in. Once we get to the precinct, I'll talk to the officer in charge. Hopefully we can assume authority and question each one while they're in custody. The captain will love it that we saved a warrant."

"Do you really think there is a killer among these neanderthals?" asked Lola.

"Maybe. One thing is for sure. Trouble follows these guys around," Garson said.

Chapter 26　　　*Know When to Hold'em*

March 29, 2007　　　Present day

The interrogation room was littered with papers on the floor while Mitch sifted through a folder. Lola sat at the table with a laptop while Garson paced carefully avoiding the piles of paper.

"Tell me one of you got something out of those interrogations. We've been at it for sixteen hours and I've got absolutely nothing to show for it! What's worse, the killer is tipped off now. He'll be on his guard, making it twice as hard to catch him!" Garson exclaimed.

"Have you told the captain yet?" Mitch asked looking up from his file.

"No. I've had enough agony for one day. He can wait until tomorrow."

"Maybe we have the wrong guys. If nobody looks guilty, it could be because no one is," answered Lola, looking frustrated and tired.

"I'm not going to accept that!" Garson slammed his fist into the table making Lola jump. "My instincts tell me that we just interviewed the killer! I just can't tell who or why."

"As I said earlier, I'm making some progress on the why," Lola motioned to the other two to stand around her. "I've studied the bank records for several of the victims and there are discrepancies,"

"What do you mean?" asked Garson. Lola pointed to the computer screen.

"Follow the debits and credits. Every month people make similar payments. Mortgage payments, car loans, utilities – the payments are consistent each month in their amount and time of month. Same as the deposits, payroll is every two weeks."

"Is there a company common to the victims?" asked Garson.

"No, but look at these withdrawals. Several times a year, thousands of dollars have been made out to cash."

"Is that really a big deal? To avoid taxes, people will often pay contractors in cash," Mitch answered.

"Maybe. But in some of the bank statements, there are also large deposits of cash as well not related to victim's salary," commented Lola

"What are these people buying or selling?" Garson asked.

"If I can find that answer, I bet I can find why they are getting killed!" answered Lola.

La Fleures Motor Inn - Montreal

"Boys, I'm making a killing tonight!" Chilly gathered up the chips on the poker table and pulled them toward him. The game was Texas Hold'em and all the players were sitting around the table in their motel room trying to work off some steam from the previous night's brawl and interrogations.

"You're pretty calm considering what we just went through," commented Taj.

"The cops were a joke. You don't really believe that someone on this hockey team is an actual killer?" Tunny queried.

"Dude! The woman who questioned me said she had evidence," Dozer responded nervously.

"Then why didn't they charge someone?" asked Presley. "If they're so sure of themselves then how come all of us are sitting here playing poker?"

"Maybe they're trying to rattle us, hoping we'll give up the guilty party," added Booker.

"What if one of us is a serial killer? Maybe using the hockey team is just his cover," gulped Rook.

"You watch too many movies," laughed Dawson, folding his cards. "Why would anybody like that waste his time hiding among us?"

"Oh, I don't know, maybe the lousy money and the dingy motel rooms is a real draw for serial killers," Brick answered looking over his cards and upping the ante.

"Mon ami! I think we are looking at this all wrong. The female officer interrogating me…." Stefan started.

"The hot one," interjected Tunny.

"That's the one. She blamed us for Tidwell's death among others. We know he was killed the night after our game in a motel room. Just retrace our steps – was any one missing that night?" Stefan asked.

"I was asleep with my wife; do you want to check my alibi?" answered Brick.

"Everyone was home. There's no way to track if someone drove to Buffalo and took Tidwell out! Anyone of you could be the killer," Tunny folded his hand.

"Now you're just playing into the cop's hands. I call," Booker laid his cards down. "Pair of Aces."

"I've got nothing."

"Pair of sixes."

"Dolly Parton!" answered Rook.

"What's your malfunction, Rook? Dolly Parton? You got boobs on the brain? Tunny yelled.

"Settle down," Booker interrupted. "Dolly Parton is a strait 9-8-7-6-5. Nine to Five. Remember the movie?"

"What are you, some kind of card shark?" Tunny asked.

"I used to watch my old man as a kid. He'd have his buddies over on the weekend and play poker into the wee hours. I wasn't allowed to play, but I always watched. Picked up a few tips. I learned that poker is like taking candy from a baby," Rook responded as he scooped up the chips and dragged them to his end of the table. "Thank you, babies."

"There's more to you than meets the eye," commented Dawson. The door to the hotel room smashed open and Coach charged in.

"What the hell is going on with you guys? I just spent three hours at the police station trying to explain to the strip club owner that the team would pay for damages. Then, as I

try to leave, the precinct captain tells me that the whole team
is under suspicion of murder!" screamed the Coach.

"Relax Coach, you're going to bust a heart valve," said Presley.

"Bust a valve!" Coach's face became red with rage. "I'd like to
bust each one of you in half! What do you think you're doing? We are
on the first winning streak of the team's franchise and you guys are
spending it in jail! Don't you know we get enough bad press!"

"Bad press might be the least of our problems if one of us is a
killer!" Taj said as he leaned back in his chair.

"Don't ever say that again!" Coach yelled making Taj fall out his
chair. "No one on this team is a killer! I'd stake my life on it!" A
couple of players snickered.

"Maybe that makes you the killer," offered Booker. Coach gave
him a look that could kill.

"I don't know about you dudes, but all of this talk about killing is
stressing me out," commented Dozer.

"The whole team needs a break," offered the Coach. "And I know
just where to send all of you."

March 31, 2008

As the sun set, Lola and Mitch drove slowly through the street filled with older rundown duplexes. A gang of teenagers watched them as they went by. Their heads swung to follow their car as they turned the block.

"I don't think they were looking at you," commented Lola.

"No, they'd have this car stripped clean in two minutes if they had a chance," Mitch responded. "Charming neighborhood. Explain again why we're here?"

"One of the victim's computers was left at a remote business and wasn't destroyed like the others."

"The smashed-up computers were definitely deliberate?" Mitch asked.

"Absolutely. And by missing this one and combining it with what we know about the cash withdrawals, it gave me something to look for. On the laptop, there was an electronic payment between the victim and a dummy corporation. It was hard to track, but after several false leads, the techies found an internet provider who provided this address for the receiver of the transaction." Lola pointed at a non-descript four story apartment building.

"What do think? Drug dealer?" Mitch questioned.

"Seems likely. If so, the victims could be clients."

"Serial killer drug dealer. What a scary combination."

"I don't think the dealer is alone. Three different methods of murder. Probably employs three different killers for clients who don't pay," nodded Lola.

"Well I'm glad we brought backup. Teams one and two are in position. We go the most direct route."

"I can't believe Garson didn't come."

"He still believes that the hockey team is involved. He is maintaining surveillance on them while waiting for our report."

"He's going to miss all the action."

"His loss. Listen, I'll go in first. You follow two steps behind," Mitch commanded while pulling the car to a stop about five houses past the suspect home.

"It's nice to see that chivalry isn't dead," mocked Lola. "But we already discussed this. I'm going in first. Suspects are always more at ease with a woman than a man. Besides, I want first crack at this killer," as Lola checked her weapon and stepped out of the car. Mitch hurried to catch up.

"Not so fast. If a video camera is watching us, I don't want it to show anything other than a couple heading home." He looked at his watch and spoke quietly into the mike. "Blue team, maintain position. Red team, cover the rear. Remember the code word, 'It sure is chilly tonight.' Nobody moves until one of us says that line."

"Affirmative," two team leaders said in unison over Mitch's earpiece. Lola and Mitch walked together on the sidewalk as he placed his arm around her waist.

"Your hand is a little low," Lola commented as the two of them went up the stairs. Mitch reached for the door.

"Just playing the part of a happy couple," Mitch smiled as they entered the lobby. To the right was a wall of beat up mailboxes and a bulletin board with notices.

To the left, graffiti was sprayed on the wall. Metal bars separated the lobby from the apartments. An elevator rested just inside the gate.

"Smile and play the part. The building has a surveillance system where residents can look down through the camera on the wall before buzzing someone in. No telling if our suspect has a permanent feed." Mitch tapped a door code and the metal gate buzzed open. The two of them walk nonchalantly through.

"No landlord," Lola asked.

"Nope. Leasing company just gave us the door code. Said the owner didn't want anything to do with a police investigation. Apparently, they have had no problems with this tenant."

"Sounds like the owner has a very hands-off approach with his tenants," commented Lola.

"As long as you pay your rent. Let's take the stairs." The two of them climbed the steps until they reached the third floor. The carpet was worn and the walls, once white, were covered with the black marks of furniture that had been moved sloppily through the halls over the years. The corner apartment, room 332 was their destination.

"Stay behind me. I don't want whoever's inside to see both of us." Mitch motioned as he knocked on the door. He flashed his badge.

"I'm still going in first," Lola commented.

"Open up, sir. We have a warrant to search your premises. You have five seconds to comply!" Five seconds went by with no response. Lola and Mitch looked at each other and stood in front of the door. "Coming in!" They kicked the door lock in unison, and it shattered under the force. They passed through the door and entered the hallway into the dark apartment. Lola reached for the light switch and flicked it up. No light came on.

"Use your flashlight," she commanded and the two of them examined a dingy kitchen. On the table was a pizza box with several slices of pepperoni. Lola touched the box. "Cold. Could be a couple of hours when this was ordered."

"Keep searching. Let's sweep the living room." Mitch went in first, his flashlight illuminating a big screen television with high-end stereo. "We definitely have our man. Who could afford these electronics in a dump like this?"

"You'd be surprised," Lola answered. "I've been to welfare homes where the kids were starving but Daddy still had tons of money for a pool table for him and his buddies."

"Fair enough. I'll search down here. If we don't find anything, I'll call in the teams to sweep for clues."

Lola climbed the stairs. Light from the windows of other apartments illuminated the bedroom. Lola entered; her flashlight danced over an unkempt bed. She sniffed as she saw a couple of porn magazines lying on the floor. As she turned to the bathroom, she was surprised by cold hard steel pressed against the side of her head.

"It sure is chilly in here tonight," she responded nonchalantly.

"It's about to get a whole lot chillier if you don't drop your weapon," a gravelly voice from the dark commanded.

"I'm a police officer. Please drop your weapon," Lola answered not lowering her gun.

"I don't care who you say you are. You're trespassing in my home and I'm starting to feel threatened. You move and I blow your head off."

"Then you'll be dead two seconds after you kill me. Now drop your weapon and let's discuss this rationally," Lola's gun moved slightly towards the voice.

"You cops barge into my home and tell me to act rationally. You people make me laugh," Lola heard the gun barrel cock into position. A red light punctured the darkness and lit up the suspect's chest. Mitch's gun went off. The gunfire was deafening as the attacker went down. The attacker's weapon dropped from his hand, landing on the bedroom floor. Lola swung her flashlight downward onto the attacker's face. He was young, mid twenties, overweight, and wearing baggy clothes. She placed her fingers on his neck.

"He's dead," she said to Mitch.

"Are you all right?" he asked.

"I'm okay. Felt like I aged a year having a gun pressed to my temple, but I'll be fine. Thanks again for saving my life. That's two I owe you," she said as she looked into his eyes.

"Maybe someday you'll return the favor," Mitch held her. They were interrupted by the sound of feet on the stairs.

"Officer! You need to come downstairs." The two of them ran down the stairs to the squad leader and passed the rest of the red team just entering the apartment. They saw a utility closet set up with a computer and monitor. A green sickly glow illuminated the darkened room. Several bank transactions appeared quickly on the screen.

"Is this what you we're looking for?" the squad leader asked.

"Maybe. We'll soon find out if it was important enough to die for," Mitch answered.

Chapter 28   *Karma Sutra?*

April 2, 2008

"Tell me why we're here again?" Tunny asked as he pulled his shorts on. The locker room was full of Assassin hockey players.

"Coach felt we needed to relax after all the problems with the police," Brick answered.

"And the fact that there is a murderer on the team," added Dawson tightening his sneakers.

"You believe that?" answered Booker. "It takes time and energy to plan a murder." "Everyone on the team is too lazy for that." Dozer walked around the corner wearing a very tight leotard. It looked very old as if he had worn it in high school. The team broke out in laughter. Dozer was puzzled.

"Dude, I can't breathe," complained Dozer.

"Ring, Ring!" Chilly pretended his cell phone was ringing. "Hello," Chilly answered his own phone. "Hey, Dozer! I just got a call from the eighties. They want their workout clothes back." The locker room roared with laughter.

"Okay, take it easy," Presley stood up from his bench and escorted Dozer to the door of the change room.

"Hey, the instructor may be a hottie and you will definitely stand out," offered Stefan and the three of them headed into the yoga studio.

"You think Stefan is right?" Rook asked Tunny as he tucked in his t-shirt.

"Let's find out," Tunny answered as the rest of the team entered the yoga studio. Two of the walls were covered with mirrors and the third wall was a window that faced the street. The instructor was wearing a form-fitting outfit and was bent over trying to adjust the music.

"Hello!" Rook smiled. The instructor turned and stood up. She was fifty something, a larger woman with a bit too much makeup. She returned Rook's response with a seductive smile.

"She's all yours," nudged Tunny.

"Everyone grab a mat from the corner," she commanded to the hockey players. "My name is Silvia and I have been teaching this class for the last twenty years. I plan to teach you how yoga will relax your body and eliminate stress from your mind. In this class, you will learn several positions that will help you reach a higher plane of consciousness."

"Trust me, there's not too many positions I can't handle," Tunny poked Dawson.

"Pardon me?" Silvia answered, not understanding Tunny's comment.

"Never mind. He's all show and no go," replied Chilly.

"Why are we learning these positions? How is this going to help my hockey game?" Dawson complained. Silvia looked at him as if she had heard this question many times before.

"The positions I'm showing you will increase your blood flow and stretch your muscles. It will make you stronger on the ice and give you greater flexibility to increase your reach. It also has other social *benefits,*" she smiled.

"Such as?" Stefan was curious.

"It will increase your sexual ability. The added flexibility will make you king of your castle." Silvia looked like someone who knew.

"Really?" Dozer was very interested.

"Don't get too excited. You have to find a partner first!" jeered Tunny. Despite their jokes, Silvia suddenly had the full attention of the hockey players. She tapped the CD changer and the studio was filled with the low background music of jazz.

"To begin, I want all of you to follow me by sitting on your mat. We will warm up your muscles with some basic stretches. Remember to stretch only as far as you feel comfortable. If it starts to hurt, I want you to stop."

The Assassins sat down and began stretching their legs and backs. The room was soon interrupted by Rook's complaints. He jumped up from his mat.

"I can't take this! Stefan is stinking the entire room up," he said while fanning the air in front of his face. Stefan was non-pulsed.

"What can I say? I feel . . . relaxed," he grinned.

"This is a common bodily function. Don't punish your fellow players who release their pent-up energies. Embrace it!" Most the players looked at each other. Brick was the first to respond.

"You probably should open a window then." Silvia promptly obliged the request. The team quickly finished the exercises while several players relaxed.

"I want all of you to sit down with your knees bent and stretch your body forward, arms out,"

She walked around the room handing each hockey player a furry stuffed animal." The first exercise is called 'grabbing the ferret.'

"Grabbing the what?" asked Taj.

"It's like a furry weasel," answered Booker.

"Why would you grab it?" asked Presley.

"Aren't they illegal?" inquired Brick. Silvia ignored all of their comments.

"Stretch your arms in front of your bodies. Now close your eyes, grab the ferret tightly as it tries to escape your grasp." The hockey players began moving their fingers pretending the stuffed animal was alive in their hands

"I got you, little furry dude!" Dozer yelled with his eyes shut.

"Watch out, I think it's trying to bite you!" Chilly poked Dozer's hand with his fingernail.

"It's attacking me!" Dozer screamed and tossed it into the air. It landed on top of Brick's stuffed ferret. Brick grabbed the second one and placed the two face to face.

"You want a piece of me! You want a piece of me!" Brick mimicked one attacking the other by going for its throat. Several other furry ferrets were thrown in all directions. Tunny looked confused.

"What's wrong?" Stefan asked.

"I can't see how this will improve my sex life!"

"Please, settle down," Silvia tried to regain control. "Please do not throw your ferrets around. If you are going to gain anything from this class, you need to take my instruction seriously." Brick was hit by another ferret. "I want you to stay in the same position for our next exercise."

"What are we petting this time?" joked Tunny.

"This time," she glared at him, "we will practice an exercise called *spread the butter*."

"Say what?" Dawson replied looking confused.

"Follow me," she motioned from the head of the room. "Take your right hand and dip it into an imaginary jar of butter. Scoop it out with your fingers and pull your hand out of the jar. Now take the butter and spread across a piece of toast in from of you. That's it! Right and left. Right and left. Go slowly, get more butter if you need it," she said like an elementary school teacher.

"What are you doing?" Presley watched Dozer scooping his hand on the floor.

"I dropped some. I didn't want it to go to waste," he replied with all seriousness.

"I'm using margarine. I'm trying be healthy," commented Stefan.

"Am I the only one that thinks this is crazy?" said Tunny in exasperation.

"Pretend you're punching someone instead of slapping butter, that should make you happy," added Chilly.

"Less talk, more spreading," Silvia commanded.

"I don't know about you," Brick said to Taj, "but I'm getting hungry."

"What's wrong? You don't like this exercise?" Booker asked Dawson.

"I just don't want all this grease to get on my hair," Dawson replied.

"And stop! This last exercise is the best and the most controversial," stated Silvia.

"Why? Do we have to choke a chicken?" Tunny joked as the rest of the team looked at Rook who glared back at them.

"No, nothing so barbaric," she answered. "The last exercise is called 'cutting the woman in half.' Please reach forward with your right hand and use your hand as a cutting tool."

"Are you being serious?" Tunny asked. "There's not, like, a camera watching us right now." Several team members looked around the room for a hidden camera.

"I do not appreciate the comments," Silvia replied. "These exercises are legitimate. If you spent less time getting caught up with the names and more time actually trying the exercises, you'd get the benefits."

"I bet in the female classes they change the name to cutting the male in half," Brick whispered.

"More like punching the male in the balls," Chilly whispered back.

"Work with me, gentlemen," Silvia yelled. "After you cut, put your arm at a ninety-degree angle to your body as far as you can reach. Once you feel the pull, I want you to repeat the motion with your left arm."
The players repeated the cutting motion with much gusto for the first few minutes resembling a karate class. Silvia walked around the room to watch the progress of her students. She stopped behind Rook.

"Nice form," she commented while looking at his backside. Rook was embarrassed at the attention.

"Cougar alert," whispered Tunny at Rook and swiped his hand like a paw with claws.

"Let's put it all together, gentleman," Silvia returned to the front of the class. "Follow my lead. All together. Pet the ferret."

"Pet the Ferret!" yelled the team.

"Spread the butter."

"Spread the butter!"

"Cut the woman in half."

"Cutting!" yelled Dozer much to the amusement of the rest of the team. Presley's cell phone rang through the studio.

"I didn't even know he had his phone," said Chilly.

"What did you think the bulge was?" joked Stefan.

"Hello?" Presley answered as he stepped back into the changing room.

"One more repetition!" Silvia commanded as she walked to the back of the room to admire her student's body of work. Because of the room's mirrors, the players watched her gaze as she checked out their bodies. Booker made a gagging reflex as if he was going to vomit.

"Okay. Take a break. Get a drink of water and we will continue in two minutes," Silvia commanded as she returned to the front of the room to change the music. Presley stepped back into the room; all the blood had drained from his face. Several players noticed and went towards him.

"What's wrong?" asked Brick. "You look like someone just died." Presley looked up at him and at the surrounding players.

"Someone just did. I got a call from the hospital. It's the Coach. He just died of a heart attack!"

Chapter 29   *Ashes to Ashes - We all Fall Down.*

April 5, 2008

The sky was overcast as the hearse pulled up to the cemetery. Six Assassin players stepped forward as the pallbearers. They placed the casket on their shoulders and proceeded to carry Coach to his final resting place. Two grandchildren accompanied his wife and daughter and they walked slowly behind the coffin. Friends and family gathered behind them, following the procession to the empty grave.

Coach was a flamboyant figure and had made many friends during his early years as a player and later as a coach. He was a polarizing figure when he was alive. People who knew him either loved him or hated him. Today, those that loved him showed up in force. To honor his memory, the entire hockey team wore their jerseys over their suits.

"I washed my jersey three times and it still stinks," complained Dawson.

"Ssshh! Keep your comments to yourself," Booker replied.

The spring air was cool and even though the snow had melted, the grass was still brown and the ground soft. Two rows of folding chairs were set out for family around the gravesite while the majority of mourners stood behind them. Coach had made a will several years ago detailing his funeral arrangements. He had requested that his casket be closed. Considering his death was the result of a heart attack, he had sparred his family a lot of grief as his face had a ghastly look of pain. A smiling photo of Coach as a hockey player was framed and placed on the podium to the left of the grave. Everyone settled into place as Presley stepped up to the microphone to give a short eulogy on behalf of the hockey team. Presley looked down at his team members while adjusting his cue cards on the podium. He cleared his throat and those around become silent

"Today we are here to commemorate the memory of Joseph "Coach" Munroe. He was known to many as a father, a husband, a hockey player, a leader, and a friend. But most of all he was a character. You might not have agreed with what he had to say, but you always noticed when he entered the room. He was larger than life.

There were times when you wanted to scream and yell at him," several people nodded and smiled, "and other times you wished he'd never leave. I feel I speak for all of my teammates when I say he will be missed. We didn't always agree with his decisions, but down deep we know he had our best interests at heart."

"Coach always had something to say. Sometimes I felt he tried to be controversial in order to challenge our way of thinking. His comments were always black and white – there was no gray in his personality and you always knew where you stood with him. Unfortunately, we took too few opportunities to thank him for all that he did for us."

"They say the sense of hearing is the first sense you use when you are born. Hearing is the last sense you use before you die. Coach could always be heard long before he entered the room and his voice will be remembered long after today. Coach, we'll miss your speeches, your angry tirades, your cheers, and your laughter. Your impact goes far beyond the game of hockey. The world will be a duller place without your presence. We will miss you old friend. Amen."

"Amen." The crowd answered back. Presley stepped down and was quickly surrounded by his teammates.

"Good speech, buddy!" said Chilly as he slapped him on the back.

"He would have liked it," commented Taj.

"I say after the funeral we all find a bar and have a drink for Coach!" said Tunny. His teammates chimed in their approval and then stood at attention as one of Coach's family members came up to deliver her speech.

Through the trees behind the crowd, three officers watched the mourners.

"There was no chance this hockey coach was murdered?" asked Garson.

"Coroner said he found nothing suspicious. The deceased was overweight, a drinker, and a smoker. His heart was a ticking time bomb that his doctor warned him about years ago," Mitch answered.

"Typical man. Never listens," commented Lola.

"So, we can rule out foul play," asked Mitch.

"Didn't fit the MO anyway. Let's go over your trip. Tell me what you got off our dead suspect at the apartment," questioned Garson.

"Timothy Ranson. Computer hacker. Worked a couple of mail fraud cons and bank transaction embezzlements. Been jailed once but went underground as soon as he was released four years ago," added Lola.

"Until now," continued Mitch. "Tech support went through his computer top to bottom. He had a fail-safe as soon as we tried to examine his files without a password. We lost half of the data before we knew we triggered it. They stopped the drive from being wiped and recovered some data. It appears a number of bank transactions were taking place between hundreds of clients, including some of our vics, with a company called Transweep. It was hard to follow the money because it was moved so many times, but it eventually ended up in a bank in the Cayman Islands."

"Completely untouchable and almost untraceable," added Lola.

"What is the money from? Stock transactions? Bank theft?" Garson asked.

"Unknown. Too much data lost to understand its source. But we did find something interesting that is connected to four of our victims. A code word was used to direct information a few days after a bank transaction was made by our victims. In each case, reference is made to a 'cleaning order' being issued for that person."

"A hit?"

"Maybe. Although why after a money transaction. It doesn't make sense."

"Maybe they didn't deliver the amount they promised? Client took offense and had them eliminated?" commented Lola.

"These weren't always wealthy people and the transaction never seemed larger than a few thousand. A hit seems over the top for the revenues."

"Where do we go from here?" asked Garson.

"There are other names on the list. Unfortunately, because of the encryption, there is no identification beyond the name. It may take some manpower and time, but we can try to track down the more unusual names to see if there are similar surnames on the Eastern Seaboard."

"Still doesn't connect how the hockey team is involved," Garson scratched his chin.

"We think we have that one figured out," Lola answered. "Someone on the team is the 'cleaner'. He must get the call from Transweep to 'clean' a specific house and uses the hockey team's travel schedule to coordinate the hits. The team is on the road a lot. Could be an easy cover to travel unsuspected and never have your name on the airline or boarding list."

Lola was interrupted by the mourners who filed past their vantage point. The funeral had ended, and most people were leaving the gravesite. The hockey team walked together behind the family to the parking lot at the far end of the cemetery. Taj looked over with a sense of recognition.

"Aren't those the cops that questioned us?" he asked Chilly. Tunny ran forward before anyone could respond. He stepped straight into Garson's face.

"You caused this! Your stupid harassment got him so worked up that he had a heart attack!" Tunny jammed his finger into Garson's chest. If it hurt, Garson showed no sign.

"Why don't you back off before I charge you with assault," answered Mitch stepping toward him. Garson held out his hand to prevent escalating the moment.

"You'd like that, wouldn't you," yelled Dawson. "Then you could bring us in again with no proof."

"All right! Everyone simmer down. I'm sure the officers have some reason for being here," Presley responded.

"Dude! You're not here to take one of us away?" stammered Dozer.

"Not without a fight," said Brick as the other players mobilized.

"Enough!" Garson yelled and held out his hands for everyone to calm down. "We are not here to arrest anyone. We came to pay our respects and to apologize." The hockey players looked at each other. "The investigation was called off. The evidence was flimsy, and the team is exonerated. No one is going to jail. I apologize for the stress that you and your teammates have been under. We did not want to contribute to your Coach's death. If you will allow us, a donation will be made on behalf of the department toward the Coach's charity."

"That sounds really nice," answered Taj. "But you make sure you follow through. He would have liked a defibulator at the arena. That will save lives."

"That's sounds fair," answers Garson. "Please accept our condolences." The anger left the players and several started walking away.

"I hope that we never see each other again," added Chilly, grabbing Tunny by the shoulders.

"Well, I wouldn't mind seeing some of you again," commented Stefan looking at Lola.

"Come on!" Booker pulled him away. The players continued walking to the parking lot while several still looked back at the three officers. The officers watched the players get into their cars and drive off.

"What was that all about? Did the Captain cancel the investigation?" Lola asked.

"He'd like to but he's busy with his own problems right now," commented Garson.

"So why tell the team that? They're going to know you're lying if they catch us on surveillance," questioned Mitch.

"They won't see us because we won't be watching them." Both Lola and Mitch looked at each other.

"I told them the investigation's off because I don't want to scare the killer underground. We need him to continue if we're going to catch him."

"But how, if we don't watch them?" asked Lola.

"Find one of the names on the database. Find their location. Send a cleaner order out. We'll stake out the location. We don't need to watch the team. The killer will come to us."

Chapter 30

Stakeout

April 12, 2007   11pm

Lights glimmered across the Niagara Falls landscape. In the distance, a tower looked over the waterfall. Patrons sat in the revolving restaurant, taking turns to view the majestic falls. Well beneath the tower, in a less glamorous side of the city, Mitch sat in a van desperately trying to avoid falling asleep. A pizza delivery car drove past, the smell of fresh food wafting through the air. Mitch's mouth began to water. *I'd love to place a takeout order right now.* His food thoughts were quickly interrupted.

"Red Team – check in," Garson's voice squeaked over the radio.

"Roger – No activity around the house," Mitch answered.

"Blue Team – Respond," the radio buzzed again.

"Will you stop calling me blue team? I'm one officer sitting in the house. By the way, this blond wig is driving me crazy!" Lola replied.

"Sorry, the last two nights we had help," Garson sighed. "All the other officers have been pulled to another case in Buffalo. We're on our own tonight."

"The Assassins have played back to back games and head out tomorrow. If one of them is a killer, they will have to strike tonight," Mitch answered.

"That's assuming he got the cleaning order we emailed out. Maybe we didn't follow the right protocol and scared the killer off," commented Lola.

"Or maybe he realized that you don't quite match his assignment. When we took over this house, I warned you that this woman had smaller *assets* than you," Mitch joked.

"Great. You think I scared the killer away because my boobs are bigger?"

"Serial killers are known for their eye to detail."

"If I can break up your witty banter for a moment, how about we return to the case?" Garson asked. Their silence confirmed their agreement.

"We're are lucky that this woman happened to be abroad in Europe for ten days and allowed us the use of her house," mentioned Mitch.

"Any idea why she was on the database list?" Lola asked.

"No, but she wasn't the most open person in her responses. Once she's back in North America, we'll make sure she gets a full interrogation. But I don't want to waste this opportunity. This is our last chance. If the killer doesn't take the bait tonight, this case is as good as dead."

2am

"Report!"

"I'm tired and I have a headache. And the movies on television are crap. How come everything on this time of night is twenty years old?" Lola complained.

"Great. Good to see our taxpayer dollars at work. Mitch, do you have anything to actually contribute to this investigation?" Garson snarled. Mitch was mesmerized by the brake lights of a car driving by. He shook his head and quickly responded.

"Nada. There has been hardly any traffic at all on this street. A couple of cars returned home and pulled into their garages. Several cars have driven though, but no one has stopped on the street. If our killer is stalking our victim, he must be doing it from one of the houses."

"Take a walk. Make sure you take Inspector with you. Going out alone will create too much suspicion," guided Garson.

"Roger that," Mitch answered and looked at the back seat. Inspector was a German shepherd, part of the local K-9 unit. Inspector quietly moved on the back seat, ready to spring into action at Mitch's command.

"Let's go, boy." Inspector could walk without a lease, but Mitch did not want to attract attention and connected a leather strap to his collar. It was a risk to be out walking so late, but the dog provided good cover. They walked down the street, meandering slowly. Mitch glanced into each window, hoping to spot something suspicious. *The killer could be using infrared. If that's the case, he could be watching me right now.*

Mitch bent down to tie his shoe and took a moment to check out a house across the street. Lights from a television occasionally flashed illuminating the front window. *Can't imagine the killer is watching the late show.* He walked to the end of the street. Inspector growled at a car going by that turned down another block. *How is the killer checking out the home? In all of the murders, none of neighbor's homes were broken into. No one had spotted anyone strange in the neighborhood previous to or on the night of the murders. The killer couldn't belong to every neighborhood. How would he stay invisible? What are we missing? If the killer doesn't show tonight, will we ever know?*

5am

With an hour and half to go before dawn, Garson looked at his radio to check in with the team one last time before calling it a night.

"Lola – report." He was met with silence. Exasperated, he yelled again. "Wake up! And I don't want to hear another report on bad movies!" Again, his response was met with silence.

"Lola, answer us!" yelled Mitch, beginning to worry. No answer. "Something's wrong. Trust me, she wouldn't fall asleep!"

"Converge! Bring in Inspector. If we're going to blow our cover, I want every available resource we have," yelled Garson.

Mitch bolted from the car. Inspector was in close pursuit with the leash dragging on the ground. They raced to the front entrance of the split entry. Mitch kicked the door open. Inspector charged into the doorway and vanished into the darkness. Mitch rushed into the living room and saw Lola's limp form slumped on the couch. He rushed to her and checked her pulse. It was very faint, and her lips were blue. Garson charged in from the rear door.

"Is she?" he asked.

"Barely."

"Call dispatch. Get an ambulance for her immediately and call for backup. I don't want you to leave her side." Garson turned as he heard a squeak from a floorboard upstairs.

"Go!" Mitch motioned his head upstairs.

"Inspector!" Garson yelled and the dog charged from the kitchen passing him on the flight of stairs. A door slammed shut. Garson charged, taking two steps at a time while Inspector barked at the bedroom door. Garson kicked the door. It held shut. He pulled out his revolver and fired at the lock. It shattered under the impact. The dog charged into the room, leaping on to the bed. A window hung open with the curtain hanging in the breeze. *Damn it – he came through from the roof!*

Garson leapt onto the bed and looked out over the roof. Through the murky darkness, he caught the silhouette of someone jumping off the roof. He turned around and dashed through the broken door. He took four steps at a time, almost stumbling at the bottom. Mitch was frantically speaking into his cell phone while holding the limp form of Lola in his lap. Garson charged out into the backyard, jumped the fence and crossed the neighbor's lawn. He heard the sound of a car starting up down the street.

That's him! Garson dashed past three houses and jumped into his unmarked car. He gunned the engine to life and raced through a stop sign while turning onto the next street.

At this time at night, with so few cars I might have a chance. He glimpsed a car's brake lights flashing red far down the street. *One chance!* His foot pressed the accelerator in the hopes of catching his quarry. *There's something on the roof of that car!* He read the writing on the sign - Casino Pizza.

Damn it! He's been in the neighborhood the whole time! He knows we're on to him. If I don't catch him now, he'll be lost to us forever!

April 13, 2007   5:30am

The streets of Niagara Falls were almost deserted. Neon lights flashed among the empty storefronts. The sun would be up soon, and the city would come alive with early morning workers. Garson contacted the Niagara Police.

"Special Agent Garson requesting assistance. Murder suspect driving red sedan with a pizza sign on roof. Suspect driving through entertainment district on Main crossing Vermont toward casino. Unable to read license, suspect too far ahead. Over." Garson looked up and narrowly missed a homeless person pushing a shopping cart full of recyclable bottles.

"Dispatch to Agent Garson. Currently short staffed. Officers are responding to shooting at Comfort Inn. Will need twenty minutes to respond."

Great. He'll be gone by then. "Understood. Please have officer responding call me for current location." Garson tossed the two-way radio onto the passenger seat. *Looks like it's just you and me,* as he looked intently at the car in front of him. Garson floored his car and the pizza vehicle responded in kind. *Guess there's no doubt you know you're being pursued. Which player are you?* The distance was too great to see the size of the driver. The killer turned onto the roadway looking down the escarpment towards the falls. He passed a taxi and gunned over a small crest.

Niagara Falls was not a large city. By car you can travel out of the city in a few minutes. Garson knew the killer wouldn't head to Customs and be stopped before heading to the US. That left few options. The killer didn't know about Garson's lack of support and would try to lose him immediately. The pizza car drove more erratically heading east out of town. Suddenly, the pizza car veered right, smashing through the gate to Marine World, the second most popular tourist attraction in the city. Marine World had a variety of sea animal attractions, with dolphins and killer whales headlining the family shows.

The parking lot was vacant. The theme park didn't open for the season until May. Garson turned the corner and smashed into the right side of the pizza car. The shock of the airbag caused disorientation for a moment. He pulled his seatbelt off and jumped out of his car with his gun drawn. He looked into the empty driver seat of the pizza car.

He saw the main sign with a map of the amusement park with its attractions. Garson looked around the parking lot and caught the silhouette of someone running through the main gates. *Looks like this is going to be a foot race.*

Garson broke into a gallop with the cool morning air gushing through his lungs. He hopped over the turnstile like an athlete jumping hurtles. *Hope this park has a night security guard.* Garson ran toward an amphitheatre and almost slipped on the wet concrete. A dolphin chirped a happy whistle towards Garson. *Maybe a I can feed this killer to the killer whales.* Ahead, the killer remained the same distance ahead of him. *Great, the guy's obviously in good shape. How am I going to close the distance?*

Almost on cue, the killer stumbled on the icy ramp way leading to the penguins. He immediately jumped up, but the distance between the two had shrunk. Garson followed the killer's shadow down the ramp into the dark tunnel. He saw the glow of penguins diving in the frigid pool of water. Ahead, he could hear the thumping of footsteps as his quarry's feet slapped on the walkway.

The tunnel ended suddenly, and the small barns of the petting zoo came into view along a dirt trail. A tree branch smacking sound told Garson that the killer was close. Frightened goats brayed at Garson as he turned a corner. The smell of manure overpowered his nostrils. His lungs demanded air and he could feel the acid building in his calves. *I've got a couple of minutes left in me before my body is going to give out.* Ahead, the light of the midway rides beckoned to him. The trail divided into a fork with right and left trails through the rides. The killer veered right toward the roller coaster.

Garson ran to the left by the midway games. He remembered the map of the amusement park at the entrance. His trail went straight to the back exit while the roller coaster pathway took longer to the back of the park. *I hope the killer failed to notice the route. There's no way I can catch him in a footrace. Hopefully this will give me the advantage. If the killer gets through to the back and to the park behind, it will be impossible for me to find him alone.*

The last of the midway games ran out as he came to the exit turnstile. He leaned against the ticket house and tried to catch his breath before his lungs exploded. *Control your breathing; the killer should be exhausted as well. Could have a weapon. Try to take him alive if you can.* The sound of running feet on a pebbled walkway told Garson his quarry was close. He drew his gun and inched closer to the edge of the building. The sound of footsteps drew closer. *Wait until he gets a bit closer so he can't get away. Then you're mine.*

"Officer Garson – we have one unit available to assist with your pursuit. Please advise of current location," the walkie-talkie on his belt squawked. *Damn It!* He flicked his radio off and jumped out onto the pathway with his gun drawn. "You're under arrest!" he yelled and looked at the empty pathway from the roller coaster. He glanced towards the midway games. The whole area was still. Garson flicked his walkie-talkie back on.

"Control, send your squad car to the rear entrance of the Marine World theme park. Suspect on foot, no determining features. Stop any person on foot in this vicinity. Suspect considered dangerous. Approach with extreme caution."

"Roger that, ETA five minutes," the walkie-talkie replied.

I blew it. Probably the only chance I'll get to capture the killer. Now that he knows we've on to him. He's a hundred miles away by daybreak. Garson sat down on a set of steps.

"Mitch – report! How is Lola?" The radio was silent for several seconds.

"Mitch here. I'm with the paramedics. Lola's getting oxygen – apparently, she has a high level of carbon monoxide in her blood. If we had waited any longer either the murderer or the lack of air would have killed her. We're taking her to the hospital, but they're predicting a full recovery. Any luck on your end?"

"Had him, lost him. Maybe for good."

"What do we do next? Should we go arrest the remaining team members?" Garson thought about the questions he posed to each of the ten players when they were being interrogated. Each one of them insisted on their innocence and there had been no evidence to implicate any of them. Yet something nagged him, something one of them said just didn't seem right. *Could he trust his instinct again?*"

"Hold off. The killer knows we're tipped off to his methods but not his identity. Tonight, is their last game of the season. I've got a feeling the killer is going to make one last appearance. And if he does, I think I know how to catch him."

"And if he doesn't show?"

"Then we'll know for sure who it is."

Chapter 32   *Killer Perspective*

April 13, 2007   6:30am

He jumped over the back fence into the park. His feet barely touched the ground and he ran into the darkness of the forest canopy. His lungs exploded and he bent over from exertion. *I've got a maximum of five minutes before his backup start searching this park. I've got to keep going.* He took a deep breath and pushed through the brush. He quickly found a trail and headed in the opposite direction of the amusement park. The sun was slowly rising on the horizon allowing him to see in the distance. He saw an abandoned ice cream shack adjacent to a playground and a parking lot appeared a hundred yards ahead of him. He came to the edge of the park and crossed the street heading up to the business district. Within a couple of minutes, he saw a taxi stand with a couple of cabbies standing by their cars talking and smoking. He gestured to one and took a seat in the back of his car. The cabbie jumped in the front, looking back at his fare and grinned.

"Crazy night of partying eh?" he smiled with a big gap in his front teeth.

"Crazy yes," the killer answered. "Can you take me to the Westwood motel?"

"You bet. I'll have you there in a few minutes." The killer slumped back and closed his eyes.

How did they know? Everything was fake! The cleaning call, the victim, the house, all a trap. The website has been compromised. From here on in, no more contact with the seller. Fortunately, the two had never met and there would be no way he could identify him. But he could feel the noose tightening around his neck. They may have stopped watching the team, but they would probably come back once the cops realized the team had a game in Niagara Falls last night. It was only a matter of time before they traced it back to him. Question was, did he go rejoin the team or take off now?

The last game of the season would be in Oshawa tonight. The fans would be excited, and the arena would be packed. The cops would be watching, but they probably still wouldn't know who to arrest. The cop never got close enough to see him – his identity was still safe. One more game. I've got one more chance to play with the guys.

The taxicab pulled into the motel parking lot. The killer saw the team bus and asked the driver to stop. He paid the fare and stepped toward the patio door he'd left unlocked. His roommate was dead asleep, and it took a freight train to wake him up. If he ever woke up in the middle of the night, he could always make up the excuse that he went to see another player. As he slid under the covers, he knew he had a couple of hours before the rest of the team woke up. With a nap on the bus ride back, he'd be ready for tonight. It was all coming to a head and he'd make sure, with his planning, that he'd come out on top.

Chapter 33 *The Final Game*

Both teams stood on their blue line awaiting the start of the game. The Oshawa arena was packed to the rafters with fans eager to watch the final game of the season. Many fans were given white t-shirts with the Assassins' logo on the front. The sea of t-shirts made the crowd look like a huge white monster. The Chicago Fire players looked around nervously, not used to this type of fan support.

"A lot of people came out to support the Coach," commented Chilly tightening his chinstrap.

"The Coach would have loved this crowd. I hope we don't let them down," answered Presley.

"Can you guys shut up? You're interrupting the national anthem!" Brick nudged Chilly.

"Her voice?" commented Tunny looking at the large woman with the microphone. "The only thing louder than her voice is her ugly flower dress," he shivered.

"Quiet," Brick responded. "When it comes to our anthem, she has a voice of an angel." Several players snickered as her voice cracked on a high note.

"Voice of an angel," mimicked Tunny as she sang the last line. The crowd clapped with respectful applause.

"Welcome to the Oshawa Auto Dome for the Central Hockey finals!" Fans screamed and cheered, to welcome the voice of the announcer. "Tonight's winner goes to the National semi-final in Portland, Oregon in two weeks. The Chicago Fire has been the league's most consistent team, finishing with a league leading point total of 54. The Oshawa Assassins are the league's Cinderella story. They were close to the league basement at Christmas and by the end of the season finished in second place with 53 points. Tonight's game is winner take all. Whoever wins gets two points and the league trophy. One final game to decide a season's worth of struggle."

The announcer allowed the crowd noise to die down to a dull roar. "There is one question you have to ask yourself." The crowd looked toward the announcer's booth. "Ladies and gentlemen – are you ready?" They screamed their approval. "Then let's get ready to rummmmbbbble!" The crowd went ballistic. It had been a long time since the Assassins were a contender. The music blared across the ice and the simulated sound of gunfire sound effects reverberated throughout the arena as the players skated for the warm-up.

From above in the announcer box, Garson surveyed the ice surface. He looked over at the announcer. "Any scratches on the Assassin team?" he asked.

"Are you kidding?" The announcer turned in his chair wearing a bright orange sequin suit jacket. "This is the game of the year. Nobody's going to miss it. Are you aware of an injury?" he leaned forward hoping for a news scoop.

"No, just checking. Can you turn around? Your suit is blinding me."

"Everyone gather 'round." Presley motioned to everyone on the bench. "Tonight, is the biggest game of the year. For some, the most important game of your career. We have a lot of people depending on us to win. Our family, our fans, but most importantly, let's do it in honor of the Coach." He held his hand out. "Are you with me?"

"For the Coach!" the team yelled in unison. The first line skated to center: Chilly, Stefan, and Taj started as forwards while Booker and Dozer played on defense.

Stefan looked at the Chicago Fire player, Arnold Avery, at center ice. Arnold preferred the nick name Double A because he was so full of energy. Many players felt he was definitely full of something.

"Good luck, mon ami!" he saluted. Arnold looked at him with disgust.

"Keep your head up, you French frog. Otherwise, I'll squish you under my skate," he snarled. The puck was dropped, and Double A was upended by a check from Chilly, who winked back at Stefan.

"The Assassins are flying tonight! After being the league's doormat at the start of the season, they are playing like a team possessed. Rumors have been swirling that this is their last season; the years of losses have finally taken their toll. This is one fan who hopes this isn't their final game." The announcer turned and saw Garson heading toward the door. "Don't go now – the game's just starting."

"Don't worry, I'll be back," Garson replied. He stepped into the hallway and walked down to ice level and the dressing rooms. The crowd drowned out the sound of his footsteps. He walked by the zamboni driver's office and grabbed the Assassins' dressing room key. *Great security – I bet he's watching the game.* He knocked on the dressing room door in case support staff were still in the room. After five seconds, he turned the key.

I'm not sure what I'll find. I don't think the killer will keep any incriminating evidence in his locker. Is a murder weapon too much to ask? The reek of sweat and hockey gear permeated the locker room. *My gear never smelled this bad in basketball.* He started on the right, looking at each player's stall, going through personal items. Watches, wallets, pictures of wives and girlfriends. He looked at the edge of a player's extra hockey skate and ran his finger down the side. *These babies are sharp; I'd hate to get cut by one of them.*

He noticed a room to the side and tried the door. *Locked – must be something good in there.* He pulled out a lock pick kit and gently tugged at the lock with a metal tool. After ten seconds, the lock popped open. *That was slow,* he smiled. Inside the windowless room was a nondescript desk with a computer and a filing cabinet. *I'll need the tech boys to go through the computer.* He pulled open an unlocked file drawer. Inside were files and contact information for most of the players, some game statistics, ledgers from game revenues, and travel schedules. *This is a dead end – I'll check in with Mitch.* Garson opened his cell phone and received a static signal. *Damn, these arena steel beams are hard on phone signals.* He walked out of the dressing room and up a flight of stairs toward an emergency exit. He hit redial.

"Mitch. How's Lola?"

"Good," Mitch's voice replied. "She was sleeping the last time I visited. They want to keep her overnight for observation."

"Have you reviewed the video footage from Marine World?"

"Not yet. It just arrived by courier and the editor is copying it to the hard drive now. If I find anything, I'll call you. What's happening at the game?"

"Game's started and everyone's here. I searched the dressing room. Go through that footage as fast as you can – I need something to narrow down my options and time's running out fast." A horn blasted through the arena bringing the crowd to its feet.

"What's that sound?"

"The first period ended. I've only got another 40 minutes of playing time left before my suspects are gone."

"Better hope for overtime," Mitch commented.

Back in the announcer's booth came an animated commentary.

"It's the end of the first period and it's a scoreless tie. Great saves made at both ends of the rink. Who will draw first blood? And now a word from tonight's sponsor. . . ."

The Assassins piled into their dressing room as the zamboni cleared the ice. Taj stepped into the room first.

"Hey, who left the light on?" he commented.

"Never mind. Would somebody try to set me up?" Dawson complained. "I was sitting in front of the net alone and nobody bothered to pass."

"Maybe if you spent less time looking at yourself in the glass, you might get a pass," sneered Tunny.

"Enough!" Presley stepped in between them. "We're playing well. The goals will come. Don't get off your game."

"He's right!" replied Chilly as he entered the dressing room. "The fans are amazing. Feed on their energy! It's so noisy, the Chicago players can't hear themselves on the bench."

"Sounds like a good reason to celebrate," Dozer reached for a beer.

"Hey. Mon ami! Wait until after the game. Don't dull your senses," commented Stefan.

"Dude, that's the problem. Ever since those police interviews, I've gone cold chicken on the weed," whined Dozer.

"The term is cold turkey," corrected Booker.

"Dude. Chicken. Turkey. Don't get all intellectual on me."

"Everybody relax. This is our night! Coach would be proud," Brick replied. The air horn blew from the ice surface signifying that the second period was ready to begin.

"It is time for us to make our reappearance," Taj flashed a smile as the team headed back to the ice.

"The second period is about to begin. Shot totals were ten for Chicago and nine for Oshawa. Both goaltenders looked strong and we'll see how they hold up to another period of pressure. We're ready to drop the puck," cheered the announcer.

"Hey Frenchie, watch me score this period! And there's nothing you or any of your lovers can do about it," Avery announced.

"Avery, I'm going love ramming this puck down your throat!" commented Taj from the left wing. Before Avery could respond, the puck was dropped for the second period.

Garson returned to the announcer's booth and sat on the couch.

"About time you came back. You're missing a hell of game," the announcer replied looking back from the action.

"Tell me something, are there any skyboxes here? Any place where the owner would sit?" Garson asked.

"Skyboxes! You got to be kidding. This place is lucky to fit five thousand people. There's no room for a skybox. If you want to know, the best seat in town is right here," he gestured around the booth.

"Then where does the owner sit?" asked Garson.

"How am I supposed to know? Frankly the team's been so bad in the past, I don't think the owner bothered to watch a game. Is it important for you to meet him?" Before Garson could answer, they were interrupted by on-ice activity. The announcer grabbed the mike.

"What a hit! The Assassins are really cleaning house!" The referee put up his hand to signify an Assassin's penalty. "Oh no! Looks like the Assassins are going to take a penalty for a clean hit. Where did they get this referee?"

"Two minutes for cross checking," said the referee as he pointed to Brick.

"Come on! You've got to be kidding. He took a dive," Chilly gestured to Double A. Avery smiled and then fell back to the ice, dramatically playing up his injury.

"Go to the box," the ref yelled, and Brick skated over and sat down in the sin bin. Tunny skated over Double A.

"You can get up now. You're a shoo-in for the award ceremonies for biggest diver in the league!" The linesman separated Tunny as Avery stood up with help from his teammates.

"I can't help it if the Assassins are a bunch of goons!" Double A yelled back.

"That's enough! You guys line up in the circle or I'll give you both a delay of game penalty," the referee growled. The teams quickly matched up. With Brick out, Booker and Dozer secured defense while Chilly and Presley played forward.

The puck was dropped, and the Chicago Fire drew it backwards to their defense. Double A rushed forward and skated toward the net. The Chicago defenseman shot the puck. It hit Chilly's stick and spun into the air. The referee looked up and accidentally tripped on a Chicago player's stick, tumbling to the ice. Double A saw the puck in the air and with his glove, smacked it into the Assassin's net. The red light went on!

"Oh, come on! The puck was hit with a hand into the net. An obvious cheat. The referee better call the goal back," the announcer cried.

"He gloved the puck into the net! That goal shouldn't count," complained Presley to the referee. The referee motioned to Presley to stay where he was and went over to talk to the only other official on the ice.

"Did you see anything? I fell on the ice and missed the goal," the referee asked.

"I couldn't see through the bodies from my vantage point," the lineman shrugged. "It looked like it bounced off some bodies and went in." Double A rushed in between them.

"Come on ref! The puck hit a leg and bounced in. Don't let these fans tell you how to make the call."

"He's lying. He intentionally gloved it in!" complained Presley.

"Okay, that's enough! Both of you!" The ref yelled back and skated to the score box. He dropped his hands to signify a goal. The crowd roared it disapproval.

"No! The referee called a goal," the announcer moaned. "How could he have missed the hand-gloved goal? If we had video replay, the goal would never have ever counted. The fans are showing their disapproval by throwing things onto the ice. Drinks, hats, I even see a lobster. Now that's an expensive toss."

The referee skated over to the scorekeeper's box and spoke to him. Seconds later, an announcement was made.

"Please refrain from tossing debris. If not stopped immediately, the game will be called and awarded to the Chicago Fire," the announcer proclaimed. The crowd booed but no more items were tossed onto the ice. Several support staff swept the ice while each team took a two-minute time out.

"You have real classy fan support in your city," Garson commented sarcastically.

"That's the great thing about democracy, special agent. When a bad call is made, everyone gets to voice their opinion. Other sports are no different."

"You're right. Hockey fans don't have a monopoly on erratic behavior," said Garson as he stepped outside of the announcer's booth to make another phone call.

"Lola, how are you doing?" Garson spoke on his cell phone as he stepped towards one of the exits of the arena.

"I'm fine," she coughed, lying on her hospital bed, "and I'm ready to get out of here!" She tugged at an IV.

"Sit tight. You almost died. Give the doctors a day to make sure you don't have any permanent damage," said Garson.

"And if I say I'm okay to return to work now?" Lola asked as she lifted her head.

"Let me rephrase that. I am ordering you to stay put. Get up before the doctors give you a clean bill of health and you're fired!"

"I'll give you one thing Garson. You're clear in your commands." Lola coughed and adjusted the pillow on her hospital bed. "What's this, a mercy call?"

"Hardly. Tell me about the cleaning orders again. I feel like I'm missing something."

"Okay. What we gleaned from the hacker was a massive number of transactions were conducted on the eastern seaboard. His computer took a small percentage, but we don't know the nature of the transactions.

"How did the orders go out?" inquired Garson.

"Email sent to a dummy address. Usually changed every couple of months. I don't know the encryption key they used to keep both sides aware of the change. Funny thing was that even though the cleaning orders to our guy were from September to April, the business was run year-round.

"Our guy might not be the only cleaner?"

"Maybe not."

"How much were the transactions for in the cleaning order?"

"Don't know. None of the transactions were tagged. Always seemed to be in even amounts, although I did notice a couple of credits of $30,000. Wasn't sure who they were for and what they paid."

"Okay, that's helpful. I've got an idea of where to look and see if that number comes up. Get some rest, I'll call you in the morning."

"You're not going to take this killer down without me?" Lola asked her anger rising.

"Not unless the killer forces my hand," he answered.

"It's the start of the third period. Score is Chicago Fire one, Oshawa Assassins no score. Besides the cheap goal in the second period, the goaltenders' play has been flawless. If the Assassins want to see the post season, they have to find the back of the net," the announcer talked over the roar of the crowd.

"It's do or die time, boys. We need to score or it's straight to the golf course." Booker proclaimed in the pre-period scrum on the Assassins' bench.

"Talk about the obvious. How about somebody feeding me in front of the net?" complained Dawson.

"Man, you are a broken record," answered Taj. Presley looked around at the faces of his fellow players

"We have to show more spirit out there!" Presley proclaimed. "Tunny, start playing with more intensity. Show the fans how much you want the game.

"Intensity!" Tunny yelled. "I'll show you losers some intensity. Rook, watch my back. I'm going to collect some heads.

"What do you want me to do? Go pick them up?" Rook said with confusion. The rest of the team laughed.

"Play back because he's going to take some risks," replied Stefan. The whistle blew signifying the start of the third period.

"Put your hands in the center," Presley commanded. Everyone put a hand in the middle of the circle.

"Assassins! Let's kill'em!" Both teams headed to the middle of the ice. Double A skated to Chilly at the face-off circle.

"Twenty minutes to go before my celebration. Don't worry though, I'll make sure to comment on your game play to the press. Maybe some team will pick you up next season. The Fire can always use a good benchwarmer," Double A smirked.

"Enjoy yourself Double A. You've got a whole summer of crying ahead of you," Chilly replied as he drew the puck back to his defense from the face-off.

"Five minutes into the third period and the face-off is in Chicago's end. The Assassins have been relentless in their attack, out shooting the Fire six to one. Chicago's goaltender is standing on his head with amazing save after save. Time is now the Assassins ultimate enemy," the announcer yelled while downing his third drink of the period. "Are the Assassins going to score?" he asked the crowd.

"Get behind me, Rook. I'm going to get this draw," commanded Presley as he went to center.

"You want me to take the shot?" Rook was confused. Most Assassin players never showed much confidence in him.

"Yes, but keep your shot low. The goaltender has a killer glove hand." Presley lined up as Double A skated into the circle.

"Time's running out. Tick, tock, tick, tock," he sneered.

"Don't polish your trophy just yet," warned Presley. The puck was dropped, and Presley pulled the puck back to Rook's stick. Double A came charging at Rook.

"Give it here, newbie!" he yelled. Rook was startled and passed the puck to Taj in the corner. Taj sped to the net but was blocked by a huge defenseman. He passed it back to Rook who snapped the puck towards the net. Double A grimaced as the puck hit his skate and deflected in the opposite direction of the goaltender's lunge. Rook watched as the puck entered the goaltender's crease and slid into the net.

"They score! The Assassins have tied the game! The puck deflected off the Chicago player and into the net. Ladies and gentlemen, we are tied!" the announcer yelled.

Rook held his hands up in celebration while the rest of the players slapped his helmet.

"You did good kid, you did real good," Brick laughed almost knocking Rook over with the strength of his slap.

"You shot that perfectly," added Taj.

"Way to go," yelled Presley. Tunny skated pass Double A.

"Thanks for the assist, loser. We couldn't have done it without you," sneered Tunny as Double A turned purple with rage. He swung his stick at Tunny and missed.

"Go back to your bench or I'll call a penalty," the referee warned Double A. One of the Chicago defenseman dragged Double A away. The Assassins players headed over to the bench.

"Gentleman, I think we have a hockey game," Chilly commented over the roar of the crowd.

"What have you got for me, Mitch?" Garson spoke into his cell phone while standing in the concourse.

"Maybe something, maybe nothing. I'm reviewing the tapes. Most of the cameras are poorly lit and your chase is pretty dark, but in one camera angle, I can make out a jacket. But the face is cut off."

"Anything interesting on the jacket?"

"There's a letter on the upper right-hand corner of the jacket but it's blurry. The techs are taking it frame by frame, but the resolution is horrible and it's almost impossible to read even when we blow the image up.

"Keep trying. As soon as you get something, you call me!"

"You got it, boss," said Mitch as he clicked his phone shut. He stared at a television screen. "What is on your jacket?" he murmured as he squinted hard at the screen.

"With one-minute left to play, the game is practically in overtime now. This game is tied at one a piece and the next goal will decide the winner. Let's make some noise for the Assassins!" The announcer screamed as the fans bellowed out their applause for their hometown.

"This is awesome, dude. The fans are loving us!" exclaimed Dozer as the team gathered around the bench by using its last time out.

"Let's give them something to really cheer about!" added Stefan slapping his stick on the ice with excitement.

"Good. Use that energy to score a goal," Presley replied.

"I want on the ice. I can feel a goal," exclaimed Dawson.

"You just want the glory," chided Tunny.

"This may be the last play of the game. Get the puck out of our end and rush their goaltender. If he sees the puck, he's going to save it. If we get some traffic in front of him, we might have a chance. Are you guys ready?" Booker advised.

"Let's kill'em!" was the team's response.

Both teams lined up for the face-off. Chilly was at center with Dawson and Tunny on the wings. Brick and Dozer held up the point. Double A skated into the circle and looked at Chilly.

"Watch me break this tie and become the hero. You can tell your kids how I saved the day," sneered Avery.

"Avery. If you score, I will bow in front of you and tell every media source that you are the best player in the league. But if we score, you have to duct tape a puck in your mouth and shut up!" Chilly yelled.

"I'd pay money to see that," Tunny laughed from the wing.

"Not going to happen. Be ready to bow," Double A answered.

The puck was dropped and Chilly brought the puck back to Brick. Brick turned backwards toward the back of the net as Double A gave chase.

"Pass it to me," Dawson screamed.

Brick shot the puck along the boards up to Tunny. Double A wasn't paying attention and skated into Brick's chest. He fell to the ice.

"Stay down big mouth. Your season is about to end!" warned Brick.

Tunny carried the puck though center ice while a huge Chicago defenseman charged at him. Tunny passed the puck to Chilly just as the defenseman gave a vicious hip check. Tunny went down onto the ice.

Chilly crossed the blue-line with ten seconds left on the clock. The crowd was yelling for him to shoot while the goaltender readied himself to stop the puck. The other Chicago defenseman lunged at Chilly. He saw an open spot in the upper right-hand corner. *If I make this shot, the scouts will pick me for sure.*

He slapped his stick on the ice and gestured towards the net. Both defenseman and goalie reacted as if the puck had been shot and committed themselves. Chilly changed direction and passed the puck to Dawson who was alone in the crease. For a second, he was so shocked by the pass, he almost forgot to shoot. The goaltender tried to recover, and Dawson quickly roofed the puck into the net. The Assassins scored!

"They did it! The Assassins have scored with three seconds left!" the announcer yelled and almost fell out of his chair from the excitement.

Dawson skated around the net and jumped on the boards. Fans everywhere tried to grab him, almost ripping the jersey off of his body. The rest of team emptied the bench and swarmed him, throwing him into the air.

"Somebody finally passed the puck," he grinned.

"The Chicago team has conceded the game and the timekeeper has run the clock. The game is over! The Assassins are divisional champs!" the announcer screamed.

Fans jumped over the boards to hug their favorite players. The ice surface swarmed with fans that were tumbling and falling on the slippery surface. Several players aimed their sticks up, as if firing a gun, to salute the fans for their support. The Chicago team skated dejectedly back to their bench. When Double A skated by, Chilly smiled and yelled.

"Don't worry, there's always next year." Double A could barely raise his head in response.

Presley skated over to the scorekeeper's box and grabbed the trophy before the victory ceremony could start. He skated around the ice holding the trophy high in the air while the fans stood and cheered. Soon the whole team was skating with Presley, each grabbing hold of the trophy. Tunny skated over to the bench and took a couple cans of beer. He skated back to the crowd of players and grabbed the trophy.

"Now this is how we celebrate!" he opened both beers and poured them into the cup. "We are the champions!" and took the first drink. Several other players grabbed the trophy and drank as well.

"This is crazy! I've never won a championship in my whole life," Rook yelled.

"You think it's crazy now. The party has just begun!" said Taj taking a huge drink from the cup.

2 hours later

The arena was dark, and the stands were filled with debris. Fans and players headed downtown for a night of debauchery and inebriation. The city police force had already been busy responding to acts of public indecency as well as noise complaints. Garson watched as the Zamboni driver locked the door behind him and left the arena.

The team headed down to the Shooting Gallery bar downtown with hundreds of fans. I know where they are going to be for the rest of the night. There's something in the financial books I want to check again. Garson worked the lock for a second time that night and entered the dressing room. He flicked on the switch and headed toward the room off to the side. The door was unlocked, and he sat down in front of the computer. He reached down to the printouts and looked the team financials over the last season. He noticed three deposits of $30,000 during the course of the year.

The killer is keeping the team afloat. His paydays keep the team running, the killer must be the owner of the team. He heard a noise behind him but before he turned, a hockey stick slammed into the back of his head. Before his world went black, Garson looked up to see his attacker wearing an Assassin's jacket. Unconsciousness gripped him before he could recognize the killer's face.

Sudden Death

The killer dragged Garson's limp body across the ice. He pulled the body up against the net and lashed his hands to either post. He checked the ropes and was confident they were secure. A huge bump swelled on the side of Garson's temple from the hockey stick. The killer slid over to the bench to lace up his skates. He threw his jersey over his gear and tightened his helmet. He placed his gloves on last and grabbed a hockey stick. He tossed a puck on the ice and skated over the blue line to take a shot. He lined up the puck and looked at his target before shooting. The puck slammed into the post and veered wide. The reverberation of the net caused Garson to regain consciousness. He raised his head; his arms were immobile. His feet slipped, gaining little traction on the ice.

"If my life is passing before me, I don't remember a hockey rink being a high point." Garson looked over at the killer. "Why don't you step out of the shadows so I can see your face?" The killer remained in shadow. "Okay, I'll try to piece this together on my own. *I've got to stall him as long as possible while I loosen these bonds.*

"The team's always lost money, even with its small payroll. Most players assumed the ownership had deep pockets; some players thought the team was used as a write-off. But you paid to keep the team afloat. You did a good job with the books. The company that owned the team had no connection with the players. When I asked around, no one had even seen the owner. People don't really ask questions as long as their paychecks keep coming. Problem was, in the last few years, the team was losing too much money. I remembered from your interview when you said that the team was a business. Only you had a *sideline business* to pay for the debt."

The killer shifted his position and brought his stick to his right side. He seemed perfectly willing to listen to Garson's explanation.

"I figured how when I found the casino chip in a victim's purse. I knew the victims weren't random murders. Your victims were gamblers – most lived alone, but even those with families kept their secret. Gamblers will do anything to hide their losses from their friends. That is, if they still had friends. I remembered the female reporter friends mentioning that she become more anti-social in the months before you killed her. Gamblers tend to drive their friends away from them."

The killer nodded his head as if the analysis of a gambler's psyche was second nature to him.

"All bets were made online, usually for several thousands of dollars at a time. Although I imagine some people got in over their head fairly quickly. You smashed the victim's computers to prevent us from tracking the bets. We initially thought you were looking for something on the computers when you really were actually hiding their transfers. After our raid of the network manager, I realized that the online gamblers were being targeted when they couldn't pay back what they owed. How am I doing so far?"

The killer took a slap shot. The puck went straight into the net narrowly missing Garson's crotch. "I'll take that as a yes," Garson gulped.

"There is one thing that bothers me. One thing that almost prevented me from tying these cases together. You killed three different ways – why use three ways to kill your victims?" Garson's request was met with silence.

"Come on, step closer. We can't have a discussion if I'm doing all the talking. I'm obviously not going anywhere. Tell me why you used different methods to kill your victims."

"Why…… Presley?"

Presley stepped out of the shadows and removed his helmet. His face was calm, but beneath his mask, he appeared to be hiding a cauldron of emotions. But now there was no longer a need to hide.

"Do you know much about hockey, Agent Garson?" Presley asked as he skated several feet to grab another puck on the ice.

"Didn't know much before the investigation. Know quite a bit now. Can't say I like the game too much," as he looked at his arms tied against the cold steel of the net.

"Sorry to hear that. You're missing quite a game. I've grown up with the sport all my life. Almost made it my religion. The decision of a game carries quite a bit a weight. My teammates and I have rituals before a game. Some don't shave during a road trip; others wear a lucky shirt. Still others call their wives for good luck. My ritual deals with the result of the game."

Keep talking. I can finally feel some give in these ropes.

"Some flip a coin to make decisions. Heads they do this, tails they do that. I don't let chance determine how my victim died. I prefer to have some input into the end result. I let the game decide my target's fate." Presley flipped the puck onto his stick while talking. "Winning, losing, or a tie is the difference between dying by gun wound, strangulation, or by stabbing."

Garson stopped trying to break his bonds as he stared in disbelief.

"You decide how to kill people by whether you win a game or not? You're sicker than I thought," Garson commented while Presley laughed.

"Kept you from figuring out it was one person for a lot of years. Suffocation was the most popular since we lost a lot of games in the early years. I thought the act of the team choking and losing while my target suffocated was very symbolic.

"And what's the symbolism of a win meaning getting shot?" Garson asked.

"If you've seen the opening to our games, you've heard the gun sound effects every time we score a goal. It shows the visiting team that we have taken a shot at them. A gun shot that scored!"

Presley took a slap shot that caught Garson square in the chest. Garson's yell filled the empty arena, but he couldn't clutch his chest because of his bound arms. "I could be playing in the nationals in two weeks if you weren't so damn persistent!"

"Nice shot," Garson groaned. "But the fault is all yours. You blew it when you attacked a fellow hockey player. Why take out Tidwell? He wasn't a gambler," asked Garson.

"No, he wasn't. And you're right. I brought this on myself." He skated closer to the net. "Up until now, my assignments were always gamblers who bet too much. Gamblers who refused to pay or couldn't pay. Many threatened to give up the operation to the police. Bad mistake. These people knew the risks and suffered the ultimate gamble. Tidwell was different story."

"He rubbed you the wrong way?" asked Garson still suffering from the chest shot.

"He rubbed everyone the wrong way. The problem was he was so good. Too good for our league. He threatened our team's chances in making it to the end. This is the team's final hurrah. He had to be removed. With all of his enemies, I thought it would be difficult for you to narrow down the suspects."

"Yet you risked everything. Was it worth it?" Garson grimaced.

"Every second. Trust me, you'll do anything to save your family. This hockey team is all that I have. The players, the only family I have. I knew it was coming to an end, but I wanted to decide when. Instead, I will have to decide how it will end for you." Presley slapped the puck again and it crunched the knuckles in Garson's left hand.

"Aaahhhh! I don't remember any of your killings including death by hockey puck!" Garson yelled. He felt his cell phone on vibration. *It must be Mitch, if only I can flip it open. I have to keep Presley talking.* "Is this a new ritual before you sacrifice me to the hockey gods?"

"Not quite. You see, I'm an innovator. You're the one loose end before I take my permanent vacation. After tonight, I'll be in a warm country with no extradition treaty."

"Your face will be everywhere; you're kidding yourself if you think we won't catch you."

"You'll never know. By the time I'm done, you'll be in no condition to tell them. Brain damage is a terrible thing." Presley brought his stick back for the killing shot to Garson's head. *Slap!* The puck careened toward Garson's face. He only had one chance.

Garson pulled on the crossbar of the net and yanked the posts out of the ice. He fell forward, bringing the net over his head as the puck sailed above him, smashing into the boards.

"You can hide under that net like a turtle but eventually you'll stick your head out!" Presley warned as he took several shots at the fallen net. The mesh of the net stopped most shots harmlessly, but one shot hit him in the arm.

"Why don't you come finish me off? Are you afraid of me? Garson yelled from under the net. *I've got to bring him in closer. A couple more shots and I'll be in too much pain to fight back.*

Presley skated in for the kill. He whacked Garson under the net with his stick.

"Thanks, Garson. I'm really enjoying this. I appreciate you dragging this out."

"Glad this is working out for you." Garson yelled back. Presley skated by again ready to hack with his stick. Garson tried to stand, pulled the net up and charged at him. He slipped on the ice and fell forward onto Presley's chest, knocking both of them down. The top of the net fell on Presley's skate cutting one of Garson's bounds. He freed his right arm away from the crossbar and tried to stand up.

"You're quite a fighter, Agent Garson. It's too bad you don't play hockey; we could use a player like you" as Presley regained his footing. Garson furiously pulled on the bonds around his left hand. He took a whack from Presley's stick as the hockey player skated around him.

"I believe that is a penalty," said Garson as he pulled his other hand free. He pushed the net away from him as he stood on the ice. "Now you've got to face me man to man," he yelled as Presley skated to the boards. Presley smiled at Garson as he picked up a remote control off the timekeeper's bench. Suddenly, the arena lights went out.

Crap! I'm blind, in incredible pain, and I'm standing on ice without any traction, with a psychopath that's trying to kill me.

Suddenly a door opened, and a flashlight broke the darkness from the far end of the rink. Its light shone up to the rafters and then reflected off the glass barrier between the ice and stands.

"Garson! Where are you? I called you several times," Mitch yelled. "Is that you on the ice?" He pulled out his gun and stepped onto the ice surface.

"Mitch – watch out! The killer is here! Call for backup!" Garson screamed. A second later, the sound of a hockey stick reverberated and the flashlight tumbled on the ice. A skate blade stopped, and a hand flicked the flashlight off. Garson's hope for help had vanished.

The arena was deathly quiet. The only sounds from the old building were creaks and moans.

Presley may have knocked out Mitch, but he heard him coming onto the ice. Otherwise he must be as blind as I am. If I can make it to the boards in the dark and climb into the stands, he'll never catch me with his skates on.

Garson stepped tentatively towards his right. He groaned slightly as he felt the pain in his leg.

Shut up you idiot. You're giving away your position! He felt the stick whack his left leg as he fell to the ice.

"You're sick, Presley. Why don't you try that again?" demanded Garson. But before he could say more, he received another slash to the head.

Great. He can see me in the dark!

Presley smiled while adjusting Taj's night goggles from the paintball game. He bit his lip not to give away his position.

I feel like hamburger meat and Presley can see my every move. I need an advantage. He felt his phone in his jacket and fumbled to open it. He hit redial, hoping the caller would pick up on the first ring. The phone clicked that it had connected. "Get help! I'm on the Autodome ice surface – the killer is. . ."

A voice emanated from the phone, interrupting Garson's plea. "I'm sorry, your call can't connect as dialed. Please try again later," the computer voice droned. The phone was quickly whacked out of his hands.

"Didn't anyone tell you that cell service was bad in this arena," laughed Presley in the darkness.

"Why don't you make this easier on both of us? Lie down on the ice and I promise you, my blade will cut your throat quickly. You'll hardly feel a thing. Trust me, I'm a professional," said Presley from Garson's right.

"As tempting as that offer is, I'll stick with the beatings. I'm a glutton for punishment," returned Garson. A hockey stick bashed his head from behind and Garson fell to the ice. His head was swimming as he tried to get up but fell hard again onto the ice. The cold surface beckoned to him to close his eyes for his last sleep. A spotlight shone at center ice, illuminating Presley with his stick in the air.

"You fought hard Garson, harder than any of my victims. But in the end, the result is the same. I hope all of this was worth it to you."

"Not really. Why don't you just skate away? I won't be going anywhere," croaked Garson knowing that he wouldn't be getting up for awhile. Presley considered the request.

"You present a good case. So far, I have only killed pathetic gamblers and an egotistical hockey player. Do I cross the line by killing a cop?"

"Spare my life and maybe you'll get time off for good behavior," coughed Garson. He spit up blood, laughing at his own joke.

"Nah. One more murder is not going to change anything but the body count." The spotlight faded and the lights in the arena slowly warmed up. There was enough light emitted for Garson to see Presley skate closer to him. "Sorry. A captain has to make tough decisions. I promise to keep your co-workers busy for years." Garson raised his head from the ice.

"You're under arrest for the murders of sixteen victims. You have the right to remain silent – which you have not exercised – any thing you say can be used against you in a court of law," Garson coughed before finishing.

"You're delusional, agent. This game has come to an end and you've lost," Presley pushed Garson's head down with his stick and readied his skate to run over Garson's throat.

"Look behind you," Garson croaked.

"Please. That is such a stupid cliché," answered Presley.

Bang! The first bullet caught Presley in his shoulder. He rolled to the right but didn't fall down. His face was a mask of anger as he realized that everything had slipped away. He turned his rage toward Garson and lifted his skate for the killing blow.

Bang! The second shot was at his knee and the force sent him writhing to the ice. A figure jumped over the boards.

"Mitch!" Garson whispered as the figure came closer to him.

"Someone even better," Lola replied. She stepped beside him, kicking Presley's stick away while giving his skates a wide berth.

"Shouldn't you be in the hospital?" coughed Garson, grateful for her timing.

"If I was, you'd be dead," she answered.

"Never mind. How did you know?"

"I wasn't sure, but Mitch said there was a letter on the jacket. In one camera angle, they were able to discern the letter C on the front of jacket. As soon as he said that, I realized that a captain has a 'C' on his jersey and figured a team jacket would have the same. Mitch told me you were still at the rink and I knew you would be in trouble. Not a minute too soon."

"What about your partner?" Garson asked.

"He has a bump the size of a goose egg on the back of his head. A guy as thickheaded as him should be fine. Now he finally owes me his life. As for you," she pointed her gun at Presley. "Your game is over!"

Chapter 35   *Winners and Losers*

April 20, 2007

Garson pushed his wheelchair down the hospital hallway away from the TV room. His ribs were wrapped, and a huge bruise covered his right eye.

"Good to see you out of bed," Mitch commented while walking down the hall toward him. "Anything good on television?"

"Just depressing news. You'd think nothing good happens watching today's news. Misery sells. How's your head?"

"Still attached. Besides a persisting headache, I'll survive," Mitch answered. Garson noticed the bag of takeout food.

"What did you bring me?" Garson asked.

"Chinese, with the wontons you like."

"Good. Bring them into my room. The head nurse gets upset when she sees me eating anything but hospital food."

"Well, this stuff's not the healthiest."

"Have you ever been in a hospital for a week before? The food is awful. For all the sitting around I do, you'd think I'd be gaining weight. Just the opposite, I've lost eight pounds."

"If you were female you wouldn't be complaining," Mitch said as handed him the bag. "Eat and relax. You've earned it."

"What about the tests on Lola?" as Garson sat on his bed.

"The hospital found a high level of carbon monoxide in her blood. If we hadn't found her when we did, it would have been lethal," Mitch answered. The coroner mentioned the last victim's skin was pinker than usual. On a second autopsy, he confirmed that this was a symptom of carbon monoxide poisoning

"We should have caught that before," Garson mentioned while eating. We looked at the obvious method of death, not realizing how he prepared them.

"When a victim is stabbed, you don't tend to look too deeply at other methods," commented Mitch.

"Doesn't matter. We should have realized that the victims never fought back because they couldn't breathe. Carbon monoxide made his victims lethargic and disoriented, so their resistance was minimal. In the hotel room for Tidwell, there was an impression on the carpet. It must have been from a small pump releasing carbon monoxide in the air. It weakened Tidwell enough for Presley to kill him without alerting the other players.

"Don't beat yourself up over missing that. You brought a killer to justice," Mitch pointed out.

"Have I? I keep thinking I've missed something. Presley was definitely the killer and the hacker you killed delivered the tools. I keep thinking that neither one was the brains of the operation. That someone else was pulling the strings."

"Give yourself a break, you've been through a lot."

"Maybe so. By the way, is Lola still watching our killer?"

"Yep, he's out of acute care and in wing B. His shoulder and knee are healing. He'll be ready for the trial."

"I thought you said she always went for the heart and head," Garson asked.

"Thank god for the killer she saved her target grouping for the practice range."

"How many of the hockey players have come to visit him?"

"I think all of them have, although they're pretty horrified by the methods he used to keep the team going."

"I just hope we've put an end to the gambling killing spree."

"Do you want to bet on it!" Mitch put a five-dollar bill down.

"No. After this case, I don't think I'll ever make a bet again," Garson smiled.

A thousand miles away in the industrial heartland of Ohio, I sat in a coffee shop with a bunch of hockey players.

"I appreciate the offer to play with you guys. After my team folded, I figured my season was done," I put down my coffee.

"No problem. Our goaltender hurt his ankle in our first playoff game and our back up is sick with the flu. You're doing us the favor," commented a large blond player named Carson.

"I still can't believe what happened to your last team," a shorter player named Victor exclaimed. "I've played some rough hockey games before, but I've never met a hockey player that kills."

"No matter how many games you play with a guy, you really don't know what he's like. Money can be a pretty powerful motivator," I replied.

"Speaking of money, we should get back to the rink for practice," Carson placed his money on the table for the coffee as the group headed outside to the parking lot. "I'll see you two in a few minutes," Carson yelled as three players jumped into his car. Victor and I turned the corner and he stared in disbelief at my brand-new truck.

"Is this yours?" he asked me.

"You bet! 350 horsepower of driving torque – fresh from the dealership. Want to drive?" I tossed the keys over to him and he grabbed them out of the air.

"Are you kidding? I'm all over this," he said as he disengaged the door lock and stepped into the front seat. "This is incredible. Who do I have to kill to get a beautiful truck like this?" he jokingly asked as he started the ignition.

"Funny you should ask," I smiled in the rearview mirror as Victor drove the truck out of the parking lot.

Post-Game Analysis

Garson was promoted to the position of Captain and oversees a team of thirty agents. His former captain was demoted as a result of the stakeout fiasco. The bank robbers are still at large.

Lola and Mitch are no longer partners with the force. They are partners in real-life, married in Niagara Falls and living in Buffalo, New York. Lola doesn't call Mitch by the name Brown anymore.

Presley is captain of the floor hockey team in jail and has led his team to three consecutive tournament wins.

Chilly played three games in the National Hockey League when several players were injured. He assisted on one goal. He retired and became a coach for a university team.

Dozer became an undercover cop and played a role in one of the biggest marijuana busts in the history of Vancouver, British Columbia.

Taj accepted money from his family and became a sports physician, helping many athletes with their injuries.

Booker became head librarian for the city of Kingston and led an after-school project to better educate young people.

Tunny became a major player in 'pay per view' hockey fights, pitting the worst brawlers of hockey against each other. Eventually it got shut down, and he later became a coach for 'Ultimate Fighting'.

Brick and his wife set up a bed and breakfast and became tour guides at a nature reserve where he hugged every visitor.

Stefan became the sales manager for a large women's lingerie company and travels across North America promoting the latest fashions.

Dawson became a spokesperson for the promotion of male cosmetics and is currently in a series of ads showcasing men's shampoo.

Rook played on a number of minor league teams before retiring and becoming a social worker. He specializes in working with troubled youth adjusting to a new environment

The goaltender's whereabouts are unknown.

Acknowledgements

I'm sure you will not be surprised by the fact that the Assassins are a fictitious team. But many of the players and experiences in this novel are based on real life hockey players.

I have had the honor of playing recreational hockey for almost a decade with a group of guys called the Halifax Kings. There are the worse bunch of rag tag, wise cracking, beer swilling, body checking, foul smelling hackers you could ever meet.

They are also the best hockey players and friends a guy could have. My thanks go out to them for their humor and dedication to the sport of hockey. Many of the characters in this book are born from these players. I appreciate them for being themselves and providing much of the material (that's hockey, not murders) in the book.

About the Author

James Kochanoff is currently in a four-book deal with Silver Leaf Books in Massachusetts. The series is a young adult dystopian fiction with the first novel "Drone World" exploring the life of a teenage girl who thinks she lives in a perfectly safe city patrolled by drones, until she tries to leave it.

He signed a contract with Toonz Animation, Asia's largest animation for an animated pilot of his novel "Men of Extreme Action." To see images from this pilot, please visit his website at
www.adventurebooks.ca

It's tough to make a career as an author. About 1% can truly make a living at it. If you enjoyed this book, please leave a review on your favorite book retailers' site and tell others about the book.